PRAISE FOR SWEPT AWAY

"Call off the search for the next great Newfoundland literary voice. With an authentic voice that's true to his roots, Darrell Duke will sweep you away to the cold heart of Placentia Bay, drop you in the middle of a lovelorn mystery, and entwine you in a quest for what truly matters. Full of the gritty reality that makes outport Newfoundland a battlefield for the heart, especially for those who grew up there and remain, Swept Away is astonishingly intimate and innocent, yet full of mischief and passion for the beauty of life and this strange, cruel world. You want a glimpse into the lives and souls of real people? Get Swept Away."

— GERARD COLLINS
Award-winning author of *The Hush Sisters* and *Finton Moon*

For: Leigh,

Thank-you!

SWEPT AWAY

DARRELL DUKE

Darrell

STAGEHEAD PUBLISHING

NEWFOUNDLAND

Library and Archives Canada Cataloging in Publication

Duke, Darrell, 1970-, author

Swept Away / Darrell Duke

Issued in print and electronic formats

ISBN: 9798499924167

1. Newfoundland and Labrador—Atlantic Canada—United States Military—History—Romance—Tragedy—20th Century 2. World War II—Freshwater, Placentia Bay, Newfoundland 3. Expropriation—Lost at sea—Resettled Communities—Newfoundland and Labrador—History—Sea Stories

COVER GIRL MODEL: MacKenzie Reading-Wakeham
COVER HAND MODEL: Jack Duke
LAYOUT & DESIGN: Lori Duke

Stagehead Publishing Ltd. Clarenville, NL, Canada A5A 1M9

FOR COUSIN JACK HOULIHAN

Whose encouragement and belief in my ways of keeping history alive continue to inspire me to do my best. Until my final written and sung word, I will remember affectionately your kindness, your great smile, and your love.

Finally

Pallid, torn flesh shines in the sun, bobbing between rocks ensnared with rope, nets, cork floats and other garbage. Still, with all my bitterness towards a god I don't know exists, I grip the oars and pray it is finally her; it *has* to be. It *is*. At last.

The skin of the naked body looks as soft and delicate as a rotten fish. Like a starved dog, I make at the revolting spectacle with a boat hook; but there's little or nothing to grab. Leaning over the side of my dory, the always-cold sea lops upon my sore legs. Due to the motion of my long-handled hook, the lump of drowned flesh and bones begins to make its way towards me. Her long hair swishes in the dirty seawater pitching against the rocks and back again at the boat. It *is* her. *Finally*, I've found My Love.

"Thanks, God! Thank ya, Lord!" I say without thought.

The backs of her arms are gone—long since food for hungry fish—and her spine is sticking out of her back like the skeleton of a dolphin or seal you'd see washed up on a beach after a storm. But I have *found* her. Found *her*. I raise my tired arms above my shoulders and offer my hands to Him, the One who's supposed to be living someplace in the sky. More praise to God and profuse apologies for having ever doubted *Him* spew from my trembling lips covered in tears and seawater.

Through great sobs and an infinite, unleashed reservoir of tears, I reach out to lift her from the evil water and into my dory designed to roll gracefully with every wave of the sea. I'd been warned about the state of a drowned body and what fish would be after doing to it. I am prepared for the worst. No matter what, the poor girl will get a decent burial and her mother won't hate me half as much because I've finally brought her daughter home—although not home the way she always meant when I'd call for My Love at their door. *Make sure ya has her home by 10 o'clock, mind*, her mother would say. Memories flood my thoughts, as I try to gently drag her body closer—long walks with My Love, gentle touches, and soft, respectable kisses in the moon's pale yet still-bright-enough light to make silhouettes of us by the end of her fence, as her mother pretended not to watch us through the white shears supposedly offering privacy to the kitchen inside.

No matter what, My Love will be home at last. Her mother's little girl. I'll get through the proper funeral and burial shenanigans and then be left to visit her grave at night when no one is around to hear my muffled screeches and bawls and apologies because everyone knows it was my fault she'd fallen overboard and drowned that day. Everyone knows I could have done something to save her.

My hands, stronger than ever now, grab hold of visible bones which manage to stay attached to the rest of her body. The unsympathetic sea deliberately drips agonizing ear-piercing drops of its filthy self from her long, matted hair. I want to stop and remove kelp and dirt and slime from her tresses, to make her feel better—give her a dose of dignity. Through the wind caught in my ears and the sounds created by sea bullying past and against everything in its way, I hear my father's voice: *Haul 'er into the boat, b'y*! So, against my strong desire to pluck kelp and weeds from her once-lovely head of hair, I listen to my dead father and get her halfway over the starboard gunwale now almost even with the surface of the sea. I'm sure the dory will swamp, but I'm hardly going to leave My Love here. Her bottom half is still beneath the sea's surface, and I hope a pack of dogfish doesn't show up and rip apart what's left of her. I gape into the water and, seeing no sign of fish, I relax a little.

She is heavy. I fall back across the seat with the hole in it for the sail mast. She slips from my grip and my left arm goes numb from the pain of lodging the back of my forearm into a thole pin. The worn, round pin used for holding an oar breaks under my weight. I shove the boat hook under one of my legs to make sure My Love doesn't slip back into the water. Then, I unfurl enough jigger twine to tie figure-eight loops. I slide one of the twine loops over an oar and the other end of the thin manilla over the remaining thole pin on that side. This will do until I get back in safely and have time to carve a new pin to replace the broken one.

With the book hook still attached to My Love, I right myself to grab her, look at her, love her. Her legs are half gone. *Jesus*! Then, I see feet at the end of the boney legs. She has shrunken—almost as if she's returned to the stature of a child. But I don't care. I have her. Finally. Again, *finally*. Her body, I mean. Her mother will lavish me with kindness and forgiveness, and I will learn to lift my head a bit in the years to follow as I make my way to the fishing stage, the wharf, the slipway, the garden, the field. I'll put up with the smell of her corpse for the sake of all that, although it would be easier to heave her back into the water—leave her where she was, where nobody would ever know she'd been. But I can hardly do the like of that.

"Thank God!" I say aloud.

Then I say it again. I also mutter a *sorry* for taking the Lord's name in vain. *What else could I say seeing what I'm seeing*, I think.

I cry great sobs of sadness while a strange version of joy provides added strength. I row around several headlands. Each hidden beach looks like the perfect place to go in and bury her. *Jesus, the stink*. I look to the sky. *Sorry*. Instead of looking *at* her, I look *over* her, into the growing horizon and now and then over my shoulder towards Freshwater in the distance. It was about here, in this area of the sea, where we'd watched and heard the Americans blow an old schooner to matchwood, for target practice, on the same day My Love was taken from me—from this world.

The sea has soothed. I pull the dory over its surface with ease. The sun shines on her hair rinsed with spray from my oars. The closer we get to our home beach, the more her hair seems to come to life. The Crevecoeur is to my right; its broken-heart-shaped hill of rock is mending before me as I rescue My Love, my no-longer-lost love, from her briny grave. The vast mount, the tallest this side of Freshwater, they say was named for a young Frenchman who'd lost his own love during an invasion by the English hundreds of years ago. Perhaps her man did the right thing by jumping off the cliff to the rocks and sea below. I wish I'd had the nerve. But now I don't have to do that.

I've managed to value my dedication to My Love by never giving up looking for her remains. Now, I'll be a hero for never avoiding my true intentions. There'll be no more doubt and mockery, for they'll know I really *did* love her. They'll say how wonderful I am for staying true to my word: that I'd look for her the rest of my life if that's what it took to find her and bring her home.

A glance upward and upon the sloped meadow of the Googly Hole reveals men, women, and children. One by one, they pause their toil of planting and weeding—growing vegetables. From their vantage point, their unquiet voices caught in the natural amphitheatre of the crescent-shaped beach announce their sight of me and my precious cargo. Or at least I imagine it's what they are thinking and saying. Maybe I'm just *hoping* they notice—a prelude to the praises I'm sure to receive upon my arrival with another of our little town's missing and presumed drowned. One by one they drop their picks, hoes, rakes, and shovels, and tether their horses to the sparse trees of the meadow. The people put extra effort into their gait to be to the beach by the time I haul the dory upon the rocks. They'll even grab hold of the boat's bow and then grasp her gunwales to make sure I am safely out of the waves—as relieved as I am that My Love's days and nights at sea have once and for all met their end.

Old men on the beach with nothing to do finally find use for the long minutes of their day since they can no longer fish for one reason or another. Audible is the idle chit-chat and the dishing out of news second-hand from their wives and daughters. The old fellows scuff as energetically as they're able. Towards the incoming spectacle they hobble. Not that they can see my prized freight, but the increasing talk of the growing crowd and the baulks of hungry gulls in pursuit of my boat tells the people this is no ordinary landing of cod.

The stench of the rotten body announces itself long before the dory comes close to the beach. Men and boys from five or six small boats tending their fish and lobster traps set on the inshore stop their work and look up. Some even leave their anchored skiffs and row in their punts for a closer look at the excitement. By the time the crowd from the meadow reaches the beach, the old men have broken out their scapulars, miraculous medals, and rosary beads. Upon receipt of the good, but disturbing news, they remove their knitted caps and crank their old heads towards Heaven, whispering every prayer they were ever made memorize.

"He found her. Be Jesus, she's been found at last."

"I always knew he'd find 'er."

"Someone should run up the hill an' tell her mudder."

"Someone's long gone t' do that."

The few women present drop to their sore, aching knees upon the wet, slippery rocks, clasping one big hand against the other in prayer. For once I don't tell them to get a bit of sense, and although my stomach is turning from the stench of My

Love's half-eaten carcass, my heart manages to swell with happiness—something I haven't known since the moments before our special stop at Sandy Beach before she was taken so long ago. But such news doesn't fade in a small town; it only grows. I turn away from the horde of people advancing towards me, hang over the side of the boat and empty the contents of the breakfast in my stomach. The women look twice as disgusted. The morbid faces of the men making their way, arms outstretched towards my boat, are whiter than usual.

"'Nough t' turn a harse from his oats," one man says, as his wife whacks him across the shoulder for his sauce.

"Shut yer big gob, b'y," she warns him.

When we land, and most hands grab the boat and haul her ashore, one of the men lets out great sobs. His cries are so loud the gulls take off in frightful flight from the rocks at either end of the beach. But they don't stay away for long. Soon, they're back and circling above us in a frenzy of squawks and bawls. The crying man's voice is still heard above the racket of the birds.

"My Jesus," he screams. "'Tis Mary! Me precious Mary."

Not until this moment does it occur to me that it isn't My Love at all, but the daughter, a little girl of the trembling man before me. She'd been taken out to sea by a scoundrel upsurge on a Sunday about two months ago while the family had tea and a rest on First Beach—just around two or three headlands from here. I want to scream at him, that it is *not* his daughter but My Love and *will ya frig right off*! But he is right. It *is* his little girl and I've found her. Not the heroic welcome I need.

This is just one of seven or eight bodies I'm after finding over the years. Hesitant, affectionate hands touch my shoulders and reluctantly pat my aching back. I can't pry my red, swollen eyes from the grieving father cradling what's left of his dead child. It isn't until now that I learn not everyone in this town lacks compassion or the decent sense to attempt understanding me and what I live with, or without—and with no end in sight, again, of finding My Love and a morsel of peace before I die. Again, I think of the French soldier unable to live without *his* love and how quick and easy it would be for *me* to run and jump from that high hill to end my suffering.

Unenthusiastic pats continue to touch my back, as the father of the lifeless child cradles his child. He slips and falls to his knees on the rocks, but he never lets go of his treasured girl. Another man carries a fish cart alongside one of his legs and sets it in front of the grieving man. With loving encouragement to do so, the father lays his little girl onto the handcart which four men, not the usual two, count to three and lift the lifeless body now covered in a woman's overcoat. A concoction of prayers for the dead child's soul become muffled with the wind and the knocking together of loose beach rocks by fumbling boots and bare feet. Women, men and children alike sob and bawl over the spectacle—a funeral procession I wish *I* was part of. My mind is as tattered as the pale flesh of that poor child. *Is it wrong that I'm shedding tears not for the little girl nor her grieving father?*

Feeling more than a fool for all the glorious moments I'd invented in my head before my arrival to this beach today, I turn my head and curse the same god I'd been praising for the past hour or more. There *is* no god—especially when I look up and see My Love's mother scrambling down the slope towards the beach where a greater crowd of people and birds has gathered. I shove the dory off and hop back aboard, grabbing the oars and hauling on them more fiercely than ever. Head down, eyes closed, I don't care where I end up. But to look in her mother's eyes is something I cannot do—one place I cannot be. Her mother's cries, on top of the grieving father of the found little one, top the shrill cries of the gulls and crows now more plentiful than ever.

No shouts of *thank you* or *wait, you're a good man, after all,* reach my ears—because they never left the mouths of those on the beach in the first place. I was and always will be a goddamn fool. It must have killed them when they thought I'd found My Love: that they might have to say *well done yourself after all this time* and how pleased her mother will be with me.

But none of the sort was ever muttered.

Before She Was Mine

Another lonely night has passed. Another long day to follow, for certain, without that lovely new Girl from up the Hill—the one I'd like to take for a wife.

Since I first laid eyes on her a few months ago, I can't stop thinking of her. It was a sad spectacle—her and her parents and little brother struggling up the hill with their meagre belongings. They'd lived in Argentia which has been taken over by the Americans who are continuing to build a large base there for their army, navy, and air force. If trucks were available, larger furniture was carried while people who couldn't fit aboard tried their best to walk alongside or at least follow. The Girl from up the Hill was every bit as gloomy as the rest, as she struggled with a trunk. I offered her a hand and she reluctantly, finally, agreed to let me help. No words were spoken until her father said, "I think this is the spot, if I'm readin' this paper right." It was there I dropped the trunk and saw nothing, but a parcel of land cleared of trees, concrete forms for a foundation, but no house. I wanted to ask of their intentions, but they were beyond miserable, but I could tell by the look of them they would survive the ordeal, sooner or later.

A month later, she stopped by our meadow where I'd been busy shoeing our horse. I released the big animal's hoof from my grip and gave the mare a little tap to let her know she could stroll the field until I was ready for her return.

"I'm sorry," she said.

I looked up and nearly died of the fright. It was like the

dreary images I'd been looking at all my life had been replaced with the most beautiful painting imaginable. She was stunning—probably wearing the same homemade dress she had on the first time I saw her, only this time it wasn't flecked with mud from truck tires spinning past her on the road.

"Hello," I managed to get out through a throatful of lumps.

"Hello!" she said back.

"Whatta ya sorry about, girl?" I asked.

"When ya helped lug the trunk up the hill for us…I wasn't very nice. I'm sorry."

"Oh, Jesus, girl," I laughed, "don't ever say yer sorry fer the like of that. We can't imagine what yer after goin' through. Is it true they burnt yeer homes?"

"'Tis," she said, sighing. "Not all o' them, but enough so we'll never get the images out of our heads. Ours was one o' the last to be burnt before the people down home formed a committee an' had a stop put to the burnin'."

"Hard stuff," I sais.

"'Tis," she said. "I b'lieve I knows yer gran'mudder. She lived not far from us. They burnt her home, too. How is she? I heard she moved here to Freshwater, too. Shockin', we haven't had a chance t' look an' see where lots of Argentia people are livin'. Where is she, anyhow, yer gran'mudder?"

"Nan is tryin' t' get settled away in an old house down the road. 'Tis not far from our house, me an' My Brother's, just across the brook an' up in an old meadow."

"I'll find her, sometime, an' drop in t' see her," the lovely girl said, and it was plain to tell she meant it.

"I'm sure that'd be nice," I said, "but I'm pretty certain she's not the same person ya might o' known in Argentia."

"Sorry t' hear," she said. "Sadly, I hear there's a lot o' that goin' on with people from down home."

"If I'm ever down the road an' see ya," I said, "I'll gladly take ya up t' Nan's, in case she needs remindin' o' who ya are."

"That'd be very nice," she said. "Well, I gotta find a way o'er to Placentia t' get a few things at the big store there."

"If I had the time," I shouldn't have said, "I'd row ya o'er in one our dories."

"That's alright, b'y," she said. "Lots to be done, I know."

I don't know how much time had passed since she left to head to the beach, but I looked to the sea from our meadow until I saw a skiff putting out the harbour. I don't imagine she had any shortage of offers for a run across the water. Sitting in a pile of hay, I sucked on a smoke and thought of her. My thoughts ran wild. *When she returns, I could run down to meet her, and take her hand as she lifts her lovely legs out of the skiff. Her smile, no doubt, paid the normal wages required for such a trip. I imagine her beauty stifling the racket of the make 'n' break engine, and her politeness draping the dirty, black smoke coughing its way out of the pipe rising from the little wooden box housing the boat's motor to help muffle the noise and to keep it out of the weather. I'll offer to carry her bag from the Trading Company, walk her up the Back Path and on up to her house.*

It hadn't been all that long ago when the Americans drove the people of Argentia and Marquise from their homelands, and soon after the local girls couldn't marry the strangers quick enough—and it shows no signs of slacking, either. In my head, it was obvious the Girl from up the Hill would be one of those, so I tried hard to keep her near me, and away from the strangers.

"Shag it," I said to My Brother. "I'm goin' down to the beach t' give her a hand with her stuff. I won't be too long."

On our way up from the beach, I carried her bags in one hand and wanted to hold her hand with the other. When I thought she wasn't looking, I'd peek into the bags. There was wool for her mother, a new knitting needle for her father's nets, even though he was too sick to fish, and a wooden toy for her little brother half dead, himself, from the consumption. Metal toy cars and trucks had been scarce since the Second World War began; the metal better off used in the making of tanks, guns, bullets, and bombs, so the governments decided, according to newspapers and radio reports.

The Girl lived almost at the top of the steep hill. She walked fast, taking big strides while I find myself conscious of my steps and more easily out of breath. I was content to lag, admiring the spring in her hind legs and they so brown and soft-looking beneath her cotton summer dress. She looked back at me, killed me with her smile until I turned yet a murkier shade of red, knowing she knew how happy I was to be scuffing behind.

That scenario played out dozens of times and, each time, I did my best to make her feel extra special.

I was born and raised here in Freshwater, and I don't mind one bit those poor families joining our little town. As far as I know, no one here is objecting to them moving here; they have to go someplace. And with jobs on The Base, it only makes sense most of them live as close to the place as they can.

"At first," the Girl from up the Hill says, "the big talk was of movin' all of us t' Herrin' Bay, up the Northeast Arm."

"I'm glad the majority o' them ended up here," I say. "If you…I mean, if *they* hadn't moved here, I'd never have…"

I stop myself from sure embarrassment and light a smoke.

"You'd never have what?" she asks, "know how t' light a smoke?"

I exhale through my nose and offer a little laugh to try and hide my humiliation.

"'Tis alright t' have a few new faces 'round here t' look at, that's all," I finally manage to say.

"Well," she says, "that's good. Thanks, fer acceptin' us into yer town."

"Don't worry," I say, "when all the mud settles down an' dries, an' grass an' weeds start takin' o'er again, everything will be lovely. 'Tis a grand spot here in the summertime, 'specially down on the beach an' in the meadows. I must get back t' work before My Brother has me head."

"No rush, b'y," she surprises me. "I can have the kettle boiled in no time, if ya like. I knows it looks small, the shed, but there's plenty o' room an' we have a spare chair."

"I'd like that very much," I say, "but I'll definitely drop back another time, if that'd be alright with ya."

"Yes, I knows ya have lots t' do," she says, "an' so do I. Hopefully, we won't have to stay in that old shed fer long. Daddy says, now that the foundation is made, it won't take long t' build a house on it."

"Yes, an' I'd gladly help with the buildin' of yeer house, but I know there are contractors doin' that an' they have their own workers."

"Thanks," she says, smiling her beautiful smile. "That's very sweet of you t' offer."

Six months must be passed, and now she's calling me *sweet*. There's hope for me yet.

At night I fight sleep like a stubborn baby and yearn for what thoughts of the Girl from up the Hill the next seconds might bring. I close my eyes just to try and see hers looking back at me. Bluer than a clear evening sky in summer they are. So blue I wonder if it's her eyes which give the sky its colour or the other way around. I'm content to believe the former. And her hair is the colour of hay at harvest—yellow and sparkling from a bar of Sunlight soap. As the sun's rays tenderly stroked it into the slightest of a wave today, the sight caressed my every sense. Her hair bounced on her small, strong-looking shoulders and down over her back I imagine feels like silk. Not that I'd ever felt silk, but I've heard it's lovely to the touch.

Why can't she be something less than perfect? I can't focus on anything but her. A complete, blissful showering of my senses she gives without the slightest of her knowing.

"Don't be so goddamn foolish," I try to convince My Brother. "I'm not in love with her."

"Go on, b'y!" he says. "Ya floated down the hill like a faerie."

I tried poorly to conceal my giddy serenity by fidgeting with the small ax next to the stove.

"Yes, b'y," I say, because I had nothing else to say to halt his mocking.

"The way ya passed by our garden, sure" he continues, "ya'd never say ya had cows t' milk an' horses t' feed."

He's right. Jesus! He's right. But what odds. I don't care. He can't stop there, either.

"As poor Mudder used t' say, God rest her soul, 'ya haven't the sense of a suckin' duck.' Don't chop the hand off yerself now, mind, wit' that ax."

My Brother is right and, again, I can't argue with him. Mother and Father often said that of me—*never had the sense of a suckin' duck*. But I'm content with my lot in life, with the scraps of information I have gathered along the way. I don't care for much—only that, right now, I *am* in love with the Girl from up the Hill and I'm brimming with encouragement to be a better person because of it. Because of *her*. I know I'm not perfect, but I also know, or at I least think, I'm a good person who'll never hurt an innocent being.

Last year, in 1941, the nearby towns of Argentia and Marquise were taken over. *Expropriation*, they call it. The American government needed the space to construct a base. It has already proven worthy of the mental and physical upheaval it has caused by the capturing of German U-boats by the Americans at the very entrance to Argentia's harbour. Despite unnecessary, often-horrific encounters because of the ruined towns, the necessary upheaval has created jobs galore for locals. That keeps away a lot of the misery for many.

"The Yanks could've gone about it better," My Brother says to add to my successful attempt to stare him away from taunting me about the Girl from up the Hill. "Instead of burnin' homes, they could've bulldozed them like they started after the Argentia crowd formed that committee and got on their case about the grief they were causin'."

"At least now we know the reason fer their rush," I say.

"True," he says. "Now go t' sleep outta it. You'll need yer strength t'morrow fer charmin' yer girlfriend."

"Girlfriend?" I say. "Jesus, b'y, I just met her."

"Ya met her almost a year ago, b'y. I knows what yer up to, me son," he laughs.

"That long? I ask. "It feels like a lot less time than that. Yeah, well; 'Night now!"

"'Night," he says, yawning.

Buttoned to the Neck

Sunlight through the windows slowly forces our eyelids to lift. I stretch to meet the day and smile about the Girl from up the Hill. Life's not so boring anymore since she's been here.

Many locals, wanting a way out of boats and off the sea their entire lives, have found their paradise working for the Americans.

"Not many 'round Freshwater in the day anymore, since The Base come," My Brother says.

"I know," I add, pouring molasses in my tea. "Even some *women* workin' there."

"'Magine," My Brother says, chomping on his toast and jam. "I 'spose yer missus will be down there next an' tangled up with one o' them good-lookin' Yanks."

"Prob'ly," I say, as if his comment hasn't ripped my guts out.

Some of the old crowd around here call the Americans *Foolish Yanks*. I believe the *foolish* part came from a time, recently, when the Americans built a pontoon bridge to span The Gut—a body of the sea separating Placentia proper from Jerseyside. Old fellows, having spent their lives fighting the tides in that location in schooners, skiffs, and dories, stood by and laughed. Some even told the Americans their idea was an unwise one, but they managed to connect Jerseyside to Placentia. No more than two weeks later, the bridge was dismantled by Mother Nature and carried up the Northeast Arm of the bay. Of course, someone had to make up a song about that—like we do with most events, good and bad.

"Let's get goin' now," I say to My Brother from my room.

"Yeah, alright!" he says, yawning.

The black flies are thick. With long-sleeved shirts buttoned all the way to our necks, the heat is enough to kill us. On our homemade handcarts, the same kind we use to lug saltfish, me and My Brother haul piles of yellow grass from meadows long cut by generations of Irish families like ours.

With a path well beaten from the beach to Larkin's Pond, we follow the brook with little water after little rain all summer. Then we see the trout. Lovely Brown Trout, mostly. There's the scattered Rainbow Trout, too, but mostly Brown. They're trapped in little pools. With no luck, from our quick hands they try to hide.

I splash a bit of water up in my face to cool down and My Brother says I'm off my head because *the Yanks* are after poisoning the water since they came here, and I'll be dead yet. He says the water from O'Keefe's Pond up on Castle Hill is the best around because the Americans don't know about it yet. That's where My Brother goes every day with two big, galvanized buckets hanging from a sturdy stick thrown across his wide shoulders. I still go to Larkin's Pond.

"I heard the Yanks are plannin' t' build a dam between that an' the other pond that flows into it," My Brother says. "An' when that happens, a dam, we won't be 'llowed t' fish out there anymore because we might *contaminate* the drinkin' water."

"Yeah, well, the crowd from Argentia and Marquise livin' here says *don't mind the Yanks; that'll never happen*, I add.

"We'll have t' see, I 'spose," he says, throwing more water over his face and neck.

The little bits of pork fat I'd carried from the house and

dropped into the pan sizzle. Grease flicks in every direction. If we were home, one of us would roll the cleaned trout in flour first, but here is different. I rip their heads off and their guts out and fling the waste. After rinsing the fish, I lay it into the pan of popping grease. With a stick from the ground, I shuffle the fish around and keep flipping them over, so they don't burn too much.

"Don't go burnin' mine now, mind," My Brother barks.

I like the taste of burnt food, but he doesn't, so I'll cook mine a bit longer than his—not that we can afford to waste time.

Sitting on the bank, eating our fried fish, and drinking warm water, we watch an old man across the way shoo his horses into a stable.

"They says he never had a wife an' that's why he's so cranky an' why no one bothers talkin' to 'im," My Brother says, munching away at his fish and bread and butter.

Thinking of what My Brother has said makes me want the Girl from up the Hill even more. We say we don't really care about most people, especially old folks, but that's not true at all. Watching the old man is just something to do while we rest and eat. But I do admire him—his determination to do what needs to be done to get through this life often drenched with drudgery and uncertainty. I like old people. I respect how they keep their thoughts to themselves, except when they're talking to their animals.

"I'd love to know what really went on in Argentia and Marquise," I say. "But the crowd from there are too traumatized t' speak of it. Either that, or they've been told not t' utter a word."

"Maybe yer missus will tell ya all about it when ye are married," he mocks.

"Shut up, b'y," I say, flicking water from the stream up into his face.

"Sorry, b'y," he says. "I know. One thing ya *can* tell is the mouths o' those forced-out people are stitched shut with sadness—ya can see it in their eyes, swollen from bawlin'."

The old man's shouts echo off the hill behind him, and all over our town.

"Some says he talks to his horse the same way the women gets on wit' the babies, an' he must be off his head to be gettin' on like that," My Brother adds.

"Maybe the horse treats him better than the missus used to," I say.

"Ya never know, b'y!" My Brother laughs.

Meadows roll up from both sides of the brook—except for where the new road was put through by the Americans, mostly to hasten the moving of the bodies from Argentia's three cemeteries. Instead of leaving two-hundred years of their ancestors beneath a runway necessary for the building and operation of The Base, most agreed it was best to dig up their relatives and friends and reinter them in the Freshwater graveyard.

"Used t' bother me—knowin' dead relatives were disturbed—but now I see the new road as one leadin' to the Girl from up the Hill."

"Ya sap, come on, b'y," My Brother says, rolling his eyes while giving me a hard smack on my back.

The long, thirsty roots of ancient trees seem to hold the earth together, quietly having burst their way through the edges of the brook and bent until their tips found water. Remnants of old, straight rock piles and crooked lines of newer ones run in every direction, indicating where it might be fit to grow a few potatoes, cabbages, and carrots.

Much of the meadow here in the middle of Freshwater has been ruined by plows and trucks hired to clear land for the building of houses to become homes for the hundreds of displaced people from Argentia and Marquise. Dogs are dirtier than ever, rolling in the deep tracks made by heavy trucks and machinery while cats hop cautiously over and across the ditch dug along one side of the road. The Americans say they'll eventually put metal culverts so people can access their properties more easily, but right now logs chopped and limbed at each landowner's expense of time and energy serve the purpose.

The black flies continue to distract our tired eyes from the lonely old man's business. They bite the skin of our hands and wrists and try to burrow into our flesh. There's no end to the smacking of our hands off our arms, necks, legs and shoulders, and our curse words increase in quantity and volume by the second. Old women, bandannas tied tightly around their necks, are beating out mats slung over fences, checking their rhubarb, or weeding their flowerbeds. Loudly and decisively, they tut-tut their disgust at our brazenness. We toss our heads, pointing our chins in their directions—almost an effort at an apology, as we shove our fly-bitten bodies off the bank to help us rise from our place of temporary comfort.

Our stomachs are satisfied. We lick our greasy lips tasty from the trout caught with ease. If only the lovely Girl from up the Hill could be caught so easily.

"Stop daydreamin', b'y; there's too much work t' be done," My Brother says, smacking me across the back of the head.

We take our first steps to leave our place of rest. With a full belly, the cast-iron pan in the brin bag slung over my shoulder is less heavy now.

Done another day's hard work, we head back down the hill. Not far from the land where we'd watched the old man work earlier, youngsters swing from an old, tall tree. Through the air, on longstanding, coarse ropes taken from rotting ships' hulls down on the beach, they scream their excitement. Flying ungracefully into the rocks and bushes below, they laugh, and they cry. Then they get up and do it again.

"Get home out of it, mind," mothers call out from homes in every direction, "before 'tis dark."

Ropes are left to dangle empty until the next fine day. On most Saturday nights the girls sit on the tires hung from trees and hold on to the ropes while their boyfriends, or fellows trying to be their boyfriends, tease and push them. A good many of them have twisted their ankles going up there in the dark and it serves them right, I suppose.

"I've no interest in goin' up there," I say, "unless the Girl from up the Hill—the good-lookin' one from Argentia—is gonna t' be there. I doubt that'll ever happen, though. She stays home with her mother an' father all the time because her father and brother are sick."

"Oh, is he?" My Brother asks, not mocking me for once.

"Yeah, he is," I say. "I'm glad in a way, as bad as that sounds—not glad her father an' brother are ailin', but glad she's not up there, in the woods, in the dark. Unless I was up there, too."

"Ya sap!" My Brothers says again, smacking me across the shoulders.

The flies follow us up the path and in through our door that never closes properly this time of year on account of the house settling back into place in the warming ground.

"Goddamn flies," we both say the same time, and laugh.

We remove our woolen, summer caps, scratch our heads like we're lousy and tear at the skin above our ears to kill or remove ravenous black flies.

Our laughter is followed by a silence and both of us know we're waiting to hear Mom say *stop taking the Lord's name in vain.* But that doesn't happen because poor Mom is dead and gone.

"What I wouldn't do t' hear her say that again—or anything fer that matter," I say, sighing.

"I know, b'y," My Brother says. "I know."

Our plaid shirts are heavy with sweat. Our fancy new machine for washing clothes is something else. It has a ringer for straining water. It runs on gas and stinks and has half the kitchen beat up from dancing off the walls and table and chairs. We get a kick out of that, even though it has torn a little hole in the canvas. Mother wouldn't appreciate it. Sometimes, when we're loaded, we'll turn it on for badness and a laugh. Mother *certainly* wouldn't have that. The clothes dry faster than ever on Mother's line in the yard now, on account of the washer's ringer. Overnight, on the strong jigger twine spanning the kitchen above the woodstove, the dampness from the evening fog leaves our clothes from off the line. In the morning we'll have nothing but the best of comfort on our bodies again to begin another day.

The low flickering of our bedside candles is the only thing between darkness and our tired eyes. The lovely breeze coming through the raised window blows over me in the bed. When I notice the moon at its largest, I hold an index finger in front of the burning wick of my candle and blow out the flame. A thread of waxy smoke is drawn out through the open window.

In the next room, My Brother snores to the top of his lungs. *Goddamn flies*, he says in his sleep while smacking his lips together. The racket is almost as bad as when the washer is spinning around the kitchen—now that I'm finally comfortable in bed and enjoying the warm draught flowing from nature through the raised window.

I like it when there's nothing but silence. I can smile without fear of mockery from My Brother and drift into whatever thoughts my mind chooses. These nights it's all about the Girl from up the Hill, and that's fine by me. I know I'll never be good enough for such a beauty, but in my dreams I'm safe from the ridicule of people—myself included. Most dreams of her end with her smiling, as if she cares about me. She's a little hesitant, but her kind eyes mirror my longing for her. For a few minutes when I wake each morning, I keep my eyes closed, hoping to catch another glimpse of her. But that never happens.

Tentest walls are a pretty good insulator against the cold, but also a great carrier of sound. When Mom and Dad were alive, we'd hear them talking low, but not low enough so we couldn't make out what they'd be saying: worrying over this and that—the weather, the traps, fish, no fish, the boat, the gardens, enough rain for the barrel to catch drinking water, not enough rain in the brook for mother to wash clothes, too much rain flooding the brook and ruining drills of vegetables in nearby fields, and would we, their boys, ever find nice girls to marry and give them grandchildren to spoil.

All those worries are ours now, except for the washing of clothes in the brook, thanks to the gas-powered ringer-washer. And no sign of a woman—at least one close enough to give grandchildren to our dead parents. My Brother is courting a nice girl from the top of our meadow. Perhaps they'll get married and have youngones someday.

Father always hoped we'd have our own boat, never thinking he'd die one day, and we'd end up with his. She's a lovely ship, too. We've replaced a few rotten ribs, but other than that, you can't beat her—the way she faces the breeze of wind that smacks you across the face when you haul her out around The Point. The sheets of reddish-brown canvas catching the breezes—the way they snap loudly with the strain put upon her spars by the wind. And the way she rolls gracefully against those swells from the backlash of waves constantly tormenting the cliffs of the coast.

"'Tis like she got claws on her belly t' grab hold o' the water, haulin' herself along," My Brother always boasts of the schooner.

The next day, alongside the fence of our meadow, the Girl from up the Hill stops to say hello. I tell her about the schooner.

"She's not what ya'd call a big boat, mind ya," I say, "but she's good as a big one."

"Sounds like a grand ship," she says.

"Sure, some Sunday, if ya like, I can take ya fer a sail on her," I say, unsure of where my nerve is coming from.

"Yes, b'y," she says. "I'd love that, sure."

"Yes," I continue, "we can heave to, have a picnic on the deck, an' watch the sun drop behind the horizon. "P'r'aps I'll even sing ya a song."

Hey eyes widen at my words, and I instantly regret letting my tongue get ahead of my mind.

"No need o' takin' the big boat, I 'spose," I say, "when we can just use one o' the three dories stacked an' lashed to the schooner's deck."

"That sounds nice, too, thanks," she says.

Her smile melts me where I stand (good thing I'm leaning on the fence).

If she knew what I'm really thinking, she'd likely be gone

running up the hill. I try to appear relaxed. If we take one of the dories, every time I have to lean ahead for the next haul on the oars, I'll be that much closer to her. And there'll be no end to the reaching because I'll have to keep rowing to get us anywhere. Unless she chooses to sit behind me, up in the bow of the boat. I'll put a grapnel there and make up some lie about how I need it to balance the weight of the boat. She won't argue with that, I suppose.

"Sly as a dog, ya are," My Brother says, after she headed back up the hill to her half-finished home-to-be.

I never should have told him.

Morning comes quickly again. I tie back the storm door, pour our tea, and wonder what kinds of foolishness will go through my head today—especially when the heat takes over.

"She have her eyes on ya, ya needn't worry," My Brother says of the Girl from up the Hill.

I hope and pray he's right. But I don't know.

"There's somet'ing wrong with you," he says. "Ya better hurry up before she catches the eye o' one o' them Yanks with the white teeth an' a shirt fer ev'ry day o' the week."

"Ah, shut up, b'y!"

No matter what we say to one another, we know there'll be no hard feelings and we can insult each other until the cows come home.

In the meadow I can't stop thinking of the Girl from up the Hill and how I'd like to invite her into our house. Then again, I'd want no part of her living here with My Brother and he better looking than me and not half so shy.

As I'm making hay near the road, her light cough grabs my attention. She lays two buckets of fresh water on each side of her feet.

"Long day, already," she says.

"'Tis," I agree, wiping my brow.

I must look like a real fool—standing with a senseless grin on my face with no clue how to talk to her.

"Some day! Some hot! Some wind!"

Surely, those grand expressions of poetry will drive her towards me, arms flailing for a grip on me—the real Oscar Wilde.

Still, she smiles. When our eyes meet, I can hardly lift the hand-carved, thick-handled pitchfork, let alone pick up hay and throw it onto the pile.

After a bit of idle talk, we bid one another a grand day.

"Have a nice day," she says. "See ya later on, maybe."

I'm in a spin. *See ya. Later on.* Well! Should I jump the fence and grab hold of her?

"Alright," I say, ashamed of my failure to say the right words.

I'm not much good at hiding behind the mound of drying grass and watching her walk away, either. When she turns around and catches me gawking at her like a cat drooling over a fledgling bird, she still smiles.

It never fails; whenever she looks at me, I get weak from her beauty. They're blue, her eyes. And her hair, yellowish, like the sun in the evening just as the fog's coming in. Or perhaps more like the faint grass of the meadows in fall. Her lips are full and curled at the ends, even when she's not smiling. My eyes cast upon the ground, and I feel sick in the guts—when she looks at me. She must think me not well in the head, especially when everyone knows she's without a man to keep her company in the evenings. I ponder if she wonders why I haven't invited her for tea, or a walk. Maybe my loose invitation to join me aboard a boat is a good start.

This is new to me, too. I've never cared about a girl in Freshwater because they were all relations. Although she doesn't get into it much when she stops by our meadow, she has hinted enough at her disgust with some of Americans she has met. She's madder with them, though, for the way they destroyed her home and her town.

"They thinks they can have whoever they wants fer a wife," she said one day. "*I* might be able t' get o'er it, but I doubt Mother an' Daddy ever will."

My selfishness found wonderful pleasure in her words, thought I wouldn't dare let on.

Nan

Some mornings to pass the time, when it's too wet to go at the hay, or just too miserable to do much else, I go over to Nan's and watch her go about her business. She has dementia. That important bit I haven't bothered to tell the Girl from up the Hill. Maybe she'll figure it out on her own, someday.

Sometimes, to Nan, it's like I'm not even there. She confuses me with the Youngfella from in the Lane, over in Placentia, where she sometimes stayed with *her* grandfather, after her husband, *my* grandfather, died.

"Me gran'fadder floated his house from Lil' Placentia in the 1880s—long before they started callin' it *Argentia*," she tells me for about the one-hundredth time.

"Yes, b'y," I act surprised. "'Magine now!"

Should I interrupt her, tell her I'm not the Youngfella from in the Lane—I'm her grandson? Nah! She's fine in her own little world. Sometimes I wish *I* had no mind. Sometimes, I also wonder if my mind has left me and everything I think and do is just made up. I guess these are the sorts of things you think about when you spend lots of time with someone losing their mind.

From certain stories she's told me, I gather Nan was happy with her husband early in their marriage. But after most of their children died, he was never that nice to her. At least, that's what she says.

"One after the other they went," she says of her dead youngsters—her eyes as vacant as her deceased husband's homemade chair.

There's one thing that seems to be a great source of contentment for her, though. She often talks of a man, a Mr. Morrissey—*The Lovely Mr. Morrissey*, she often calls him while speaking of his gallant ways. I believe she secretly loved him.

"He knew yer gran'fadder from down home, in Lil' Placentia," Nan says. "Tradin' fish fer supplies an' got t' be friends in them long line-ups on the wharf. A nice man, he was. Never spoke t' me any different than he'd talk wit' a man. I wonder if he's still alive?"

"I don't know, Nan, sorry," I say.

"Ya knows the way most men can easily talk down t' women, yet depend upon 'em fer ev'ry little thing?"

"I 'spose," I say, unsure of the right reply.

"Well, he wasn't like that, Mr. Morrissey."

"Very good," I say.

She refers to my dead grandfather as the *Crooked Auld Bastard*, or *Himself* which is usually a proper insult coming from those who use such names for people with proper birth names—as if they can't stand them and wouldn't lower themselves to utter their real names. I'd like to know more about him in case I ever have children of my own one day—something to tell them—but I never know how Nan's going to react when I bring him up. So, most times, I don't bother.

I don't know, for sure, if the things she speaks of ever happened or if they are just things she'd wished had happened—now that she's not herself anymore. But she's all I have left in a way: my only link to the past. So, every moment with her, whether her mind is lucid or not, is a treasure. The day will come, I know, when she'll be cold in the ground up on the hill, alongside her family, old friends, and neighbours from

Argentia and Marquise, Himself included.

"He could've had his own plot," Nan says, "but that would mean upkeep an' maybe even one day the expense of a headstone. Not likely. Memory of 'im is headstone enough."

"Yer alive, Nan, girl," I say, trying to change her mood, "an' that's plenty o' reason t' smile."

"I 'spose, b'y," she says, tossing her head.

Nan hasn't been right since her Argentia home was burnt. Still, she's luckier than most of the folks of those towns who are hove together like rats in old shacks and people's leaky sheds and half-rotten barns—all waiting for houses promised them by the British and American governments.

"Compensation they calls it," Nan says, looking straight into my eyes. "Huh! Fer drivin' us away from our home."

"There's a big war happenin' again, Nan," I say, regretting my words the moment they fell out of my mouth. "To prepare against the mad German, Hitler, an' his armies an' navy lurkin' beneath the surface o' the sea in what they calls *submarines*."

"Sure, yer just as bad as them, if ya b'lieves the like o' that," she scowls.

"I'm only sayin' what I read in the Daily News."

I end my sentence there. There's no point in trying to persuade her, otherwise. I let out a little laugh, trying to disarm her reasonable, angry stance. The only hope of her mad rant stopping is for her mind to slip to another place and time. I feel bad for wishing that, but I don't want to spend my whole visit arguing worthlessly with someone I love who may or may not be here tomorrow. I decide to try one last line to see if she'll bother understanding. Then again, I have no right trying to convince an old woman there's really a good reason for strangers burning her home to the ground and then driving her away from all she'd ever known. But I give it another shot, anyway.

"They says our 22s fer gettin' birds an' even our shotguns fer moose would never stand up t' the big guns the Germans uses. I don't know; I hope we never has t' find out."

As I'm talking about guns and Germans, I can almost see Nan's mind float out the window.

"Who's that out there?" she asks, looking back at me.

"Where, Nan?" I ask. "I don't see anyone."

"Out 'longside the fence, b'y," she says, as if there's something wrong with me for not seeing what she sees.

"Oh, that's only Mr. Bruce from next door," I lie—her neighbour from Argentia long dead—hoping she'll go along with me and relax.

"That's not Mr. Bruce, b'y!" she says, tut-tutting. "Jesus Christ! Get yer eyes checked, b'y! I b'lieves ya needs spectacles, ya crooked auld bastard."

Knowing she sees her dead husband now and not me, I'm not sure what I should say. I got what I wished for and now I wish we were talking about Germans and guns again, even if I wasn't getting a sensible response from her.

"Oh!" I stammer, "it must be one of his youngfellas then; I can't really see through the steam on the pane."

"No, b'y!" she says, a little nicer this time. "They're not belonged t' anyone 'round here. They're comin' in the lane. Go t' the door, luh, an' see what they wants. Go on, now! An' don't go invitin' strangers in; I've nothing t' give 'em. Queer time o' the day fer anyone t' be comin' to yer door."

In the few moments it takes me to get up from the table, walk out to the porch, open the door, close it again and come back into the kitchen, Nan is asleep on the daybed. Her delicate legs are hanging halfway over the side. She's out cold. I pick up her crocheted quilt at the end of the bed, unfold it and place it gently over her little body half covering her Mammy's quilts and blankets. Nan never stirs.

She must have gone to the side window to see if she could see who she thought was out in the yard. To get a good look out that window, you must kneel on the daybed and lean forward with your hands resting on the wide sill. When she heard me closing the door, she must have turned to get back to the table, afraid I'd think she was being a news bag. Instead, the softness of the quilted daybed and its comforting feather pillow lulled her into its soothing embrace.

It is during times like this when I try to realize the wanderings of her thoughts. It must be exhausting for her in every way, the poor, old soul. I'm glad I don't have to tell her there's no one outside.

She's been reliving that awful day since—when the Americans came to tell her she had to leave her home for good, then set it ablaze as she was leaving. She was hardly *not* going to look back at it.

"The Crooked Auld Bastard," Nan begins, "That was as useless…never made it out o' Lil' Placentia alive."

"Oh!" I say, acting surprised at the information.

"He was sick when the demolition of the place began," Nan says, "an' his sister, God rest her soul, said his heart couldn't stand the madness. He died sittin' on the step o' our place. He could see an' hear an' smell the gas an' flames, see, an' his heart wasn't able for it."

"Jesus, Nan," that's hard stuff," I say. "I didn't know."

"Well," she says, banging her fist off the table, "he was

certainly no good t' me alive an' he's twice as useless dead—the Crooked Auld Bastard."

I understand her reason, not that it's a *good* reason, for hating her husband—for *dying* amid such upheaval. She was left to gather most of their sparse possessions before being forced into a shed in Marquise which, by that time, hadn't been ruined. Nan resented the fact *he* got to be buried in one of Argentia's graveyards where a few generations of both their families lay in peace. Until now, that is. She still cursed on him when they skidded in the muddy road with his body amongst other bodies and human remains aboard a big, loud truck on its way to the graveyard up the hill.

"No pleasin' that one," My Brother always said of Nan.

An old widow had died—one of the Kellys—descended from the first Irish people who first settled in Freshwater. She was a lovely, strong, and smart woman, I've been told. Nan knew a distant cousin of the deceased woman and was able to get the newly vacated home. It is anything but new, but good enough for Nan's needs. Me and My Brother often say Nan certainly had her mind then, and that not all that long ago. At first, she refused to come up here and stay with us, so she made do in temporary shelters in Marquise, like lots of other displaced people, until she could no longer stand the humiliation, the degradation. *I felt like a cornered rat, alt'gedder, in that place*, she often says. *The Yanks had tore away all the land around it an' 'tis a wonder it didn't fall into the bog like everyt'ing else down there.*

"Sick an' tired of it all, b'y," she says, laughing—although I know she is anything but happy. "I dreams 'bout it a lot, ya know. I sees the big bulldozer—its great big Jesus metal bucket knockin' down the walls of our house 'fore they set fire to it. I'll ne'er get o'er it."

"I know, Nan. I know."

By the time a local committee convened at Argentia and convinced the Americans to, at least, bulldoze homes, the emotional damage had been done. For many, like Nan, it's doubtful the bitterness will ever go away.

"How would ya know?" she barks. "Ya weren't there! Ya had t' go an' die, ya useless good-fer-nutting."

"Ya told me 'bout it lots, that's all."

"Oh," she says, searching the walls and ceiling for proof she knows what I say is true. She tosses her head in disgust. "I 'spose, b'y."

The old house is way too vast—no need of her having such a big place, stairs, and all, at her age and in her poor state of mind.

"I goes t' bed ev'ry night, b'y, like ev'ryone else, why?" she says.

"Ya seems tired, that's all," I say.

I don't bother to say, but she mustn't sleep much. She's always sitting up prim and proper in her rocking chair, like she's expecting company and is ready to pour the boiling kettle at a moment's notice.

She tells me of things she did today, or yesterday, or what she plans to do once I'm seen to. I never ask her for anything. Sometimes, a week passes before I get a chance to stop over here for a decent visit. I just enjoy the change, the break from the wind and salty spray beating the face off me down on the beach or out on the sea.

"Me tea buns didn't turn out right—not fit t' eat," she says, almost embarrassed. "Throw 'em out if ya like."

"Go on, Nan, girl," I say, laughing. "Yer baked buns, raisins or not, are the best ever I had."

I feel safe talking about my feelings for the Girl from up the

Hill around Nan because I know she won't often remember the next day. Or at least that's what I think.

Daybed

Pain in my shoulders tells of rain. It could be days away, but not likely that far off. We need rain. The pain will leave then. At least, *that* pain. It might be my nerves, too. I daydream of walking in the rain with the Girl from up the Hill, of lying with her in the sunned meadow behind her house—where no one could see us.

Uncle Din is drunk, passed out on the daybed again. Herself, his wife, bawls out from their doorway up the hill, wondering where he is, and why the wood isn't yet clove up and brought in the porch.

"Ya need never t'ink you'll be gettin' in 'longside me this night, eidder," she roars out. "An' God help ya if ya tries."

Me and My Brother laugh our heads off. Uncle Din stirs, grunts, turns over to face us at our kitchen table chairs and laughs before a fit of coughing.

"Wha's she after sayin' now, b'ys?" he asks, tossing his head.

"Same ole stuff," My Brother says.

Uncle Din nurses a mouthful of liquor, swallows it, smiles, rolls his eyes, and falls back to sleep.

I wonder if the Girl from up the Hill hears Herself and what she thinks.

"Not like Uncle Din's the only drunk man in Freshwater," My Brother says, laughing. "Don't fret!"

We joke, imagining what Herself does to Uncle Din when he finally makes it up the hill and staggers in the door. We imagine her waiting, savage, with her rolling pin ready to beat him with—her hair right wild from pulling on it, and she is fuming, trampling the floorboards. Their poor youngsters. Still, we laugh.

We say we're glad we are where we are. Uncle Din mumbles the same, and how he can't understand why she gets so mad. Then, I'm sure I'd never drink like him if I was lucky enough to marry the girl I'd like to have.

"Jesus Christ, sure, the Yanks are givin' it away," he mumbles, smiling over the seemingly endless supply of booze. "'Tis not like before an' all we had was moonshine," he goes on, "'cept fer the scattered bottle o' rum from St. Pierre an' ya needs a letter from the Man Above t' get that."

When Uncle Din gets up and says put the kettle on, we sit together at the table, the three of us, and talk.

"I heared the American Government signed a lease t' be here, down in Argentia, fer ninety-nine year," Uncle Din says.

Me and My Brother must have been thinking the same thing when we burst out laughing, trying to guess how much Uncle Din will be after drinking by the time the Americans leave. We're pretty sure Herself will have him killed long before that lease runs out.

"Wha?" Uncle Din says.

With one last gulp, he finishes his drink and pushes himself away from the table. He gets up, grabs his knitted cap from the back of a chair where he'd tossed it earlier, and heads to the door.

"Alright," he says, waving one of his big hands at the air.

That's how Uncle Din says good-bye, *alright.*

Another night half gone, with a few hours left to dream about how I can make that lovely Girl from up the Hill all mine.

Someday, I think, smiling to myself. My restlessness in the squeaky bed disturbs My Brother. Rather than cursing me this time, he laughs.

"Ya better act quick, b'y, before she runs off an' marries one o' them good-lookin' Yanks wit' the white teet' an' fancy shirts an' foolish pants wit' no wrinkles."

"P'raps I'll get the nerve t'morrow," I say.

"Mind now," he says. "Go t' sleep outta it, b'y."

Dreams of Old

Now and then in Nan's mind, her house is mad alive with the voices of her children—punishment, someone once told her, for not going to church anymore. *Don't be so foolish*, she tells herself, *'tis only the wind.* She rocks away in an old chair, paying little mind to the steaming kettle.

She wonders if in her dreams tonight she'll walk into her childhood home in Argentia. Not that *she* calls it *Argentia.* It will always be Little Placentia to her.

"Some never liked the name, *Lil' Placentia*," she says, "but I always thought it special. Got a lovely ring to it, haven't it?"

"It does," I agree.

"'Tis never where it really is," she says of her house. "I don't understand that—dreams. 'Tis always down in Marquise, where I can look across the harbour an' see the back o' Daddy's fish store. Queer t'ings, dreams."

She frets most nights, half afraid her dreams will take her to the strange house in Marquise and she won't be able to make her way across Marquise Neck and back to Argentia because the tide is up.

"'Tis hard t' tell what's a dream an' what's not, anymore," she says, sighing.

Nan was twelve when her father died.

"That must be handy on eighty year ago now, I 'spose," she guesses.

She was most fond of and closest to her grandfather. In her

dreams, he never comes out of the parlour. He doesn't even talk to her. His dirty looks bring her shame, and she wishes he'd be the way he really was when he was living—gentle, kind, forgiving of her being a child doing childish things. They used to go by boat to the woods around a place called *The Sound* from Little Placentia, just the two of them, walk up into the woods and take rabbits from his slips.

"We loved bein' t'gedder," she says. "Oh my! I still finds it hard t' call home *Argentia*," she says, half laughing. "No odds what they calls it now, is there, b'y? I hear 'tis in an awful way down there."

People think her strange because it has been called Argentia for a long time.

"What odds about what they think, Nan," I say. "And what odds what's it's called now. 'Twill never be the same, anyhow."

"'Twas the best place in the world fer bakeapples one time," she recalls. "I wonder if there are any left down there, now? Plenty o' rabbits, too."

"I heard ya can't get near the marshes for the wire fences with barbed-wire on top," I say.

As if she has forgotten about bakeapples, she mentions her grandfather again. He was clearly her favourite, by far, it seems. He always roughed up her hair, grinning his toothless grin in exchange for her shy smile.

"I can see 'im now," she says, smiling her own toothless grin, "standin' in the doorway to the stairs, hands 'pon his lower back wit' curse words t' match his pain from t'ousands o' days standin' in a dory, hand-linin' an' haulin' trawls. Then he'd scuff his way to the daybed an' *heave to*, as he'd say, fer a spell. No trouble t' miss 'im."

Once, she dreamt her grandfather told her details of an old

story she'd been longing to know of. She added it to the long list of stories kept stored in her head and would never again get to dish out details to company every night in her Argentia kitchen—the way she did for more than fifty or sixty years.

"I 'spose they'll never visit here like they did down home, will they?" she asks.

"I think they will, Nan," I say. "When everyone gets settled into their new homes an' gets used to their surroundings."

"That'd be nice," she says.

"Yes," I try to cheer her up, "ya knows people will want t' know where yer livin' an' how yer gettin' on."

"Mostly, though," she says, "in me dreams, me gran'fadder stands straight-faced an' wordless. How I wishes fer once he'd be the way he was he when he was alive. Hates auld dreams."

"Hope ya has happy dreams t'night, Nan," I say, standing to haul on my coat.

"Please, God," she says.

I'm dying to tell her about how I'll be at a party this Saturday night at the Girl from up the Hill's house, now that it's finally fit for them to live in. I decide telling Nan will only add to my time here and I need a good night's rest to spend tomorrow sawing wood, leaving time to shave and wash.

"'Night, Nan. See ya t'morrow."

"Mind yerself on the step," she says. "'Tis awfully black out there; yer liable t' break yer neck."

At Last

Though most Argentia and Marquise folks may have left their hearts in their hometowns, with pride and a hard-earned sense of entitlement, ferociously they carried with them their divine right for a good time—the singing, dancing, drinking, storytelling, recitations, and spontaneous skits—it all happened on Saturday nights. It still does.

I was apprehensive at first about going to the Girl from up the Hill's house, but I was hardly going to stay home. I was relieved their new home was completed, but sad for them that the father never lived to see it finished. In a way, it wasn't unlike my grandfather's story—dying on the steps of his Argentia home as strangers doused the clapboard with gasoline while hurrying his family to leave forever. The Girl from up the Hill's father had been sick for ages and no one is surprised he is in the graveyard alongside the remains of other family members and friends.

"At least we didn't have t' dig him up an' have t' re-bury him down the road there like so many other families," I overhear the mother telling another woman.

As the night wears on and the drink provides me with unnatural courage, the more I long for the Girl from up the Hill to be in my arms. It all plays out in my tired head—when the crowd leaves, and all hands, old and young alike are seen to, showed to their beds or to a space on the floor: the ones too drunk to send out into the spring gale of raw wind and bitter cold, if they behave themselves, everyone agrees—she'll long for me the same as I long for her. Only God knows what might happen after that, so I pray.

The Girl from up the Hill seems to try everything in her knowing to get me to leave, there'll be another night. But perhaps that's just my bad mind. She seems so scared of something. But I'm sure it will be worth the wait—the agonizing she's put me through since I first set eyes on her.

She comes to me, her eyes tired, but aglow with that sparkle: the one which lured me to her in the first place, long before she ever knew I existed. Her head of yellow, messy-from-dancing, yet-full-of-life hair falls to the right with the direction of her tired head. Still, she makes her way towards me, across the kitchen. My heart strikes my chest for a way out of my shirt. My mouth goes dry, as my twisted tongue attempts to inconspicuously lick the inside of my mouth sewn shut with mortification and doubly sealed by my bad nerves. I try to appear normal while looking around the kitchen like an idiot while my now-drier-than-ever tongue searches without blessing for a morsel of saliva to keep me from choking to death and ruining the newness of their home with the remembrance of my pathetic demise.

"Ya can go t' bed now, Mother," she says in a sympathetic tone to her mother who's standing at the bottom of the stairs and who has made up a bed for herself on the settle (the Americans call them *chesterfields*).

The mother hasn't slept in her own bedroom since her husband died. She says nothing, only barely tosses her head in acknowledgment and looks at me with disapproving eyes—yet with hint enough of acceptance or understanding of how I might really feel about her little girl. She's seen us talking lots down by our meadow gate, and surely, she'll never forget my willingness to drop my work and help them with their belongings that first long day of their arrival at Freshwater.

"Mug-up?" she asks in a tone begging please don't say yes, I haven't the strength nor the desire to tend on you.

"No, that's alright," I say, and I mean it.

The last thing I want is to sit across the table from the Girl from up the Hill with a mug of scalding hot tea to spill, trembling more than I already am with desire.

It doesn't seem that long ago when I got the nerve to mosey up to her—thanks to the fact the bottom fell out of the brown paper bag from the Trading Company as she was lugging it up the Back Path. It wasn't like she didn't know I watched her every move, up and down the hill. It is a small town; it always will be.

"Fancy a hand there?" I asked like a moron.

"I 'spose," she said, half-crooked at first.

Hadn't I been arse over kettle in love with her, I would have thought *Pick the goddamn things up yourself, then.*

I took an empty, somewhat-clean flour sack from the back pocket of my overalls and got down on all fours like an idiot—an idiot madly in love and happy to be at her feet at last. I put the tins of beans in first, then the wool she'd bought for her mother, a little toy of some sort for her sick little brother, and no net-knitting needle for her father who lay barely cold in his grave on the hill.

Her father being dead surely has something to do with me being invited to her house for this party, although it's not like he was ever ignorant to me. He always said hello to me in the mornings on his way down to his boat. He never lived long enough to find a berth for his cod trap. I'd be in one of my usual spots—in the meadow alongside the dirt road tending to our cows and horse, or down on the beach getting our boat ready to go out and set trawls or check our trap. Once, he asked me why me and My Brother bothered keeping a trap in that spot because of the current there. Yes, it was often pummeled by random, unexpected waves which ripped around The Point, and we've spent many hours pounding the steel frame of the cod trap's leader back into shape, but its bounty is often worth the extra work. We could have placed it elsewhere, but our family has used that spot for a leader to a trap for the past three or four generations—it serves us well, and we aren't about to let it go to another crowd.

"'Tis worth the beatin' it takes from riptides an' storms," I told him. "The fish takes to it; we've never been hungry."

"That's good," he said, smiling, and he meant both his words and smile.

I know those rocks as well as I know anything and I'm used to keeping a dory steady and away from the cliff, so the boat doesn't get beat up. But, yes, her father was a kind, considerate man, the kind who wouldn't pass you without greeting you.

Codding myself is what I was at most of the time, especially during the winter, shoveling snow to make a path to the barn where I did little all day long—only carving her name into the stalls and posts because God knows she'd never have reason to set foot in there and notice it. I did less in spring because it's still winter in Newfoundland—waiting for the ground to thaw, waiting for the ice to leave the harbour. Waiting.

I have to say, I have missed him, her father: walking down the road, full of the confidence I knew he'd bestowed upon the girl of my dreams, his daughter. I admired that, *confidence*, in anyone. My Brother got all the self-assurance in our family, what's left of us. I wish I'd scrounged a bit of it, myself, along the way.

Maybe now is my turn. My chance. Now, it's just me and her: the Girl from up the Hill, the Prettiest Girl in Freshwater, and all the other designations of fondness my heart has secretly bequeathed her existence.

"I b'lieve the poor old kettle could use a break," I say, trying to sound witty.

"Yes, b'y, I'd say yer right," she says, forcing a laugh. "'Tis late. Do ya wanna come up to me room fer a while?"

With those words from her lips, I go numb. I'll never forget it. It's like the glass in her mother's window has stopped rattling above the table, and like her mother can't hear us from the small front room where she pretends to be sleeping. I wonder why she's inviting me to her room, but I'm not about to ask and chance frigging it up.

Death in Her Kitchen

I wonder if she can hear my heart pounding against my good shirt, partly sweaty from dancing to the accordion half the night. I was conscious not to dance too much, for that reason, for *this* reason—should it ever come to this—unless *she* was the one grabbing me by the arm and swinging me around the floor. I dare say I'd have danced till I dropped.

I was perpetually disappointed at not having her as my own, and I died a thousand deaths every time another fellow whipped her up from a chair to dance. At those moments I was glad to be wearing only a suit half damp, my Sunday best—nothing a few minutes standing against the dying heat of the big kitchen stove wouldn't cure. Fast-moving feet danced in perfect rhythm to the notes of the accordion player, a Smith from Marquise, while striking curse words were conceived on the spot as ankles banged off the heavy steel frame of the daybed full of coats and fellows passed out.

For some reason, my ears flutter and I wonder if she has noticed. Surely, my face is redder than ever now. I pray the low light of the late night or early morning, whatever time it is, hides that. Suddenly, my throat is as dry as the brook trickling through the middle of Freshwater at the height of summer. I have to bite my tongue to get enough spit to run into my throat before I can answer. I pretend to be fiddling around with the lifter and one of the dampers of the stove while she waits for my reply. Then I proceed to tuck my shirt into my pants, like you'd do when no one is around.

She laughs.

"Well, b'y," she sounds put off, "I won't be askin' ya a second time."

The beauty of her lips knocks me back, the way they curl at the ends, even more so when she smiles. The low light of the kerosene lantern between us, next to the dirty bowls not long ago full of turkey-neck soup, drags shadows across her face now more precious than ever. She drops her head in anticipation of an answer, but her lips hold onto that smile, as if she knows my reply—if I don't soon drop dead with fright.

Feeling dry and fresher the heat of the stove, I rest my elbows on the table. Still, I say nothing. She continues to smile. I can go the way of self-doubt and its subsequent pity or feel guilty for being there at such a late hour. But tomorrow, *today*, is Sunday: a day of rest for her, for me, for the whole town. All we have to do is go to Mass in the morning—always a great spectacle and sure to be a good laugh with all hands still drunk from the night before, the giggles from the youngsters and old alike when the priest, hung-over himself, takes his sweet time lapping wine from the fancy chalice. Then, after a beer or two at the club, priest and all, the day will be ours.

The sun is getting stronger each day, although the wind is still icy—but there can hardly be a better combination than cold and a beautiful girl. Uncle Din would say, *If God made any better, He kept it for Himself.* Each morning I say a little prayer to encourage the sun's warmth to hold off: lots of time for days too hot to do anything and for the flies to feast on us. The cold is more likely to suggest to the Girl from up the Hill that she'd be better off in my arms, rather than outdoors bivering and forced home without me.

It seems like forever for ample air to be dragged into my lungs in order for me to get enough wind to force out a word or two. My mind wonders how to utter a phrase without looking more stupid than I already do. Then I feel the air, a bit more relaxed, easing its way from my chest to, God help me, my mouth. I keep my lips closed for a moment while my tongue flips underneath itself for a crumb of wetness. There's no fear of me spitting at her, at least. It's a good thing. Still, I can't get a word out. Painfully, I try to swallow the excuse for moisture tormenting my mouth.

Instead, I slide my left hand across the flowery tablecloth—the soft material I'd chased only two weeks ago into Dunphy's Meadow like a dog chasing a butterfly. I caught hold of it and sauntered to the Back Path like I'd saved someone's life. Then, without a scrap of couth, I stuffed the colourful cloth into the sack. It's a wonder she's allowing me here at all.

At the table, I want to extend my right hand to her, but the lantern and dirty dishes are in the way. The left hand will have to do. I'm careful not to shove the lantern too close to her mother's drapes, afraid I'll set fire to the house and then there'll be nothing but screaming and running and no forgiveness and certainly no chance of a *real* kiss. Her eyes leave mine and wait for my hand's journey to end. I keep looking back and forth between my own hand, seemingly with intentions of its own, and her charming face. Watching my hand is akin to observing another creature—an animal with its own thoughts and will and destination. At least something here has a bit of nerve.

When she starts to move her hand towards mine, my mouth goes completely dry again and my top lip sticks to my teeth. I feel like my horse—the way it looks at me first thing in the morning when it's parched. I'm about to panic but, as discreetly as possible, I try to find my tongue again—to entice it to stir for the greater good of mankind and jam it between my teeth without looking like I might be about to take a bite out of her hand once I catch hold of it.

My hand finally reaches its intended spot and I manage to pry my teeth apart enough to give my tongue a good bite, to get some juices flowing again. At the same time, inspired by the drink no doubt, I imagine my face looks as grim as one of those pious old women in church who scowl at you like you've no business under the roof of the House of God and, perhaps, they're right. But I manage to keep my smirk and sure-to-follow laugh out of sight. I swallow, just in time, when our hands meet. It feels like a life-long journey has ended. It is clearly a gulp, not a swallow, but I am *touching* the love of my life. I don't care about anything else. I am really touching *her*. Now what?

The moment our fingers entwine, her eyes move slowly up my best shirt until they latch onto my eyes which must have look like they've seen a ghost. Her smile grows and, with more vigor than ever, my heart beats frantically. I look down to make sure my heart is still where it's supposed to be—that I'm not bleeding all over her mother's good tablecloth I'd heard her complain cost seventy cents or more. I expect the Girl from up the Hill to call me thoughtless for not yet answering, but she seems content just holding my hand.

As we watch each other, I take a deeper breath and squeeze her fingers. I imagine she sees my fingers as extensions of my tethered heart, as they try to say what my tongue cannot. When she squeezes back, it starts all over—the dry mouth. My beet-red ears are ready to take flight and get me out of the awkwardness I'm unquestionably bestowing upon myself. But her smile never wanes, and I feel sort of calm.

"Well?" she says.

Her smile is bigger than ever, as the first bits of daylight play lazily behind the closed drapes of the window next to us. Tiny flecks of light gradually bring her lovely hair back to life. She doesn't care about that, her hair in a state, and I couldn't love her more for it. Tiredness tugs at the exquisite, pale skin beneath her blue eyes whose colour intensifies with every allowance of light given up by the thick drapes. If I could, I'd tell the sun to go back to bed out of it and to leave us be. But I know time isn't a thing to be wasted, ever. Especially now. I keep my focus on her eyes and relish the warmth and every vibration offered by her hand.

"Yer mother?" I ask, trying to seem like I care who's in the house.

"She knows," she whispers. "'Tis alright."

Her eyes appear more caring with each long passing second. It's as though ten years has passed since she'd first said it, that her mother knows. Knows *what*? The pope, himself, could be warming his bare feet on the oven door and I couldn't care less. I'm as close to Heaven as I'll ever be.

Courage overtakes me and I stand fast to my beliefs and true feelings. For the first time in my life, even though fate still screams she won't be mine forever, I don't listen. Why should I? Some people never live long enough to have a moment like this, and if they do, they probably make a fine mess of it. But she seems sure of something and is doing a lovely job, once again, of keeping my heart from exploding.

She knows what? I think to myself, again. What's *okay?* Have I been that obvious? I suppose so and say to myself *what odds, it's too late now and God knows I'll never have this chance again.* I guess something in my face changes, and I look as though I know what she means, what her mother means. She lets go of my hand.

My world falls apart. I've fooled up, again. It's all over.

I try to find my legs so I can make a sheepish getaway through the back door.

"What are ya doin?" she asks, smiling.

I sit again, confused.

She had only let go of me so she could slide her chair back as quietly as possible.

She gets up from the table and makes her way to me. I stay seated, not knowing what to do, as she stands above me, looking through me. She reaches for my hand again. This time, she takes them both and lets herself fall back, as inviting me to stand. I do. Then, realizing the height I have over her, I sit again, sort of sideways on the chair. I gently take her close to me. The back of my head is numb with fright, but still, I hold on to her.

"Have a drink, b'y," she says, laughing a little, anxious to continue whatever is happening.

The last thing I need is another drink, afraid I'll end up like Uncle Din with her bawling at me night and day. I am surely convinced I look the part of the poor parched horse in the morning, but she's too nice to say.

From a glass jug she pours water into a tumbler. I sip at it, and it saves me from further humiliation. I decide to waste no more time. I keep hold of her left hand and let go of the right. I move my right hand slowly up the arm of her white wool sweater and touch her neck. I stop to take another sip of water.

My hand breaks out in sweat the moment I feel her hair. I'm afraid she'll think I'm dirty or something, and then tell me to go away. *Don't ever come back*. But she doesn't say a word, only keeps her full lips in that smile which has long since owned my heart and keeps me around like a starving, simple, stray dog.

Her eyes remain focused on mine. Her dimples—the ones I've melted over a million times—are just shadows in the sluggish light of the day's dawning. How I want to touch them with my fingers and thumb, to see if they are still there, if it is possible for anything God has made to be this flawless, this comforting. But I'm afraid it might be strange to her. I have no idea if she's ever been this close to another. Perhaps she'll change her mind last minute. But she doesn't.

Until this moment, I thought there was nothing more spectacular, more real, more vibrant, than the shimmering sea illuminated by a full moon, Larkin's Pond first thing in the morning, trout breaching its silky surface, and the smell of alders as me and My Brother muck along the railway bed wondering what would ever become of Freshwater with all the new people moved in—those decimated by Hitler's worrisome words against this side of the world. No longer are we just *us*, easy-going, hard fighting, forgiving, loving drunks on Saturday nights. All of a sudden, the rest of the world knows where we live. And *that* scares me. Scares all of us. But that fear, the sea, the pond, the track all disappears because she's near me. I can smell her skin and I long to taste it, her. The little, wonderful now-half-evil smirk never leaves her luscious lips, as I tremble between folly and anxious awareness of the esteemed moment.

I wonder to myself if it's okay to look away, to admire her hair at such closeness, or move my head nearer and study the contours of her well-toned shoulders peeking through the attractive knitted sweater, feel her neck and watch my fingers move slowly along it. But I don't. I'm scared to look away from the eyes I've been dreaming about for so long. What if I look away and it disturbs her? Hurts her feelings. She isn't one for saying how she feels mind you, but those eyes tell it all. And now I can't believe what they're saying. At least I pray to Holy God that she's really thinking what I'm thinking. Confession to the priest in the dark, fousty box in a back room of the church will liberate me from my sinful thoughts.

Her hair caresses the back of my trembling hand. As hard as I try to move my eyes to her lovely head, I can't; yet her hair's softness is every bit as precious and pleasing as I'd fantasized it would be. It hangs around her little round face, and she is more fine-looking than anyone could dream of. The feel of the skin of her neck reminds me of the rubber bands you put around lobster claws, but I can hardly tell her that. It is soft yet bound with elasticity. My mouth, no longer a desert, yearns to find a way to lure her head down closer to mine, but again I'm afraid of messing up—I'd messed up my lifetime, and this is a chance not to. I choose to remain the coward I am and see if she'll do anything about things that I cannot seem to bring myself to instigate.

When she blinks, my heart hits my chest again. I gulp. She smiles. My heart hits the walls of my soul this time. I feel faint. More water. I'd practiced my smile in the little mirror My Brother keeps by the kitchen sink. I try to remember how I think I look best. Then I'm afraid I'll screw it up and make one of the queer faces I use to get My Brother to laugh when it's just me and him and sometimes Uncle Din, too—people who understand each other and know their town and the people in it and the best ones to make fun—lots of material because someone's always doing something off their head in Freshwater.

When my thoughts leave the mirror, my rehearsed smiles, and my regular funny faces for My Brother and Uncle Din, she—the Girl from up the Hill—is still right there. Never stirred. I feel I've been away with my reflections so long she'd have gone to bed out of it long ago, and I'd be left trying to find my way out the back porch in the lingering drunkenness of what's been the longest Saturday night of my life.

My heart bounces around again, as she lowers herself to her knees—never letting go of my hand or moving so my other hand will slip from her shoulder, her neck, her perfect, honeyed hair. *What the hell is she doing?* I'll never ask.

View of the Valley

Still knelt in front of me, she's holding my hand, and looking into my tired eyes that must be blurting how foolishly in love with her I am. Instead of the long-awaited meeting of our lips, she smiles a little more, just when I couldn't have imagined it being better, more pleasing. She lays her beautiful head across my lap. Her left arm moves up around my waist, inside my shirt a little. My mouth goes dry again. I reach for the tumbler and let the last drop of water lugged in from her mother's well that night trickle past the thousand lumps in my throat.

At what point do you tell someone you love them? Never. Not at this point anyway. I'm not *that* stupid. But supposing she's never known the true love of anyone but her parents and little brother, she must feel the eternal adoration every spec of my being casts upon her—especially this night.

When she pulls back and invites me to stand, I know it's all over; I've finally messed up any chance I might have had of winning her true affection. I waited too long, and her patience has run out. In my mind I am moping across the floor, heading out the back door.

"Wait!" she says. "I have to go the outhouse t' make me water; I'll be right back."

"If ya don't mind," I ask, "can I follow ya? Not to the outhouse, mind, but anywhere in the garden."

She bursts out laughing at my awkwardness.

"Yes b'y," she says, her lips never once letting go of that smile. "Go where ya like."

As she goes into the outhouse, the light from the kerosene lantern she's holding parts with her leave. There's plenty of light for me from the fading night sky, as I stand behind the bushes and relieve the jug of water I'd downed in my state of anxiety.

The line I once imagined impossible to cross lies scuffed and crumpled on her mother's kitchen floor. The feeling left on my lap and upon my hands and arms picks at my being in a playful way. The darkness often casing my thoughts swiftly vanishes behind all the dippers and virgins and lions and whatever else they've named the impossible clusters of stars in the clearest sky ever. Then, as quickly as that, the constellations seep backwards into the night from which they came. In their place is the most lovely, unforgettable morning I've ever known.

What a relief, I think, smiling, *she doesn't want me to leave*. The cleanest air I've ever taken into my lungs restores my newfound confidence and purges my mind and body of its self-inflicted feebleness.

Yes, the air is heavenly: spruce needles, wet from last night's cold rain, freshly cut hay from the many meadows of our growing, yet still-little town, the salt air from the sea now calm and inviting, waiting to flaunt its beauty to those who'll walk to Mass in a couple of hours, the chill running down my spine at the knowing I am awake for once and not dreaming, and for some reason, I feel it will be okay—the rest of this day.

No more do I fear my neediness will give her reason to drive me away like a lost cow or sheep. The darkness sliding below the horizon takes with it the eerie shadows which not long ago covered the sea and hills. Our harbour full of boats on collar boasts untold exquisiteness, and even though it's a Sunday, and no fishing will be carried out, it's awfully tempting. The rows of freshly painted white picket fences separating the well-kept front yards of houses, mostly saltboxes, across the road stretch in the growing light to welcome this day of rest. My heart continues to pound with untold excitement, as I peer from behind a cluster of young spruce trees, Septembers Mists, alders, and rosebushes.

Old women and old men in their Sunday best, all driven from Argentia and Marquise not all that long ago, putter around their homes, killing time before worshipping the Lord down in the church, gently pulling weeds while adoring their flowers and plants. The women, their just-so hair beneath bandanas, wear neatly pressed blouses and skirts. The men, robust and wise, glow in all their finery: double-breasted waistcoats, tweed vests and straight-as-whip ties. Their knitted salt and pepper caps will stay on their heads until placed in their hands at Mass. The freshly polished, black shoes of those women and men glisten in the rising light while morning dew clings stubbornly to the grass.

Though I keep my body turned in the direction of the wooded hill out of respect, should someone notice me, I can't turn my head away from that spectacle of simplicity. Between two homes across the way I watch shadows slog themselves past clotheslines tied around trees and kept up by longers. Behind those trees are cliffs two-hundred feet or more above rocks and sea—the hidden Sandy Beach where I've always dreamt of hiding from the world with just the Girl from up the Hill by my side. The long lots of land holding the relatively new homes have been marked and divided into lots drawn for Freshwater's new-fangled residents; the head of each household's name has been written alongside the lot number. *'Tisn't Argentia or Marquise*, I've heard many of them say, but it's hard for them not to appreciate the sights from these heights—a different world, altogether, because Argentia, especially, had been moderately flat in comparison to Freshwater.

I size up the top of Castle Hill, the ruins of a French fortress overlooking our beach, the town of Freshwater, itself—the place the French named *La Fontaine*—and the entrance to our harbour.

Fingers of fog, thicker than woodsmoke, reach in over the beach and crawl up the valley of the original Freshwater—*The Valley*, the new crowd call it, rightfully. The thick spruce of Castle Hill will soon disappear in the white of nature's damp, pale blanket. Just as quickly, the hill reappears, as if the fog had never existed. For these, and many other imaginings inspired by the view from this peak, I begin to understand the difference in demeanor of those who live up here and beyond. The farther down the hill you go, the saucier the youngones are, the rougher the men are, and the strong, hard-working women make no bones about not tolerating nonsense.

"Ya done?" she calls out in a loud whisper, startling me from the useless thoughts of my wandering mind.

"Yeah," I call back.

"God, b'y!" she whispers loudly. "Keep it down, 'fraid ya wake Mother."

"Sorry, girl," I say, unphased by anything—I still feel all will be fine.

From the barrel in her mother's porch, we wash our hands with soap and water before drying them with a fresh towel the Girl from up the Hill proudly admits she has made. She then takes me by the hand, through the kitchen, now cool; the dirty dishes can wait, the same for the pot on the stove with enough water from the kettle poured into it to keep the leftovers from burning onto the bottom from the lingering heat of the stove.

We pass *all* that, as my heart kicks against my chest again. She leads me up the stairs. I snicker to myself, thinking what My Brother will say. If he thought I'd floated down the road before, surely, he'll say I must have flown up the stairs this morning and could pass him on the strength of my new-fangled wings while hurrying to get in and out of Mass.

Prayin' to Die

Nan is asleep on the daybed. She dreams she's over at her grandfather's home in Placentia.

Creeping around to the small rooms, she pretends to close all the windows, so the nippers won't eat her tonight. Blue-arsed flies lie bottom-up on every sill—dormant until the natural heat wakes them again. She leaves them be.

At each stop she enjoys another look outside—across the bay to Red Island, over to Castle Hill where the French and English kept their biggest guns hundreds of years ago and up the Southeast Arm where men once raced in rowboats while women and children cheered from the shoreline of The Blockhouse.

Looking down, she gazes upon the many trees of her back garden. The moon plays up the yellow grass and the dark lines and patches of earth—once drills of vegetables. The damson tree, the apple trees and gooseberry bushes hide behind two lovely poplars while a fence of rosebushes reminds her of a thick fishing net unfurled to dry. Looking at the top of the porch, she remembers when it was just a linney allowing rain to run off and into the barrel. The wooden staves and metal rings of the barrels are on the ground of both sides of the step. She tut-tuts at the countless times she has tried to put the pieces back together but could never manage to do it. When the Youngfella from in the Lane drops in again, she knows the barrel will be put back together right and it will, once again, serve a purpose.

It's cold in bed, and she wishes it was years ago and Himself was still alive with a desire to keep her warm for longer than his own selfish two or three minutes. She wishes most of her children hadn't died one after the other from tuberculosis. Then, perhaps, Himself wouldn't have given up his smile. Hardly spoke afterwards, he never—except to grumble. What was she supposed to say back? So, she said nothing. Not even when he died. Neither did she wish him back—unless he had the youngones with him and they were running madly, having fun, in and out of the house: not sick in her arms or suffocating in their damp beds of feathers or straw.

She wishes she didn't have to see Himself tear the cap from his head and throw it on the back of the chair every day and night. She wishes never to see him at all when he's not even there. She had always heard tell of old people losing their minds, but never imagined herself old, let alone losing her mind. It was once so sharp; she'd helped half the youngsters in Little Placentia get though their school primers.

She sees no point to it all anymore. She continues looking out the bedroom window. Twisting her neck upright, she wishes the Big Dipper would fall on her—get her the hell out of this place.

Making splits and shavings is hard on her back and there are times she'd sooner be dead than having to bother with preparing a fire. She doesn't have money to buy a bit of salt beef and, even if she did, there's no one around to help her eat it. Her fretting knows no bounds.

Waking from her dream, she wipes drool from the side of her mouth; the thought of salt beef does that to her, asleep or awake. She stands, tucking her hankie back into the pocket of her apron before untying the cotton straps at the bottom on its back. She then lifts the apron over her head. The pain of a bad disc in her neck sends a hot, sharp-shooting pain down over her right shoulder blade and up the back of her head. She hooks the apron on the back of one of the chairs, then reaches to turn the damper key flat across the stove's flue leading into the chimney. She leans in over the table and looks out the window for one last glimpse at the night's version of the outdoors before she leaves the kitchen.

"'Tis fog to the ground again t'night," she says to no one.

Memories of Argentia occupy her slow steps over the uneven stairs. In her big, freshly clothed bed in the small, musty room upstairs she takes a deep breath and wonders what it would be like to die. The smell of her Argentia home burning is forever trapped in her lungs—the very thought makes her cough.

The old Freshwater house continues to groan its tune of death while the wind whirrs up and down the still-smoking chimney and into the cooling stovepipe. The rusty flue in the kitchen stovepipe below—the one she'd just turned—is pushed or pulled by the rising wind. The scraping sound immediately erases her thoughts.

The moment she lies on her feather pillow and closes her eyes, she again thinks of being dead. Someone, perhaps even a crowd, would be by tomorrow evening, after noticing she hadn't been to Mass. They'll open the windows to let out her soul. Not that she'd go far. This is all she knows, really, and it's just as well to stay here with the rest of the poor souls who lived and died down home over the past two-hundred years. Then she remembers she doesn't go to Mass anymore and figures she's liable to be dead for a year before anyone finds her. People would just as soon talk about her not going to Mass, instead of wondering if she's sick or dead.

Now that she's dead, perhaps she'll get up and go down to the parlour and her grandfather might explain to her the matter of his ways in her dreams. What a relief that would be—to sit with him the way he once was.

"Yes, me dear," her grandfather says, "there were people here to yer wake who did not'ing only talk about ya behind yer back when ya were alive, sayin' how strange ya were: dressed in black from head t' foot all them years o'er the Crooked Auld Bastard who was never that nice to ya in the first place—as if ya were the only woman 'round here dressed in black all the time an' yer poor auld husband, *God rest his soul*, they said, was no worse than the rest of the striels 'round here scroungin' the waters fer a fish."

Her grandfather's voice in her head is stolen by the rattling of the windowpane. She thinks about the things they'll likely continue to say about her when she's dead. She supposes she'll meet Himself down in the kitchen and all he'll say is *Goddamn gover'mint! Goddamn fish*, same as he always did.

Worked Some Hard

It's morning again. How I wish My Love was alongside me here in the bed, but that won't happen until we get married. My Brother finally married the missus he'd been courting for ages. Together, we cut enough wood and built a saltbox house up in the other end of our meadow for the big family they one day hope to have.

The other day marked a full year since that first kiss and that long, frightening walk up My Love's mother's stairs.

I step out into the yard and stretch towards whatever this day might have to throw at me. The wind is small and the sun big over the back garden where I'll spend the day cleaving and piling firewood. Like a well-needed rest, My Love sneaks up behind me and covers my eyes. She smells *fit t' eat*, as My Brother says.

"Nan," she says, "just told me she remembers ev'ry year pickin' damsons down home, in Argentia—only she calls it *Lil' Placentia*, as ya know. I wish we had a damson tree t' bring her some, or maybe she'd even manage t' pick a few plums, herself."

I love how My Love calls Nan *Nan*, even though she's not *her* real nan—*she's* buried, supposedly, amongst the mess of bodies and human parts hove into that big hole up on the hill a couple of years ago. I also love how My Love seems to care about Nan as much as I do.

"Ye'll make lovely babies fer me t' rock, the two o' ye—good-lookin', ye are," Nan said a while ago, embarrassing the life out of both of us.

And, of course, she couldn't leave it at that.

"'Tis not like I'm gonna be 'round forever, ya know! Ye married yet?" she added, laughing.

"Not yet," My Love answered.

Yet, I thought to myself, looking away and smirking.

"You were by Nan's already t'day?" I ask, looking into her eyes reflecting the rising sun's illumination of the cloudless sky.

The warming air dissolves the morning dew rising from the ground like steam from a kettle.

"Yes, b'y!" she says, her smile making me sweat more than any number of times swinging the heavy ax could.

"What's she sayin' t'day?" I ask.

"Oh, she talked about yer gran'fadder an' how miserable he is. But I think that's only Nan's pain—for losin' so many children, fer the way he became after all those heartaches."

"Yes, I 'spose," I say. "Makes sense."

"I mean," My Love goes on, "'tisn't like we'd ever know half o' what she feels. I know I'll never get over Daddy dyin'—breaks me heart. But 'tis God's will, Mother says, an' she finds comfort in that, somehow. I know I'd be some gone in the head if anyt'ing ever happened t' you."

I lodge the big ax into the chopping block and turn towards My Love.

"Jesus!" I say, putting both my arms around her waist, "don't be sayin' the like o' that. Not'ing's ever gonna happen t' me."

"I know, me darlin'," she says, lightly pecking my scruffy face, "but ya do spend most o' yer time out on the sea an' we know what that's able fer."

"Yes, I know," I say, "but ya knows I've been out in a boat since I was able t' stand on me own two feet."

"Yes," she half shouts, "but ya can't swim t' save yerself."

"Yes," I mock her a little, "but when have ya ever heard tell o' me fallin' overboard?"

"I 'spose," she says, pretending to bang on my chest. "I 'spose ya'd miss *me* if *I* ever went away, would ya?"

"Sure, where ya goin'?" I say, half afraid of her answer. "I 'spose I'd be after losin' ya long 'go t' one o' them handsome strangers if that's what ya had in mind."

"I 'spose ya would've," she says, taking one of my hands and dancing in front of me, as if we were at a fancy occasion. "Ya should look in that little bit o' glass above yer kitchen sink one o' these days an' see the fine-lookin' specimen of a man ya are, yerself!"

"Go on, girl!" I say, blushing almost as much as when Nan mentioned us having youngones of our own.

"No, b'y!" she laughs. "Ya need never t'ink yer not more ruggedly fine than the crowd from Amerikay…'cause ya are. So, now!"

I want to say to her the same things she's said to me—how lost I'd be without her—but I don't possess the same nerve. The people of Argentia and Marquise seem to have a better grip on themselves than us—self-assurance. Maybe it was because they've survived such an ordeal. Or, perhaps, they were always that way. Either way, luckily for me, My Love's words and smile tell all we both need to know—that we'll be together the rest of our lives and no number of good-looking men, no matter where they're from, will stand a chance at driving a wedge between us.

"What else was Nan sayin' t'day?" I ask.

"Oh, the usual, ya know. The Crooked Auld Bastard spent yesterday cursing on the goddamn branches of the goddamn tree and the goddamn damsons that are more goddamn trouble than they are goddamn worth, with the goddamn pits on top of it."

"Oh, she went back there, did she?" I ask, laughing.

"She did," she says, "an' the next minute she praised the sun an' all its goodness, an' how lovely the damsons appeared in the warm light. Then she switched back to Himself again. 'On his breaks from complainin', Nan said, 'he walked to the maple tree wit' its leaves all yellow an' catchin' the sun an' all o' his attention: a rare thing all to itself.' Then she said, one time she thought fer sure he was smilin', but it was only a shadow 'cross his face—the *Crooked Auld Bastard.* Oh my, I nearly died."

We both laugh at Nan's recollections of my grandfather. Whether they're true or not, we'll never know, but they can be quite entertaining—for the most part, anyway.

Fall came quickly, as it always does.

After a week or so of clearing bramble and alders and tall grass from the back of Nan's meadow, I can't believe my eyes—a damson tree in all its glory—tiny plums almost purple and beginning to glisten in the sun's light. The dying, turning-blonde grass below the tree reveals where many damsons have fallen on account of the wind. It's a dream-come-true. But perhaps Nan couldn't be bothered.

I'm happy she has proved me wrong. Within a couple of days, we are traversing the sloped meadow towards the rediscovered fruit tree.

"Maybe 'tis been here for the past hundred years or more," I say, excitedly.

"Or maybe 'tis way older," adds My Love. "Maybe it was planted by the Portuguese or French before the English an' Irish ever got here."

No matter how it got here, we are content with our find. Nan surprises us as we trudge our way to the old life-giving tree.

She instructs as to the proper ways to remove the little plums and we oblige—happy as larks to see her off her chair or the daybed and out of the house.

"That's a lovely wan," she says with an impish grin. "Have a bite, girl."

My Love chomps into it like it's a kipper at breakfast and her pretty face contorts into a different one altogether. Nan laughs mischievously, and that's how we learn of the bitterness damsons are known for. For badness, I bite into one, too, and add to my distorted face a concoction of sounds to indicate to Nan my stomach is turning. It's grand to see and hear her really laugh.

At night we sit to her table for hours removing pits from the damsons until our backs and necks can no longer stand it.

When we return the next day, there are eight sealed bottles of burgundy jam sitting just so on the shelf above Nan's water barrel.

"Good fer yer guts," she says, smiling. "Nuttin' better than damson jam fer the stomach."

That night, holding My Love's hand, we are about to cross the longers spanning the ditch to Nan's meadow when we see Nan up near the big trees close to the circle where an old cellar once stood.

"We should leave her be," My Love says.

I agree. We back away slowly, as to not scare Nan, and make our way down the path to the beach.

There, we sit on the rocks at the far end of the beach where men set their lobster traps on the sandy ocean floor and haul herring from nets strung from skiff to skiff when it's not blowing too hard. From the hard, cold granite beneath us, we watch the stars flicker and dance over Placentia. They sparkle behind the long finger of land holding Point Verde Light across the bay and rest upon the beautifully silhouetted, sloped cliffs of the Crevecoeur to our right.

"I wonder if one o' those stars might be Daddy," My Love says quietly, "…lettin' me know he'll never be far away?"

"I'm sure he is always watchin' o'er ya," I say, wiping tears from her face with my fingers.

"If I ever died before you," My Love whispers, snuggling deeper into my cable-knit sweater, "you'd find me twinklin' fer *you* in the sky."

"Jesus, girl!" I say. "Don't be sayin' the like o' that!"

"Why not?" she asks. "'Tis true, fer 'tis you I'll always adore. Just look up, an' I'll give ya a sign. Don't forget now, mind."

She hits me lightly on one of my shoulders while laughing, as I become long lost in the cradle of her love—her love for me. *Adore.* That's the closest she's ever come to telling me she loves me. Defenseless, without the proper words to respond to her kindness, I imagine my soul melting and pouring over the pitted remnants of the cliffs beneath us. Into the cold, dark sea slide words I'd rehearsed to properly say—things she probably longs to hear.

"I'd do the same fer you," I manage to get out.

She finds a way to get closer to me, looks up, liquefies what's left of my needy heart and assassinates the rest of my being with a kiss I'll never forget.

"Ya knows I'd never let ya go," I whisper.

"I know," she says, squeezing my arm through my thick sweater. "I know."

Back up the road, in her meadow, Nan strolls. And even though she's been here a few years, her surroundings seem new to her. It's the damson tree which finally convinced her to take a chance and go outside. Her rare strolls to the beach are different. Once she was settled away in that old house, after the trauma of Argentia, she swore she'd never set foot outdoors again. At least the water at the beach is connected to Argentia—that's how she justifies having the stomach to traverse the road. Everyone she knows understands and they never suggest anything to upset her wishes. She's hardly the only one in the same state. It's a big step for her, for all of us.

The gentle sound of falling leaves touching branches below them and then connecting with the dry grass by Nan's feet soothes her aching senses. Like the days and nights of her long life, each leaf provokes a memory or wish—how little Baby Isaac reacted to the falling leaves, the fun he'd have looking for frogs in the perfectly-round circle of the root cellar now a pond from the hill's water run-off. *Buds*, he'd say each morning for the sparrows, juncos, blue and gray jays, and red-breasted robins—their bellies plump with new babies. He loved looking out the windows at the busy, feathered creatures gathering worms and grubs for their babies in spring and summer—the saucy, noisy crows chasing the smaller birds, and the rare times a bird would land on a windowsill to give him a good look at nature's little wonders.

"Poor Isaac," Nan always says, as if he was the only child she's ever lost.

With each step throughout the meadow, Nan's old shoes kick up leaves galore, sending them flying on erratic draughts of wind. She leans against an old shed with its rotten clapboard and lets her tired head fall back until it rests on her back and shoulders. She watches the clouds blow past the full moon and wonders if the dark patches on the moon are land or water, or nothing at all. And, if it *is* water, what would it be like if all that water were to fall to the earth?

This first day and night of having ventured to her meadow has stirred her appetite. She'd just as soon stay outside, but her body says otherwise. She longs for a mug-up before bed.

Maybe because she has moved more today than she has in years, she's more easily overcome with heat from the stove. She lets the fire go out and raises a couple of windows to air out the house on account of the unusually warm fall wind. Perhaps the cold spurt has passed, and fall will be decent for a spell—the way it happens every so many years, confusing people, animals, insects, and birds alike.

Nan rocks and rocks in Mammy's chair until nodding off into a pile of dreams. Now and then she wakes to shed a tear for certain souls gone before her—ones she's seen so vividly in her dreams, heard their voices, felt their touches—ones she loved, ones who loved her.

During one of her awake moments, she gets up to slip on her goat rubbers over the shoes she scarcely takes off in the house. She's going over the meadow below the church in Argentia and is excited to visit her Aunt Mary. Nan is just about out her door when she remembers Aunt Mary has been dead for about five or ten years, perhaps longer…not to mention the fact Nan's in Freshwater and not Argentia. For another moment of lucidity, she has vivid flashbacks of standing back-on to the wind, the big green savage of a sea hurtling itself along the corrugated crags of the island of Merasheen and barreling past Red Island. The thunderous roars echoing off the far-away cliffs reach her ears amongst a constant barrage of nature's noises.

Nan turns her head, so she won't have to witness men shoveling rocks and smaller dirt and muck onto the freshly made box concealing forever Aunt Mary's body—the sound is bad enough. The priest hardly takes a breath doing his anointed duty of forgiving Aunt Mary for her lifetime of possible sins and his knowing of all the ways she'll find to make up with God for her transgressions while she was alive. Trying to focus on the rounded, bare top of Fox Island barely visible behind the heaving sea, Nan's hearing dies from the harsh whispers of the salty air and upon the words of one of her uncles, Aunt Mary's brother. *Lard Jaysus*, he complains, *if cookin' an' bakin' an' rearin' youngones an' tendin' to the flakes put her in the Big Fella's bad books, then surely, be Jaysus, I'll be goin' straight t' hell.* Nan's uncle's rant soon brings a dignified cough from the throat of the priest, as he edges his way toward the unaccepting, grieving man.

"Jack!" the priest pretends to whisper, "I really wish you wouldn't refer to Holy God as *The Big Fella*; it is disrespectful, especially at such a time."

As quickly as she stood bivering on the bog of Argentia, Nan finds herself overcome with the heat from the hearth in Aunt Mary's tiny parlour—the opening showing its fire to both the small front room and the kitchen on the other side.

The hurt, even though for a moment she recognizes she's in Freshwater, is as strong as the day she first looked at Aunt Mary dead in her coffin. Aunt Mary wasn't sitting in her pink chair with the fancy wooden decorations, knitting and gossiping and asking for another drop of tea in her cup. Nor was she reading a week-old Evening Telegram next to the hearth made with beach rocks. Nor was she gawking past the dog irons holding her pot, pan and kettle, and into the kitchen when she heard someone come in. No, she did none of those things. She was lying in her Sunday dress; her chilly, white hands wrapped in her cold, black rosary beads, in a lovely pine box made by her brothers.

A faded photograph of Aunt Mary and Uncle Tom, taken the day they were married in Little Placentia, stands behind a slight layer of rare dust in the frame. How many mornings had Nan watched Aunt Mary give that framed glass a wipe after lighting the hearth? Now, it rests inside the open lid of a coffin. Someone would wipe it. Two tarnished coppers cover Aunt Mary's eyes once lively and full of questions: the same eyes capable of telling you off when you were anything unbecoming of what she thought you should've or could've been. Those same, all-knowing eyes once welcomed family, friends, and shipwrecked sailors alike with warmth. Those bright eyes were now closed forever. She was gone from this life.

The next day when me and My Love stop into Nan's, she tells us every detail of that dream—at least the parts she can recall. My Love pours three mugs of tea from the kettle always boiling, then sits closest to Nan and places both her tiny strong hands over one of Nan's.

"I'm not even sure if Aunt Mary's house is still there, anymore," Nan says. "Down by the Job Brudder's place, right? The Trading Company 'tis now."

"Great Aunt Mary lived in Little Placentia, Nan," I sheepishly correct her. "Not Placentia proper."

"Yes, b'y, that's right," Nan quickly realizes. "Don't mind me, b'ys. Long night again."

"'Tis alright, Nan," My Love says, soothingly.

If such a thing is possible, in this moment I love My Love even more.

"Ya better hold on to this wan," Nan says, looking at me, as if there'd ever been another.

"I will, Nan. I will," I say.

"The damsons wore me out," she says, yawning.

"Some good, though," I laugh, gently tapping her little arm resting on her flowery tablecloth. "Anyway, Nan, have a spell on the daybed now; we're goin' out in the dory fer a picnic t'morrow afternoon. I got a few things t' do this evenin' an' t'night."

"Like bailin' the rainwater outta her?" My Love says sarcastically of the boat half full of rain from the past two days of irregular, lashing showers.

"Not hard t' tell where that wan's from?" Nan says, winking at My Love. "Bless yer heart! My God, sure, how many yarns did meself an' yer gran'mudder have o'er-right the fences separatin' our prattie gardens an' 'tween the longers o' the taller fences keepin' the harses in. A lovely woman, yer gran'mudder was. Ya reminds me o' her, ya know—somet'ing about ya. Sure, ye're the spit o' yer poor fadder, the poor divil who, himself, is the spit o' yer gran'mudder, sure. He's not well, someone said?"

"He died, I'm afraid, Nan," My Love says, her head hanging as if she was in the middle of the rosary.

"Tell 'im I have 'im in me prayers," Nan says.

"She said he died, Nan," I feel compelled to butt in.

"Oh, my Jesus, he never," Nan gasps. "I'm awfully sorry, me darlin'."

"'Tis okay, Nan, thanks," My Love responds. "He's better off dead than sick an' sufferin'."

How I want to cry out loud—a bawl for My Love's misery over her dead father, and a big screech for poor Nan who's here one minute and gone to some other time in her life the next. I do neither. *Men don't cry*, so I've heard a lifetime. I suppose to myself I'm not much of a man, then.

We have to go. Tomorrow will be a big one. I have foolish expectations of what might go on out in the boat where no one can see us because it'll be a Sunday and most people will be home drunk in their kitchens, singing, giving recitations, crying, re-telling the same stories, trying to get over their hangovers from the parties sure to be happening in every second house here in Freshwater this night. I know if My Brother hadn't married and moved out, and if my wildest dreams of being the true love of My Love's life never happened, I'd be drooling in my homebrew or rum at the end of someone's daybed or kitchen table this night, too.

"At least we got plenty o' damsons," Nan says, trying to stall our leave.

"Yes," My Love says, sympathetic to Nan's loneliness, "I'll be back t'morrow night, if Mother isn't too bad, an' we'll make anudder batch o' jam, sure."

"God love ya, me darlin'," Nan whispers while taking both My Love's hands into her own. "You've yer gran'mudder's hands, ya know?"

"Go on?" My Love says.

"Yes, girl," Nan says. "Meself an' yer gran'mudder must o' turned o'er t'ousands an' t'ousands o' saltfish on the flakes in Sampson's Cove. We had some yarns, night and day. Lots o' times, sure, we'd be asked t' go 'cross the way t' Marquise to tend to the flakes there—the men'd be after bringin' in that much fish. Don't t'ink I never knew ev'ry nook an' cranny, welt, scrape, cut an' bruise on yer gran'mudder's hands, workin' 'longside her a lifetime. We worked some hard, us women."

"Yes," My Love says, enthusiastically, "I've always heard how busy ye always were down home."

The enthusiasm on My Love's face quickly turns to a look of panic, knowing it's time for her to be up the hill, home with her mother, especially should her mother need help in getting to and from the outhouse. My Love also must make sure there's enough newspaper there to wipe themselves. The Americans are generous like that—they save their leftover newspapers and magazines and drop them off to their new friends in Freshwater and other nearby towns.

The Last Night

"Yer a good girl," Nan says, tears in her eyes, looking into My Love's.

"No need t' be upset, Nan, girl" I say, reaching one of my hands over the tablecloth until it rested upon theirs, still stacked in a mound of affection. "Sure, we'll be back t'morow after supper."

Nan says nothing. Softly, she slides her hand out from our little hill of hands, and leisurely pushes herself, chair and all, back from the table and gets up. She lifts a finger to My Love's pretty face, as if to say, *don't ask questions; I'll be right back.* Nan scuffs past the stove and turns right into the little nook leading to the tiny parlour where no one ever goes—except for wakes and for a drop of brandy with fruitcake at Christmastime.

"I'm sorry," says My Love in a whisper, afraid of insulting Nan, "but I really got t' go home."

My nod tells her I understand.

"Nan? Ya alright?"

She doesn't answer, but we can hear her rustling through her grandfather's trunk—the place she kept the few material items she values most in this world: the two coppers used to cover the eyes of the many dead she has seen, her father's scapular he'd received at his First Holy Communion (the ink inscription reads 183-*something*: the ink long dipped from a small glass jar is too smudged to decipher the last number), bronze medals of honour and bravery once awarded to my grandfather—the Crooked Auld Bastard (Nan failed to talk about the horrors he might have seen at Gallipoli from the fall of 1915 to the first month of the following year—then how he was sent to the Western Front in France the next spring), and a bunch of other material items Nan deems worthy of keeping.

The trunk closes. We hear its metal latch as it clasps into the hole where the skeleton key dangles mostly unused from a discoloured strand of used trawl line.

Nan slides the trunk back in under the table beneath the mantel piece and makes her way back to us in the kitchen. I stand to greet her.

"Sit down, child," she says.

"But, Nan," I try to say before she hushes me and points to the wooden chair where certainly my arse cheeks have carved their very own hollows.

Ignoring me, Nan once again takes the anxious hands of My Love. She shuffles her fingers and finally opens the palm of her left hand. Though the light is low, the flicker from the newly lit kerosene lantern catches glimpses of something round and shiny—a ring. Nan fumbles through each of My Love's fingers until she seems satisfied to stop at one which will best hold the jewelry.

"Oh my God!" My Love exclaims.

Where did that come from? I want to ask but choose to leave the moment to whatever it is Nan has in mind.

"'Tis so lovely!" My Love says.

"'Twas Mammy's weddin' ring," Nan says, proudly. "Do it feel good on that finger?"

"Feels lovely," My Love says, "but I really have t' go, Nan. Poor Mother prob'ly needs me now; I have t' go, sorry."

"I understand, child," Nan says, smiling, more serene than

ever. "Ya likes it then?"

"The ring?" My Love asks. "Yes, girl. 'Tis one o' the nicest rings I've ever seen. Not that I've seen many. Yer some lucky t' have yer mammy's weddin' ring."

"Does it hurt yer finger?" Nan asks.

"No, Nan; not at all."

"Well," Nan says, crying a little, "I want ya t' have it."

"Alright, Nan, t'anks, but I have t' go. I'll bring it back t'morrow, 'kay?"

"No, child," Nan says, sounding sadder than ever. "Keep it on yer finger forever, an' if *he* (looking at me) ever gets the nerve t' ask ya, ye'll be married an' that's one less thing ye'll need t' fret over—a ring."

"Sure, Nan," My Love pleas, "ya knows I can't do the like o' that—take yer mammy's ring. Now, here."

Nan gently takes My Love's hand and removes the little band of gold. She holds it to the window which offers little light, then passes the ring to me.

"Hold it next to the lamp," she orders. "Read out what it says."

I turn the ring carefully, afraid of losing it and having to watch it roll under the daybed, becoming an instant nightmare because I'd lost it down the perfectly round hole chewed through the floor by the rats. I turn the circular brass knob on the lamp, rising the cloth wick bringing with it more flame—the shadows flickering on the pale walls get bigger. I squeeze the ring between the thumb and index finger of my left hand; inside the ring, I see something.

"There's letters there," I say, eagerly.

"Mammy's initials," Nan says, matter-of-factly. "Pop had it

done fer her in S'n John's, Mammy told me."

"B. C.," I read aloud. "B.C.? Nan, I thought Mammy's name was Lizzie, short fer *Elizabeth*."

"If ya ever had t' take the friggin' t'ing, ya'd know what was on it an' why," Nan scowls, half-jokingly.

My Love looks puzzled, and rightfully so.

"No," Nan laughs, "'tis only *you* he ever loved, so the ring I tried givin' t' him a dozen times in the past year or so."

I feel no bigger than the ring, maybe smaller, as I envision myself sliding under the table and out of view of both women—perhaps into the rat hole. I've never had the guts to tell My Love I really love her (not that she doesn't already know), and now here's Nan saying it for me.

"Sweet Jesus!" I say, under my breath.

Nan and My Love laugh out loud.

"'Tis okay, Sweetheart," My Love says, winking. "Maybe the nerve will come upon ya t'morrow, now that we have a ring."

I feel myself get a bit taller again in the chair. I manage a forced laugh, although I am embarrassed beyond repair.

"Speakin' o' the ring," My Love quickly moves the topic away from my horrid state of mortification. "Can I see the initials?"

I pass her the ring and watch her hold it and turn it to get the most out of the lantern's light.

"Yes, b'y," she says. "Look at that—B.C.—how lovely. She must have treasured it some, yer mammy."

"That's what most people thought," Nan says, as coherent as if her mind had never gone its own way ages before. "Ya knows how ev'rywan calls someone named *Elizabeth* 'Bet',' 'Betty', 'Liz' or 'Lizzie'?"

"Yeah," we answer the same time.

"Well," Nan says, "Mammy's real name was Bet'any—Bet'any Clancy—straight from Tipperary when her parents decided t' flee Ireland, not long before the Great Hunger.

Me and My Love exchange stumped glances at the details of Nan's recollection.

"But why B.C.?" asks My Love. "Wouldn't she prefer her married last name on her weddin' ring?"

"That's what Mammy always said Pop said, too," Nan laughs. "But Pop, he was born in Marquise, see…well, knowin' how the English treated the Irish in their own country, an' then Mammy's fam'ly bein' forced t' leave…well, he t'ought havin' Mammy's real initials on the ring would always remind her o' where it was she come from…so she could tell her children—the way she told me an' the rest o' me brudders an' sisters, God rest their souls."

"Bethany," says My Love. "What a lovely name! Maybe if we ever have a girl, that's what we'll call her—Bethany."

My Love looks at me when she says that, and I get half nervous, not knowing whether she's hinting we can do things to make babies happen and when. Again, I nod in agreement, say nothing, only think what odds about a ring and let's go get our family started.

"'Tis a lovely name, 'ndeed," agrees Nan. "Ya don't hear tell o' anyone 'round here wit' a name like that, do ya?"

"No," we both agree.

"Sure, there's got t' be another person in yer family who'd appreciate the ring, though, Nan," My Love says in earnest.

"Me darlin', yer the closest t'ing I have to a daughter in me life an' this belongs wit' you."

I want to ask, *what about My Brother's wife*, but I know the answer—she doesn't visit Nan enough to earn her respect and admiration the way Nan adores My Love. Who could blame her?

"Keep that on yer finger now till the day ya dies," Nan says, tears welling again in her eyes. "Ya have me permission t' be buried wit' it, unless ye have a daughter o' yeer own someday, a new little Bet'any, an' you'd just as soon leave it fer her. Now, show!"

The back of Nan's hand rests on the table, awaiting My Love's. Nan slides the ring back on the same finger, slying her eyes at me—making sure I'm paying attention.

"Oh, Nan!" My Love says in a crying, but happy voice. "Yer some sweet an' thoughtful. I will. I'll keep it on me finger forever, an' I'll always remember ya."

It's as though Nan has laid out our lives for us and, all of a sudden, I picture me and My Love married with a wee little one named Bethany who won't be a Betty or a Lizzie or anything but *Bethany*—the stunning spit of My Love she'll be and perhaps the child will have enough of my brazenness to ensure she'll have no trouble standing up for herself in this changing world of ours.

The real tears blurring My Love's vision tell me more than I feel I'm capable of handling. Or at least what her heart and soul are truly capable of conjuring. The way she looks at me adds at least ten years to our romantic existence. I imagine our walk up the hill this night will be the warmest feeling we've ever sensed.

On the way to her home, My Love says little, only how sweet Nan is.

"I wonder why Nan chose *now* to present me with such a precious gift?" My Love asks.

"I don't know," I say.

Before I leave her at her mother's backstep, our hug feels closer than ever, and life suddenly seems different—different in the best way possible—even if we aren't sure what that might mean and neither of us feels it necessary to bother with words. Our goodnight kiss closes the gap on the typical night fog. Her mouth is warmer than ever. She keeps her forehead to mine while lifting her hand containing the surprise gift from Nan. I'd heard gold tarnishes, so perhaps Nan polished the ring occasionally. My Love holds that hand and turns it. The sliver of moonlight peeking through the windblown fog brings new life to the old gold.

"Ya know the first thing Mother's gonna ask, don't ya," she says, softly.

"Just tell her the truth," I say, although I want to drop to my knees this very second and ask her to be my wife.

Tomorrow I'll manage to do that if my nerves don't get the best of me.

"I 'spose," she says. "Did Nan really offer this t' ya since ya met me?"

I'm enshrouded in humiliation and tenseness, as quick as flames take over the inside of a woodstove once everything has caught fire. Does she think I didn't take the ring because I think she isn't the one I really want to keep for a wife? Does she think she's just a passing fancy and why would I bother taking my great grandmother's wedding ring for the likes of her? No! She'd never think those things. Right away, I feel ashamed for thinking such thoughts. After all, the fact we're an item is common knowledge, and neither of us ever had reason to believe we have cause to look sideways at another. We are happy; though, I'm not sure how to answer her question.

"Well?" she asks. "'Tis, okay; I knows ya wants me an' no

one else."

Her words of truth break the tension I've created in my mind, and my strewn thoughts fumble for the swiftest excuse to help put an end to this potential catastrophe.

"Yeah," I begin, "she's been fond o' ya long before I ever brought ya t' her place. For the first year, after ye came here from Argentia, all I did was tell her about ya. She'd never seen me so hopeful about anyt'ing an' eager t' make somet'ing, another person, me own."

"Ah," My Love sighs. "If only I'd taken yer hints sooner. I'm so sorry. I liked ya from the start, too, ya know."

"Ya did?" I ask. "Jesus! Thanks, fer makin' me suffer. I was a hundred percent sure the likes o' you would never have anyt'ing t' do with the likes o' me. 'Specially wit' My Brother tellin' me ev'ry day ya'd soon be gone off, married t' one o' them good-lookin' Yanks."

"Sure, I'm after tellin' ya neither o' them could ever hold a candle t' ya."

"Well," I sigh, "now ya knows why I never took the ring—I thought I'd be makin' a bigger fool o' meself than I already thought I was."

"'Tis alright," she says, looking up into my tired eyes. "We have it now, sure."

With that, she takes my right hand from her waist and entwines our fingers. The night has brought cold to the ring. She opens her hand while still entwined in mine and turns *our* hands, so the ring glistens in the now-visible full moon. She gives me the biggest hug she's ever given me. I melt down through the boards of her mother's backstep. The dropping black curtain of night is yet high enough to reveal the loveliest red sky a sailor could dream of for the next day—especially a sailor with a doryload of love for the most precious creature God has ever lent to this earth.

"Jesus," I say, without thinking, of course.

"Wha?" she asks.

"Ya told Nan you'll never take the ring off, right?"

"Yeah, why?" she asks.

"What about in Mass t'morrow mornin'? Ya knows people will see the ring an' will be talkin'."

"Sure, what odds what they says," she laughs. "I'll say, 'yes, b'ys, we're gettin' married; haven't ye heard?'"

Again, what's left of my soul wrapped in disbelief slithers on its own accord somewhere below us, and I'm struck by this reality—this dream-come-true: perhaps she is really waiting for me to ask for her hand in marriage, and maybe it's more to do with her father dying, but what odds—she'll still be my wife. How happy Mother would be if she could hear all this. Perhaps she can and is smiling down upon us this instant. Father always said, *sure the only thing we knows is that we knows fook all.* That's becoming clearer every day and night—a wise man, my father. Here and now, I make my mind up—I will, indeed, ask My Love to marry me tomorrow out in the tranquility and sanctity of my dory.

I wonder if she is wondering if I'm going to propose marriage this instant and I feel as senseless as the night we first kissed.

"See ya at Mass?" I ask.

"See ya at Mass, yeah," she says, sighing.

"I'll bail the dory now, so she's nice an' dry by t'morrow afternoon," I say. "Bring a quilt fer yer legs in case the wind comes up—better safe than sorry. I have one Mother made, but ya'd probably like to have yer own."

"I will," she says. "I have the perfect one, too. Should I take this ring off in case I lose it?"

"Remember what Nan said, mind!" I laugh. "Plus, like ya already said, it might give 'em somet'ing t' talk about."

"Oh, yes, that's right," My Love laughs. "I have t' leave it on fer always, regardless. Fine by me."

Regardless. What does she mean by that? If my heart was ever going to burst out of my chest, it would be now. *Jesus*! I think. Do I fall before her right now, or is it too late and would I be making a holy show of myself because she'd just say *not now*, or *never*, because her father's not long dead and she has better things to do than marry the likes of me?

"Fine by me, too," I manage to get out between gulps.

I laugh to myself about the faces my horse makes when he's parched until My Love asks am I alright in the head.

"I'll tell ya about it, sometime, I swear," I say.

"T'morrow?" she asks, laying her head against my pounding chest.

"T'morrow," I say. "Certainly, t'morrow."

"Best kind," she says. "'Kay, I gotta go in, b'y. See ya at the rails."

"I'll be watchin' ya on yer way up t' Communion," I laugh.

"Sure, haven't ya always watched me on me way t' Communion?" she grins, titling her head to one side.

"Could ya blame me?" I ask.

"Go on, b'y," she says, laughing.

She wraps her arms around my neck and presses her lips to mine.

"T'morrow," she says, slowly letting go of me—Nan's ring leaving a new feeling on my being as it drags gracefully over my trembling, calloused hand.

On the way up the road from the beach, after bailing the boat of rainwater, I stop alongside the church to stretch. The grasses of the meadow alongside the Back Path swish slightly while bending to the night's gentle breeze. I reach one arm crossways and hold its elbow with the other hand. I squeeze my hands, as if I'm trying to get a grip on one of the millions of stars dazzling for eternity above me. Then, I do the same with the other arm. I don't feel much relief at this moment, but the stretching always helps. When I finally lay down in bed tonight, muscles will flicker in my neck and down my back—giving my body a fresh start for tomorrow.

I can't get the ring out of my head, and I wonder if, right now, My Love, is lying in her own bed squinting to see the glint of the gold wrapping her finger. Is she restless, waiting for my nervousness to batter and for a new courage to present itself in the way of asking for her precious hand in marriage? *Just as well*, I think I've convinced myself. *Just imagine*, I can hear poor Mother saying, *he's finally gonna be married. 'Bout time*, Father adds, slurping his tea. These thoughts make me miss my parents more, and it kills me to know they're not here to receive the good news. I turn my back to the church and contemplate climbing the Back Path and stepping back onto the rear bridge of My Love's home to make sure my feelings are not far-fetched, and I won't make a mockery of myself in the dory tomorrow. But I won't do that. I can't. It's too late.

I wonder if My Love has fallen asleep and is dreaming of being my wife—imagine, after all this time and it has finally come to this. Or, I hope it has come to this—where I get a chance to ask her to be mine forever and we'll have a place of our own with youngones running in and out the door winter and summer, and us watching one another grow old, with each day and night adding layers to our love. Or is she down at the kitchen table, dipping a raisin bun in tea and telling her mother things might change forever tomorrow, if she gets her way. Her mother might not take her seriously.

Perhaps My Love is knelt, leaning in over her mother on the front room couch and telling her how good I am to her, what a decent fisherman I am and how good the past year's seasons have been to my traps, trawls, and jiggers. I imagine her mother raising her tired arms to hold My Love's darling face, to say she wishes us nothing but the best—how content her father would be if he was alive, God rest his soul, and they both blessing themselves while shedding tears.

Instead, I turn my body back in the direction of the road leading up over the hill of myriad paths to my own home. As always, in every second or third house I pass there are times (*parties*, some now call them) happening. Part of me is dying to burst in on them all, have a drink, sing a song, and summon the nerve to tell all hands about the big day tomorrow—just me and My Love out on the sea, not far from shore, but far enough to be out of earshot of most people out on a Sunday for nothing but a bit of news.

Then I'm drawn straight up the road by the customary compulsion to check on Nan one last time before I *really* go home for the night.

The Knowing

"'T'ought ya were gone fer the night," Nan says.

My light knocking and entering doesn't bother her the least.

"Ya should hook that hook into the latch on yer door, Nan."

"Fer wha?" she asks. "Not like they'd come in here fer anyt'ing—certainly not me."

Her laugh disarms me, and I decide what odds about her unlocked door—she's right. No one's going to bother traipsing in off the road and up through a meadow lit only by the moon sometimes and navigated solely by familiar feet. The young crowd around here call Nan's place the Haunted House—nothing to do with Nan—because it was empty before she moved in. And no doubt word of the eerie abode has reached the ears of newcomers to Freshwater, and no one would have the nerve to go near the place, anyhow.

"Haunted?" Nan laughs. "'Twould be haunted if the Crooked Auld Bastard was here. God knows, he haunted me a lifetime. He's still at it."

"Ah, Nan, girl," I say, "'Tis not all that bad, sure."

"No, b'y," she laughs. "'Tis not always he comes 'round, an' when he do, I can handle him. Now! What about that lovely girl? Sure, she's right gone o'er ya; can't ya tell?"

"I 'spose, Nan, girl," I say, my blushed face veiled by the dim light of the room.

"Jesus, b'y," she says, "I knows yer not blind; ya had t' see her face light up when I put Mammy's ring on her finger."

"Yes, anyone could see the difference in her, an' she acted different after that—when we left 'til we bid goodnight at her mother's backstep."

"Well?" Nan asks, seriously. "I'm not gonna be 'round forever, ya know. I could make it to the church fer yeer weddin' if I could get a run in one o' them fancy carts an' wheels."

"Cars an' trucks, Nan," I laugh. "Yes, they're alright when the road is dry, but they're not half as good as a horse when it comes t' gettin' o'er humps an' outta them deep ruts caused by cars an' trucks in the first place."

"Never ya mind all yer talk 'bout cars an' trucks," she scorns. "I'm not that stunned, b'y; I knows the difference. I don't care if they heaves me into a wheelbarrow an' rolls me o'er the humps an' through the ruts, as long as I don't miss the big weddin'."

"What if My Love only likes the ring 'cause 'tis shiny," I say, "an' she never wore a ring before? Maybe it makes her feel special or important?"

"Ya knows she's not like that!" Nan ridicules. "She's from Lil' Placentia an' Lil' Placentia women don't have big ways about 'em; they got more sense than that. That girl, me son, is dyin' fer ya t' ask fer her hand in marriage. Get a bitta sense, b'y, an' ask the poor child before some Yank she don't have t' worry 'bout drownin' six days a week asks her before ya! Alotta women would give up their lives o' frettin' o'er their fishermen husbands fer the chance t' marry one o' them fine-lookin' friggers from The States—don't be coddin' yerself. Go ask her, b'y."

"Alright! Alright! Nan," I say. "Yer right! Yer right! By the Jesus, I'll ask t'morrow, so I will—you'll see. An' all their talk about her flashy ring in church in the mornin' will come true in the afternoon. It'll be some long wait fer the prying ones waitin' t' hear if I'm after askin' her or not."

"What odds about anyone else. Good, b'y!" Nan says, slowly reaching her tired old arm across the table and gently squeezing my hand. "'Tis the best fer ya—the two o' ye. I can tell ye are meant t' be t'gedder the rest o' yeer lives. I would o' given anyt'ing fer a chance at real love like the two o' ye have, an' perhaps I might o' had it if the goddamn tuberculosis hadn't stole all our youngones, except yer poor mudder, God rest her soul. An 'praps the…"

"Nice man from the Cape Shore," I finish her sentence.

"Ya remembers," she says with a distant smile, her thoughts immediately sent back to her pleasant visits with the kind Mr. Morrissey.

"I think ya had lots o' love in yer lifetime, Nan. Maybe ya can't always remember the good times 'cause o' all the bad, but I guarantee ya, you had good times—I can see it still in yer lovely Irish eyes."

"That's nice o' ya t' say," she says, again squeezing my hand. "If I don't mind sayin' so, meself, the Clancys were a fine brood o' women, 'ccordin' to the pictures we used t' get from Tipperary. An' me uncles, Mammy's brudders, were fine an' handsome themselves. Anyhow, 'tis late an' ya better get plenty o' rest before yer big day t'morrow."

I bid her goodnight and head out the door and down across her yard. As much as I often enjoy Nan's thoughts when they take off on the wind, more so I value moments, days and nights like this, when her mind is clear as a bell. I'll think of Nan more than ever tomorrow morning while most of the town is lulled in their varying states of sickness from tonight's drink towards the Madonna—the old bell they lugged from the church in Argentia, in the churchyard ringing to wake the dead. *As clear as a bell* and *Nan.* That's what I'll think of after the panic from vexing all night starts to leave my body and my weary mind.

It's morning again. The big day. The BIG day! Jesus! My nerves. I carefully remove Father's straight razor from its leather pouch and shave stubble from my face. I wash my hair in the kitchen sink and slick it back with my hands; it will be untamed and half curly before I'm halfway to Mass. Too nervous to bother with tea, although my guts are rumbling for a couple of slices of homemade bread made especially for me by My Love. I take the bent wire clothes hanger from its nail in the wall and remove a damper from the stove. With my good knife, I slice bread on the table. I then lay it on the wire before sliding the works over the open flames. When it's burnt enough for my liking on one side, I take it off and smear a bit of blueberry jam across the toast.

When my face and mouth are clean, I open the door to take on the day.

"I'll be back t' let ye out after Mass," I tell the hens and the rooster, as I head down over the bank to cross the brook.

The long spring's cold has quickly been replaced with warmth from the day's sun, as the many grasses adorning the remaining meadows of Freshwater reach for the sun's growing heat and light. Bright green leaves of birch trees merrily lend their blossoming freshness to the daylight, even if the fog is in. The intense yellow of dandelion poke their heads into every opening available to my eyes. Even the garbage half filling the ditch running the length of the road is no match for the strength of the brightly coloured weeds. Sting nettles cling to my good socks and pants, as I take shortcuts through meadows to make sure I don't end up beneath the interrogative gaze of the priest—you'd never say it was the same man who's more than likely going to be sitting next to you in the club for a quick beer or three or four or five before the beef and cabbage is ready and on our tables and wherever he'll expectedly be invited to eat.

When I amble up the hardwood aisle of the church, as if I'm looking for just any pew at all, my hearts pumps faster than ever when my eyes catch hold of My Love. She's sitting alongside her mother and her younger brother. It looks as if there's room for me. Suddenly, one of the ushers lightly takes a sleeve of my Sunday best suit of clothes and guides me to the pew directly behind My Love. At first, I resist. Then I go with my gut feeling and follow the nice man's lead. I turn red as a beet when her mother's eyes clasp me lost in thought while gawking expressionlessly into the mass of yellow curls dangling from My Love's drying head of hair.

Her mother graciously nods me out of my trance, enough so that My Love turns to see me. Her smile, capable of illuminating the many stained-glass windows of this holy building at night, sends a feebleness to my knees I'd never thought possible. I tighten the grip of my hands on the back of her pew, as I plank myself down on the bench I've kindly been forced onto—one of the very pews rescued from the church in Argentia. My Love and her mother look quite relaxed, and I imagine they must feel a bit at home, at least, with familiar wood beneath them. When sunlight flashes through the multi-coloured stained cut-glass of a nearby window, I see the glossiness of My Love's mother's eyes—she's thinking of and praying for her dead husband, not to mention her sick boy with his tired head resting on her Sunday overcoat.

My Loves raises her right hand over the shoulder of her Sunday dress. Her pale fingers snake slowly through her shiny hair. There it is, the ring—great grandmother's ring—no, *her* ring. My Love's ring. *Our* ring? My eyes dare to leave the wonderous sight for a split second while I look above the colossal stone altar and to the ashen, large porcelain Jesus hanging wretchedly from a big, black wooden cross. I shed a tear for the pain He's surely feeling—the nails in His hands and a bigger one through His crossed feet. Imagine people being that cruel. My selfish mind swiftly ignores *His* pain and I ask His blessing for what I'm about to do this today. Sunday is supposed to be a day of rest, we've been taught our lifetimes, but how are you supposed to ask the love of your life to marry you during the week while you're lugging hay, feeding horses and cows and chickens and sheep, and tearing yourself up for a boatload of cod the merchant will give you next to nothing for? *Sorry, Jesus,* I think, *but it's going to have to be a Sunday—this Sunday—the day I ask My Love for her hand in mine for all time.*

My Love's slight cough rips my eyes from poor Jesus on the cross and back to where her ringed finger still clings to her shoulder. Her little brother makes faces at me, and I make worse ones back at him until I'm caught. Her mother's sly eyes momentarily lock onto mine which quickly latch back onto her daughter's hand. She knows, Jesus (*Sorry, Jesus,* I think, looking up at Him in all his misery), she knows. She knows about the ring, and what if I'm not good enough for her precious daughter? Do I need *her* permission to ask?

Men dying from the cough of too many cheap cigarettes off The Base and the stench of booze in the warming air is enough to turn my stomach. I shake my head, swallow, and look at her mother who's still looking my way. I look to my side to make sure she's not looking at someone else, but there's no one looking back at us. I swallow again and every bit of strength God allows me carries my right hand forward until it touches My Love's ringed hand. Surprisingly, the instant my hand touches hers, she doesn't flinch. Instead, she turns her pretty face towards mine and the weight of want in her eyes nearly pushes me beneath the pew. I'm weak and sliding towards her. She thinks I'm being romantic or funny, I suppose, but I'm fainting. My fall into decline is cushioned by the softness of the hassock under my knees. Her mother coughs her disapproval, but I decide to be a man for once. I use the disguise of my weakened body to lean into My Love's hair—just long enough to kiss her hand, ring, and all.

Somewhere in the distance a bell has tolled, and I imagine I am entering Heaven (and perhaps I am). The potency of frankincense is getting stronger. I hear a thin chain swing before a sharp sting comes to the back of my right ear. I jump back to the way I'm supposed to be sitting and look up to see the priest gaping down at me. He's poisoned by my behaviour, and vicious over my audacity and my blatant disrespect in the House of God.

Titters come from all around—a great bit of news for the townspeople, but I don't care—even from My Love's mother. As embarrassed as I *could* be, I couldn't care less because I feel this day will change my life forever. Even better, I know her mother has the humour about her, and it must have been my bad mind which assured me she'd never want my kind marrying her child. I toss my head towards her mother, as if to say *sorry for carrying on the way I am in Mass.* The priest flicking my ear doesn't bother me much either; he does that for a pastime to people he feels deserve it. He doesn't need much of an excuse. When the collective snickering quells, My Love turns around and reaches back.

"Give me yer hand," she whispers.

"Wha?" I say.

"Give me yer hand, b'y?"

My eyes widen at her request, especially with her mother looking on.

"Come here," My Love says.

"Come where?" I ask.

"Here, b'y," she laughs. "Up here."

"But…"

"But nothing," she says.

With the entire congregation looking on, I lean forward on the back of her pew. I step out into the aisle. Whispers quickly fill the foul-smelling air until the priest's harsh, deliberate cough quietens most of them. I avoid his stare and squeeze in alongside My Love. When she takes my hand, I want to hold her, kiss her, but I'm drawn to see what kind of a face her mother is wearing. I close my eyes and open them, twice, to make sure the smile on her mother's face is real and not imaginary. My Love lays her lovely head of hair on my left shoulder, entwines her fingers, ring and all, tightly with mine. At this moment, I couldn't care less if the priest drowns in the wine from the chalice, chokes on the stale Holy Communion bread and falls in a pile on the altar—someone will look after him; I have my own to take care of. I give Jesus on the cross another look, then feel bad for looking at a man so miserable and I so content.

Away With the Faeries

Full of fishcakes, scrunchions and two mugs of tea, Nan looks out the window to see if I'm coming. She's dying to hear of the goings-on in Mass this morning. She goes to grab the rosary beads hanging from a nail drove into the wall next to where she sits to the kitchen table—an extra nail used to keep the old wallboard from exposing the rotting studded walls of the two-story structure. But she stops. Hypocritical, she knows it would be to pretend to worship a god she's certain doesn't exist, so she hauls her hand back to its resting spot upon the flowered tablecloth. Yet she'd never consider throwing out or giving away Mammy's praying beads.

She once joked that *her* face should be on rosary beads—herself having been paid a special visit by the pope, himself, and canonized a saint for putting up with the Crooked Auld Bastard for so many years.

The coo-coo clock stopped at some point during the night—*an omen*, she thinks. She'll get me to reset the clock when I stop in after Mass and ask me to pray nothing bad will become of this day or night. She knows I go to the church because I was made go there a lifetime and most people just do what everyone else does, but there's a better chance, she knows, of me getting a prayer through to the heavens than a heathen like herself.

Nan slides her chair back, stands and walks to the stove. She checks the fire and there's still plenty of wood in there to burn. She must have filled it not long ago but doesn't remember. Satisfied with the amount of warmth in the low-ceilinged kitchen, she turns toward the daybed. She sits down, kicks off her shoes and falls back, sideways, onto the quilts Mammy sewed so long ago. Nan admires the patterns adorning each square of material sewn with care onto the once-white backing of two quilts. Tracing her fingers over reevens of thread sticking out here and there like whiskers on an old man's face, she pictures Mammy squeezed into her barrel chair—pastel brown and always against the wall by the door leading to the back porch of the old house where wood, water, flour, and molasses were stored. The steam from the beef and cabbage bubbling in the aluminum boiler rattles the pot's lid, but Mammy's eyes never leave her work—another quilt to help keep her family warm.

Nan's weary mind leans toward sleep, but good rest is out of her grasp. About six gallons of damsons lay in cold water in two boilers on the table—too much work to do today, after spending most of yesterday on her hands and knees picking the little plums from the grass. The fall's quick end brought high winds and early frost, and the damsons were sent flying in every direction in the back garden.

A thin film of ice has returned to the step and Nan's soul is poisoned at the sight of it. She swings back and lets the water fly from the boiler. The wet ground full of leaves catches the water, and she quickly turns back through the door of the house. She hauls the storm door to and gives the big heavy door a bang to make sure it is closed all the way.

Night creeps in in its usual manner. As pain strikes her body without pause, Nan prays for death. Sleep is nowhere to be found, so she goes back downstairs—only this time, the kitchen isn't that of her childhood home; it's that of her married-life house.

"Jesus!" she says, "I'll see damson pits in me sleep fer a month. An' talk about pain in me neck—bent o'er the boiler, pickin' out hun'reds o' pits one be one."

"Stop complainin', girl," the Crooked Auld Bastard says, "an' get out an' bring in an armload o' wood! Make yerself useful!"

"I've half a mind t' scald ya wit' the bubblin' jam on the stove," she barks back at his sauce, "but I wouldn't waste it on the likes o' you after spendin' so much trouble makin' it ready."

To get away from the sight and smell of Himself, Nan slips on her goat rubbers and heads out through the porch. As she turns to latch the storm door, a quick gust of fall wind smacks her in the face. Then, as quickly as that, the night becomes calm.

The moon hangs full in the branches of the nearly-dead pines in the backyard—its light casting shadows upon the garden. It is rare to see a tall, straight pine since schooners became popular less than a hundred years ago—the trees used for sail masts and spars. Old Man Kelly must have decided he liked the trees where they are and cut straight trees elsewhere for the necessity of shipbuilding.

The old shed stretches out across the ground where potatoes and carrots and turnip and cabbages bigger than your head once grew. It's nice to have something to keep her mind off things, but the cold soon gnaws at her back and snaps at her right hip. She'd just as soon haul the rusty ax out of the rotten stump, once a chopping block, and cut her head off than go in the house and listen to Himself and how the world is always against him.

After a few walks around the backyard, Nan holds her breath and bites her tongue. She enters the kitchen through the squeaky porch door. No bitching and complaining is heard; Himself must be asleep. Relieved, she sits in Mammy's chair and relishes the stove's heat.

"Oh, Jesus, I forgot the wood," she says, looking over, expecting a dirty look.

She sees only the chair Himself *used* to sit on—the seat empty of the selfish fool and his bitter tongue. She breathes another sigh of reprieve knowing he's not there, or anywhere she hopes. She nods off.

In her dream, Nan is out in her grandfather's garden over on The Blockhouse in Placentia. She's walking amongst the rotten leaves, kicking them up from the grass. It's cold. The loudness of the crisp leaves muffles the waves of silence. A sliver is missing from the top right corner of the moon. The red rim warning of a poor day tomorrow explains the awful pain in the middle of her back.

From the chopping block she looks up. As quick as that, the trees have been left naked again for the harsh winter to come with its assortment of abuse: ice to cover her windows so she can't see out and the frozen step where she's sure to fall, great surges of the sea to toss boulders up to her front door, and the late December flood for which her grandfather no longer bothers leaving the house.

Winter—it always saddens Nan to see trees without leaves. But if leaves were there all the time, she supposes, she might never pay mind to them. She listens to the waves battering and tossing beach rocks across the way and is glad for the sound—happy to have her hearing. She hears the baby crying and wonders what she, herself, is doing out in the cold, fussing over the trees that are perfect—the way God made them. The looming shadows of The Isaacs across The Reach confuse her, as she's sure she's in Placentia—dreams within dreams, something she's come to live with. Somehow, she knows her thoughts *are* scattered and to not panic over sudden changes her mind is liable to invent.

Into the room to the right of the stairs she goes and lifts little Isaac from his crib. She looks out the window of the hall and admires the moon's radiant vein on Little Placentia's harbour. Isaac stops crying for a few seconds, hugging into the warm space between his mother's neck and shoulder. He'll soon be ten months old. The child gasps for air and when he finds it, he lets out a bawl to wake the devil. Nan walks back and forth, along the rail of the stairs, singing a nursery rhyme Mammy used to sing to all *her* youngones. Isaac stops crying. Nan takes him back to the window.

"Where are the birds, Isaac?" she asks.

Isaac smiles, showing a few teeth, and lightly taps the cold windowpane with one of his little hands.

"Buds!" he tries to shout but is quickly robbed of his breath.

He starts to choke and is almost blue in the face by the time his mother squeezes his chest, shaking his air passage open. He begins a fit of hacking and coughing while a spell of bawling overtakes Nan. Isaac is drenched in sweat from head to toe. He closes his eyes again. She takes him down to the kitchen and holds him over the boiler of hot water on the table to allow steam to find its way into his little lungs. Nan remains quiet. Himself is walking swiftly in and out of every room howling, *Goddamn TB*! *Goddamn TB*! She doesn't blame him and says nothing only *Shush*.

Later that night, on the way back down to the kitchen, Isaac dies in Nan's arms. Himself loses his mind over the tragedy and must be forced to the floor by Nan's grandfather.

"No, 'ndeeed yer not havin' any o' me whiskey!" Nan's grandfather tells Himself. "That's all we needs now is you carryin' on worse than ya are!"

Nan rocks little Isaac in the chair, rubbing him all over. She prays the heat will bring him back to life, even though she knows too well the distinct cold of a dead child's body. Isaac was the second last of their six children. She sings an old nursery rhyme for the last time while holding Isaac's gray, clammy face into her own.

Himself comes out from the parlour. He falls at Nan's knees and, for the first time, never cries over losing a child. Nan knows this is it. Wherever Himself is gone in his head this night, it's obvious he isn't coming back. With a slight nod of his head and a slow blinking of his eyes, he beckons to hold his little boy. Nan carefully hands Isaac to his father. He carries the lifeless child in his big arms and walks to the window.

"Where are the birds, Isaac?" he asks.

Nan roars from the grief and falls backward into Mammy's barrel chair.

Nan's grandfather goes to the shed in the backyard to bring in the pine box he made for Isaac two weeks earlier—building coffins isn't something people want to do in the throes of losing a loved one, especially a child. When Himself can no longer stand to the window with Isaac, he brings the child back to his mother. Nan sets about undressing her baby and washes him for the last time. She lifts the stove's big damper and stuffs Isaac's clothes into the fire with the poker.

Nan gets up from the old chopping block; her legs are numb and tingling with sleep and cold. Her heart is beyond grateful the time of losing Isaac is long past. The next time she goes up to cut the grass on her grandfather's grave, she'll tell him she never stops thinking of him. She has never had the nerve to visit Isaac's grave in Little Placentia, and she's half relieved to hear the oldest cemeteries are so full that they'll soon be clearing bog for a third one. Somehow, this brings her relief, as if no one else will ever pass over the graves of her other children buried in the sodden ground.

Nan looks back to the house, her home—no longer that cauldron of revulsion with the Crooked Auld Bastard finally out of his misery and buried. *Is the loneliness any better*, she wonders? It is. Yet she hopes Himself and Isaac and Isaac's dead siblings are walking, holding hands, and laughing. She tries to imagine Isaac older and saying *birds* instead of *buds*.

For a split second, she hears a bang. Then footsteps.

"Oh, Mr. Morrissey! What a fright ya give me! I t'ought ya were dead, b'y," Nan says laughing, brushing the snow from the backside of her coat, and kicking the heels of her boots off the hard ground.

"No, me dear," he says, laughing, "As far as I know, I'm still alive, girl."

Mr. Morrissey extends a big hand down to help her up.

"It must be years since I see ya," Nan says, right out of breath and not over the fact he's not dead.

"Anyhow, Missus, I got an old car. Me brudder in S'n John's died an' left 'er t' me."

"A car?" Nan says, looking up at his face, as handsome as she remembers, even more so in the moon's lively light. "I was never in one o' them."

"Sure, that can't be true, missus."

"Aye!"

"Well, girl, come on!" he says, hurrying around the car to open her door.

"P'raps we'll go in fer a mug-up. I've some lovely Christmas cake I'll cut early on yer account."

"I won't go fast, missus, don't fret."

"I can't leave, 'fraid someone will come," she says, knowing they could drive across Newfoundland and back and no one would be after visiting, but she won't dare say.

"One little run down the road, come on, girl. We'll be gone

no time."

Nan thinks back to what the Youngfella from in the Lane used to tell her about all the things the young crowd does in the cars. She supposes Mr. Morrissey wouldn't want to do the like of that with her. She's glad Himself never had a car. *Jesus, 'twas all bad enough*, she mutters to herself, half laughing at her thought.

"Wha?" Mr. Morrissey asks.

"Nuttin', b'y," she says, laughing. "Don't mind me; I 'spose I'm a bit nervous, is all."

"I can drive her as good as I can handle me horse," he assures her.

From inside the car, Nan watches the stars play hide and seek behind drifting clouds. It's freezing out, but not in here. She can't get over it. Of all the times she has watched the water and birds and sky and hills from the beach this time of year, never has she done so without the bitter wind driving her back across the road and into the house. She never saw the point in sitting in a car, missing the true sounds of nature, until now. It is different. No water seeps from her eyes and across her cheeks from the wind's bite. The irritating bawls of the gulls and crows fighting are dimmed, and she's able to watch them circle the white caps and snatch fish from the water without much distraction—except, perhaps, for Mr. Morrissey, who has the prate and won't stop talking and telling stories. But Nan just loves to listen to words, especially those free of condemnation, orders, self-doubt, and pity. Sure, she can do both. And she does.

She still can't get over the fact Mr. Morrissey isn't dead. She enjoys the never-ending show put off by the seabirds—with the conniving crows doing little of the work, only watching and waiting for the gulls to land with their catches. Then the fighting begins. The merciless crows never care a bit for one young gull with a broken wing, having been taken by the wind into the cast iron crab winch—a big iron wheel used to haul boats from the water. Part of Nan wants badly to jump from the car and throw rocks at the crows, but she knows she has no right interfering with the work of God, or Mother Nature, whichever is master.

Mr. Morrissey's soft, pleasant voice keeps her in the car and lost in tales of rumrunners and Al Capone and St. Pierre and the Wild Cape Shore—that endless wall of splendid cliffs of jagged rock wigged in meadows of green, as green as her grandfather said Ireland is, and the great caves for hiding booze and tobacco concealed at high tide. *If I had to know*, she had like to say, *I would've told Himself about the caves full o' booze an' smokes an' as sure as there's shit in a cat, he would've went lookin' fer the caves an' wit' any luck, never come back*. But since she feels luck has a way of avoiding her, too, she doesn't bother to say. She's just glad he's finally gone.

Nan imagines Mr. Morrissey is home now, in Custlett, in his little bungalow painted bright orange. He has raised his windows to let out the heat. Nan suspects he has seen a ghost or two, perhaps even the devil, himself, and he'll have lots to tell next time he visits. The Cape Shore crowd have the best stories. She supposes he has his chunk of boiled raisin cake eaten by now and is enjoying another mug of tea.

A rooster's crow wakes Nan from her latest dream. The squawks of hens shifting in preparation of laying bring Nan from half asleep to mostly awake. The shadows on her walls tell her it's about five-thirty in the morning. Maybe quarter to six. She tosses her head at the knowing she won't be seeing Mr. Morrissey today. Or any day for that matter.

Hates auld dreams, she mutters.

Old Man and His Dory

From her morning nap on the daybed, a loud noise frightens Nan—likely one of them *big ugly trucks*, as she calls them, bringing fill to make new roads here in Freshwater. When she looks out the window, she sees the other side of Castle Hill and realizes she's over at her grandfather's place, on The Blockhouse. The old home rumbles with the loose, beach-rocked ground below it. Nan looks down to make sure she has her rubbers on. She does. She runs to the kitchen door leading to the back porch, opens it and lunges towards the heavy door to the outside. As she's opening the storm door, a strange noise is heard—it is seawater rushing through the rosebushes. The thorny plants hold their place in the onslaught of the sea gone mad. A surge of frothy pale-green water comes roaring around both sides of the house and splashes up over the step, onto her coat, over the tops of her rubbers and onto her feet. The sight, alone, is enough to bring weakness to most of her body. She manages to close the heavy door just in time, and the rail allows her someplace to grip, to keep her from being swept away by the flood. There's no time to close the storm door. It bangs off the rotting clapboard of the house, its unsteady hinges allowing it to jerk up and down from the strength of the violent sea. She turns to witness the angry sea stomping around the yard. The moment the water temporarily retreats, Nan turns the knob and pushes the heavy door open again. As she's slamming it shut, she watches the return of the sea's savage scend swirl around the step, making its way to the door. She runs in through the kitchen and turns left, into the parlour, for a better look. Her grandfather's dory swings out from its mooring—the step's iron rail—and the boat bangs against the house.

Nan heads back to the porch. Her rubber boots splash through saltwater covering the spruce planked floor. She leans and grabs a yaffle of wood from the box, then hurries back into the kitchen. A stream of water now forms a widening river on the canvas of the narrow kitchen. The mauling of the house's creosote shores and long wooden spans by snarling water beneath the floorboards nearly frightens the life out of her. She spills the wood onto the floor, then scrambles to save it from as much wetness as possible. The canvas lifts in spots where the edges of the floorboards are rotten. Water pushes through. Nan is startled more than ever. The sea has never come this high, but she makes fast for upstairs, just in case. First, she goes to a bedroom window and can't tell if the ground is white with snow or the foaming sea. She goes across the hall to Isaac's room and leans against the window.

"Where are the birds, Isaac?" she says and looks down, into the face of her baby boy.

"Buds!" Isaac says.

"All the birds are up on the hill, in the trees, Isaac—stayin' away 'til the vexed water runs back t' the sea."

"Buds," he says again.

"Yes, me darlin', *buds*," Nan says, rubbing the child's sweating head.

Nan leaves the room. Isaac clings tightly to the back of her neck and her arm, as they go along the stair rail to the front window. The water is swirling around the road, louder than ever now, heaving rocks of all sizes in every direction. Nan squints at the window. Through the salty ocean spray and dirty foam whipped up by the wind and sea, she's barely able to make out her grandfather in his dory. He's trying to make his way down the road to see if neighbours need a hand. He's standing, and

Nan doesn't understand how he doesn't fall overboard, the way the boat is being tossed about. She never worries, for it's the happiest her grandfather is—when he's taking on the sea. "A wanerful way t' pass the time," he'll say when he comes in for his tea.

Surely, her grandfather has lost his mind. He is standing with both his arms raised above his head. It looks as if he's smiling. Nan lays Isaac back in his crib and goes back to the window. She raises the pane, despite the ocean's spray flying at her.

"Is that all ya got?" her grandfather roars to the heavens.

Nan returns to the crib and picks up a smiling Isaac again. They head back to the window Nan had been forced to close. They turn to head downstairs.

They are just turned away when the sound of the water leaving the land brings her back to the window. She gasps, figuring it's the end of the old man when she sees him, dory and all, being stolen by the fuming ebbing tide. His back is to the sea, as if he's having one last look at the old house that he'd painstakingly floated from Little Placentia to have a less-crowded harbour to fish from. One second the dory is on its nose, with her grandfather gripping the risings holding the boat's seats in place. The next moment the boat is nearly on its side with her grandfather standing, feet on the water side of the dory and his wide shoulders snug into the other. His oars are nowhere to be seen. Nan and Isaac go down the narrow stairs.

As quick as that, Nan bursts out laughing, frightening little Isaac, when she sees the dory left stranded in the muddy road. Her grandfather is cursing and swearing because he doesn't have logs to help roll the heavy boat all the way back into the yard, to her mooring at the step. His woodpile has been taken by the sea and dispersed throughout the town and the ocean.

Nan titters again, noticing one of the nine-foot oars standing upright in the sturdy rosebushes, the other under her grandfather's arm.

Tomorrow, the townspeople will gather for the big clean up, and men will brood over their losses of boats and flakes and stages. While the men are moping around the house and not yet back fishing, the women will pray for a quick return to normal. Himself is drunk and stumbling down the stairs.

"Wha's all the goddamn racket about?" he slurs.

"If ya were any good, ya'd know an' ya'd be awake an' out lendin' a hand wit' me," Nan's grandfather says firmly through laboured breath.

It isn't like Himself to be drunk, not while Isaac is alive. For a second or two, Nan shakes herself from this, one of the many bad dreams reigning her existence. She looks out the window. With nothing or no one looking back at her, Nan sinks back into Mammy's comfy quilt and the awful dream. Laying Isaac back in his crib, she winces from the pain in her shoulders. She goes to kiss his head, only to see no one in her stiff arms. The crib isn't even there. Himself had burned almost everything belonged to the dead youngsters after Isaac died.

"No need o' havin' more reminders than those trapped in our hearts an' minds," he said.

Nan hated to admit he was right, but she couldn't deny that.

That night, Nan creeps down to the kitchen, unsure if Himself is drunk, alive, or dead. And what of her grandfather? The flood? No one is in the kitchen, or the parlour. There's no smell of booze, or feelings of ill spirits in the house. She peeks out the side kitchen window at the frozen ground still white and sparkling with snow. She opens the back door to see her grandfather's rotten dory, what's left of it, still tied to the step—scarcely a trace of oil paint left on her wide, pine planks and split, mahogany gunwales. The seats are just bits of crumbling wood soiling the inside of the boat once handled and cared for like a treasured child. Weeds grow wildly from the mulched wood of the old vessel. Nan misses her grandfather.

"T'anks be t' Jesus," she says when I open the kitchen door and startle her from her long, morning nap.

"Now, Nan," I laugh, "there's hardly a need t' compare me t' Him."

"How was Mass?" she asks, as if she hadn't just spent days and nights in Little Placentia and at The Blockhouse with family members long gone. "Did ya sit wit' her? Was her mudder there, too? Did yer darlin' show off Mammy's ring?"

"Nan, girl," I laugh, "take a spell, girl, with the questions; I'll get t' all of it. I needs a drink."

"Ya never went to the club after Mass?"

"I never, an' I'm not talkin' 'bout booze; I'm parched fer a drop o' water, that's all."

"Oh?" she says, surprised I wasn't at the club.

I take a mug from the lowest board on her wall and dip it into the barrel in the porch.

"Mind the water on the floor," Nan says.

"What water? Do ya have a leak? I can go up on the roof an' have a look, if ya like, before we head out fer our special row."

"Don't mind me, b'y," she says. "I had that dream again—about me gran'fadder's house floodin' o'er on the beach, an' got confused, I 'spose."

"Oh, alright," I say, walking over to Nan and gently tapping her on the shoulder.

I take a seat to her table and shift my chair so I'm facing her half sitting up on the daybed.

"So...do I ask t' see an' hold Mammy's ring, then ask her t' marry me?"

"I 'spose, b'y," she says, casually. "I 'spose it don't matter how ya asks her; she'll be waitin'. I guarantee ya that much—I told ya about the stars beamin' from her eyes last night once the thought o' marriage settled 'pon her."

"Show me yer hands, Nan?"

"What fer?" she asks, as if I've lost my mind, altogether.

Nan slowly moves her crooked arms in front of her body and lets them rest upon her thighs.

"What, b'y?" she sighs.

"Yer weddin' ring; where is it?"

"What odds 'bout that," she scowls.

"I just wanted t' make sure I places the ring on the right finger, that's all," I say, unsure myself the words just uttered came from *my* voice.

"Lard Jesus," Nan says, disgusted, "I never told a soul, but before they closed an' nailed the lid on Himself's coffin, I slipped the ring off an' let it fall down alongside his suit o' clothes; I wanted n'er part o' him t' remind me o' the torturin' he give me all them years."

"I'm sorry, Nan. I shouldn't have asked; I just wanted t'…."

"That's alright, me child," she says, warmly. "I knows ya wants t' do the right thing an' not t' make a mock'ry o' the works. The ring, ya puts in on her left hand—the finger next to her pinkie."

"Best kind. Thanks, Nan. I'll be sure t' make sure she's leanin' into me in the middle o' the dory— 'fraid the ring'll fall into the water."

"Ya better not come back here if the like o' that happens," Nan laughs, but I know she's dead serious.

"That won't happen, Nan, girl," I say, smiling.

My stomach rumbles from the hunger, but I've a feeling if I eat it will come back up quicker than it went down.

"You'll do the best kind, me dear," Nan says, reaching out and grabbing my right hand. "Just be yerself an' it'll all go the way ya wants it to. An' by the Jesus, if I don't see ye after supper, there'll be some racket t'morrow! Ya knows I'll be here waitin' t' hear the news—an' ev'ry detail, too."

"Don't worry, Nan, we'll be by, as always. Plus, we gotta finish cleanin' the damsons before they goes soft."

"Shag the damsons," Nan says, laughing.

"It would be nice t' not t' have t' go at 'em, but ya knows they'll spoil if we don't do it sooner than later."

"I know, b'y," the tired old woman agrees.

"Just foolish dreams, Nan, girl; that's all."

"I 'spose, b'y," she says. "Anyhow, go on now an' get yer affairs in order; there's a lovely young woman waitin' fer yer hand—the same as *you* wants."

"Okay, Nan. I know she'll wear that ring the rest of her life."

"She will," Nan says. "An' may her life, an' yours, be long an' prosp'rous. Ye have many years left, an' after t'day, ya can call them years *forever*."

That Day

The sea is dead calm, except for the scattered youngster skipping flat stones across the water of its smooth surface or throwing long, skinny rocks high into the air—the Deadman's Dive—when they hit, a rapid, electrifying sucking sound may be heard. It's heavy competition, mostly among boys.

Groups of little girls in their Sunday dresses and shoeless feet tread lightly along the sand at low tide, bending to pick up beach glass—smooth bits of broken bottles, two-hundred-year-old glass floats (green, mostly), and marbles a fraction their original size, among other *treasures*—so much on the beach for all ages to enjoy. The excitement of the youngones usually entices us to join in on the fun of skipping or throwing rocks, or to help young eyes find old things. But I can't get past the look My Love held in her eyes during Mass this morning, and I make no offers to join in on the sure delight.

With the oars just out of the stage and laid in across the seats of the dory, I hear My Love's skirt swishing through the tall grasses carpeting the hill. She makes her way alongside the great, wooden slipway of giant logs fit together on a slant into the sea for the landing and launching of boats big and small. Each spring the slip is kept in place by hulks of men with homemade mallets, newly creosoted wooden logs and blocks and extra-large forged spikes.

I want to pretend I'm too busy to notice her, but any chance to steal a glance, no matter the distance between us, is hard to resist. An ornate basket made by her father and festooned with embroidered cloth fashioned by her mother's fingers is tucked alongside her slender, hard-worked body—her arm cupping the basket's handle is raised just enough to keep it from tipping. I'm anxious to see and taste what foods might be inside. No doubt she, and perhaps her mother, were busy baking between Mass and now, or maybe she stayed up late last night, kept wide awake by her longing for whatever this day might bring, and made my favourite biscuits—shortcake.

My Love looks serious until she notices me gawking at her. Then, her smile lights up the nooks and crannies of the cove where the sun is blocked by tall, jagged rocks or trees. I lean against the dory's bow, flicking the painter rope with my fingers. A four-foot-long book hook dangles from my right hand. When she steps off the lush path and her good shoes shift the small rocks of the beach, a shiver races up my spine. My ears tingle and goosebumps cover the skin beneath the raised hair on my arms. Even though I'd shaved my neck extra carefully for this day, the tingling sensation is no less.

Older fellows on the beach stop whatever they are pretending to be doing and stand in the doors of their stages. They lean against their overturned boats and crane their necks with odd expressions of caution—as though they're trying to see through the fog while navigating a schooner. Their looks remind me of stories Father used to tell us about his adventures at sea—a dory crossing their ship's path, or a cliff, sunker or a clump of ice hiding within striking distance of his schooner's bow. The old men continue to suck on their stubby bottles of beer, never taking their eyes off the marvelous spectacle adorning the beach—My Love. The presence of humans here never fails to bait a flock of crying gulls and other lively seabirds to the sky above us.

"Some racket," I say to My Love, as she approaches.

"Sure, they don't know 'tis a Sunday," she laughs at my

comment about the birds. "I'm sure they won't starve fer the sake o' one day. We'll have t' give 'em a crust o' bread, I 'spose."

"Now, girl," I say, "ya can't be wastin' food on old gulls. They're liable t' take the ring right off yer finger."

"The only way that's comin' off is if you takes it off," she giggles. "I 'spose yer right about the bread, though…that's not to say I have fresh bread in this basket or anyt'ing. How're ya gettin' on?"

"Girl, if I survived this mornin' in Mass," I laugh sheepishly to try and hide my embarrassment, "I'll get through the rest o' this day."

"Ah, 'twasn't that bad, b'y," she says, trying to pretend I hadn't made a proper spectacle of myself.

"I 'spose, girl."

"I have a confession t' make, fadder," she laughs.

"What's that, my child?" I respond in mockery.

"This mornin' at Mass was the best day o' me life."

Her eyes never leave mine and I'm sent someplace, in or out of my mind, surely, I've never been. Perhaps I'm feeling the virtuousness of genuine love, and it's all because of the ring. At first glance, little has changed about My Love—her eyes, as ever, offer their colour to the spirited, stunning sky of blue showing itself now and then through the dissipating fog—but she's not the same woman she was, even yesterday.

"Show," I say, reaching for the basket. "Smells like shortbread biscuits t' me."

"Never ya mind, now," she says, swinging the basket away from me. "No lookin', mind!"

"No lookin', I swear," I say, laughing.

She hands me the basket and I lay it on the seat of the boat's stern. The skin of her exposed forearms is softer than ever, as I hold it in my hands. I caress her arms, my thumbs on the softer underside of them and my fingers moving gently over the well-toned muscles of the other sides. Her shoes scuff the rocks separating our feet, and she lets her forehead land gracefully against mine.

"Give it to 'er, b'y!" an old man bawls out from the door of his stage.

I want to tell him to batter, but My Love's laughter removes any bitterness the old man's ignorance has stirred in me. The snickering of other old men on the beach tugs at my wild side, too, but My Love's eyes quickly tether me back to her soul—rapidly dissolving their pitiful voices. I move my hands up to her head and softly embrace the sides of her face. Her closed mouth smiles at me, *for* me, and I wonder if I'll have the strength to push the dory out into the water.

"I'm glad ya did what ya did this mornin'," I say. "I had a lot goin' through me mind an' I wasn't payin' attention t' what I was at—let alone where I was to."

"An' what were ya so caught up in, ya didn't know yer head from yer arse?" she asks, laughing.

With her beautiful face still cupped in my hands, I lay my lips against hers and we remain as one for a few moments. Her top, thin lip fits perfectly between mine. I open my eyes to see her eyes opening, too. We both smile, but don't dare separate. She lets the weight of her head and body fall into me and we kiss passionately, as if we were up in the meadow at night, or at her mother's back doorstep out of the line of sight of nosey neighbours. I slide my hands down the sides of her arms now clutched firmly around my waist, until I reach *her* hands. I grasp them as gently as possible, wishing to Jesus we are anywhere but where we are. The trembling fingers of my left hand fumble until my thumb and index finger are cradling the ring. I squeeze her precious hand and she returns the gesture with an even tighter hold. Our kiss intensifies. She takes the deepest breath I've ever heard, as we know it's time to shove the dory out into the water and upon the sea where we can escape the growing snickers from young and old alike. Even the gulls are louder than ever.

"Jesus Christ, b'y!" a voice roars out, interrupting the deepest moment we've ever shared. "If you soon don't give it to 'er, I will!"

"Go home; yer mudder got hot buns fer ya!" My Love yells at the saucy old man.

"Yes, go home outta it, b'y!" I add, the two of us laughing our heads off—I couldn't hold it in any longer.

Aside from a few grumbles, most of the ignorant old men disappear quietly into their warped stages once used by them to clean and salt fish they'd caught. I understand their predicament; if they were able, their boats wouldn't be rotting, bottom-up, and they'd be preparing for tomorrow morning's trip back upon the sea in search of the next meal. Not that the odd fellow might not still bawl obscenities our way, but the feeling of loss of livelihoods wouldn't be so prevalent here on a such a lovely Sunday afternoon.

"Alright," I say, "hop in. I'll hold yer hand."

My Love's hand is hot and dry against my clammy one, as I help steady her. She mindfully sits her behind on the gunwale facing the Googly Hole meadow—all the men and curious boys are in the other direction, to her back. I pretend to close my eyes, as I squint at her brown legs; you'd never say she had any relation to Ireland—but her family was ferociously determined never to lose sight of their Irish roots and customs. I remember Nan saying how her grandfather used to talk of a dark-skinned people of ancient Ireland: The *Black Irish*, he called them. And, yes, many of them had blue eyes—the colour of My Love's.

She makes it into the dory with ease. When I let go of her hand, she grabs the basket and tucks it in the end of the boat. The grapnel I've intentionally put in the boat's bow keeps her from putting the basket there. Unknowingly, or not, she's forced to sit on the seat in front of me.

"Ya have t' sit here," I say, "cause the boat'll be off balance if ya don't, see."

"Fine wit' me," she says, smiling.

"Now," I say, "when I gets her out an' hops aboard, you sit on my seat, the middle one, 'til I'm up 'longside ya. Then take hold o' the gunnel on yer right an' make yer way to yer seat."

Again, we're interrupted by the harsh voice of a grumpy old man.

"Whattaya doin' here, *Yank*?"

We look up to see an American friend of ours strolling towards us. He pays no mind to the cheek of the old man.

"Hey!" our friend calls out.

"Yes, b'y," I return. "What are ya at t'day?"

He smiles and hastens his steps in our direction.

"Got yer cam'ra, I see," I say, smiling. "Nice day fer a few snaps."

"'Tis," he says with a little laugh.

"Ah, yer catchin' on," I commend his attempt at speaking our language.

"Tryin' me best, boy," he tries again.

"Yer doin' the best kind, me friend," I say.

"T'anks," he says, laughing harder now. "Lovely day."

"'Tis, 'ndeed," My Love says, having moved up to her seat and facing us. "How are ya?"

"Very good, thank you, ma'am," he says, smiling his charming smile. "Heading out?"

"Yes," I say. "Couldn't ask fer a nicer one."

"That's for sure," he says. "Mind if I take your photo?"

"Not me, b'y," I say. "Maybe the missus can give ya a smile."

"I don't care, b'y," she says.

"Great!" he says. "It'll just take a sec, and then I'll let you both enjoy the rest of this magnificent day. The fog burning off in the background makes for a great shot, thank you."

My Love poses perfectly for the box-shaped camera while our friend stoops and leans in over the dory.

"Nice," he says.

The camera goes *click*.

"Thank-you, again, ma'am."

"Thank *you*," she returns his politeness.

"You are more than welcome," he says.

"That'll be nice," I say. "I've never seen a new picture of her."

"It certainly will be," he says. "You'll treasure this the rest of your lives. Can't beat a photo for keeping memories alive. I'll drop it up to you as soon as I can. Our dark room at McAndrew is down now for some reason or another."

"Best kind, me son," I say, offering a quick handshake to the photographer.

"Great!" he says. "Well, enjoy your day. Be careful out there. I don't have to tell you how moody that sea is."

"We will, thanks," My Love says.

"Yes, we will," I add. "Have a good one, yerself."

Our friend makes his way back up out of the beach, toward the meadow above The Point.

"Now," I say, returning my gaze to My Love. "Just as well fer ya t' stay in yer seat; I'll manage from here."

She takes a deep breath and for a few seconds I wonder if she's ever going to let it out. As I grab and steady the oars, I watch her taking in the beauty around her—the quartz veins threading the cliffs of granite below the sloped meadow where youngsters run, roll and play, the long grass drooping contently in the midday heat and probably glad for the break against scythes and sickles, horses playing and stressing nervous cows, half-grown-in sheep gawking motionlessly, except for their chawing on grass like a fellow enjoying his tobacco, and whatever else she views as beautiful. All I see is *her*—more beautiful than all those things combined, than all the fish in the sea, than the beautiful lines of planked wooden boats, both upright and afloat or turned bottom up on the beach (even rotting wood and scaling, flaking oil paint has appeal), and prettier than the sun burning up the fog and allowing us to take in all we see and adore.

"Daddy would love it here t'day," she says. "Oh, how he loved his Sundays. Who don't, I 'spose."

"'Specially this one," I blurt out, instantly regretting opening my mouth.

"Yes, 'tis certainly a grand day, isn't it," she says. "No different than all the other Sundays we've gone fer a row, I 'spose, though," she says, feigning curiousity.

I dig the oars into the rocks of the seabed and shove the dory from the shore. A racket comes from behind My Love. She crosses her legs, and although her Sunday skirt is long, I catch a glimpse of the skin just above her knee.

"Jesus, Mary 'n' Joseph," I mutter.

"Wha?" she asks.

"Oh, ah, I, ah," I stammer. "I thought I forgot the boat hook, but I sees it now."

"Sure!" she says, winking, looking past me.

Before I can come up with another excuse for my nervous outburst, I turn to see what she's looking at.

"Sorry, missus," a boy about twelve years of age says. "Want us t' give ye a good shove? We're not very big, but we're strong; ye'll see."

"I'll give 'er a good shove," another dirty old man bawls out from nearby.

"Go home outta it, b'y," I sing out, "an' let yer wife put up wit' yer sauce!"

I smile at My Love, so she might think I'm joking. She's laughing.

"Are all the b'ys from Freshwater as saucy as him?" she asks the little boy.

"I'm not," he answers, "but most are."

"I see," she says, twirling her hair with a finger and pretending to give me a sly look.

No reply comes from the lippy man, as he walks around and sits on his overturned boat, irritable and facing the meadow of the Dead Man's Cave. Part of me wishes it is three-hundred years ago and I'm a French soldier stationed on the garrison once occupying the meadow so I can pick off the saucy prick with a musket ball. But I keep my anger to myself—too many important matters to focus on.

"Don't mind him," the young boy says to My Love.

"Ah, I knows yer not the cutest now," she says.

The young boy's face instantly flushes into some shade of red or purple, as his friend giggles.

"Cute, alright," I mutter.

"Wha?" My Love asks.

"Nevermind, I was takin' 'bout the dog up there," I lie.

My Love looks up and the boys turn around.

"I don't see a dog," she says.

"What dog?" asks the *cute* boy.

"Never ya mind, now!" I say, trying not to sound as insecure as I feel. "He took off into the trees."

Imagine, feeling insecure over youngsters favouring the same beauty I admire.

"Alright, b'ys," I say smiling, "on the count o' t'ree, ye shove an' I'll push the oars off the bottom. Hold onto yer seat or the gunnels, My *Love*."

The boys burst out laughing at my designation for the best thing that's ever happened to me. I look at My Love. Her smile immediately disarms me, and I regain focus on the big day ahead.

"Alright," I say.

"One, two, t'ree!" we all shout at once.

The boys grunt, standing past their knees in the cool water, while waving to My Love. *If I was ten or twelve*, I think, *I'd be no different in the presence of something so masterfully stunning*. I laugh to myself, remembering the times before the people of Argentia and Marquise stumbled into Freshwater—I thought nothing more lovely than the lines and curves of a wooden boat.

"Ya alright, me son?" My Love asks, her genuine laughter lost a little in the splashing of the oars as they graze the top of the sea.

"Yes, girl. I couldn't be happier," I say. "We'll take 'er out 'round The Point an' maybe pull into Sandy Beach fer a bite t' eat, if ya like."

"Whatever ya wants t' do," she says, cheerfully. "How 'bout we goes out in the middle o' the bay first, between Point Verde Light an' First Beach?"

"Can't see why not," I answer her. "The water is as slick as oil t'day; might as well take advantage of it."

Swept Away

In the distance, enormous sails gracefully guide a schooner toward Merasheen Bank.

"Strange t' see schooners out on a Sunday," My Love says.

"'Tis," I say. "I've a feelin' I knows what's goin' on, though."

Two other schooners are parallel to the gigantic cliffs of Red Island. The words are no sooner out of my lips when a loud bang rings out, shaking loose the still air.

"Jesus Christ!" My Love says, disgusted. "Do they have t' be at that *all* the time?

"Takes away from our *day o' rest*, don't it," I agree.

"I'm sure there's t'ousands o' men in Newfunland who'd love t' have a schooner of their own but could never afford it, an' there's the Americans gettin' 'em fer chickenfeed an' blowin' 'em up fer target practice."

I can easily begin a rant of my own, but time is too precious and the quicker she's satisfied with how far we've rowed, the better—the faster we'll get to Sandy Beach. Those thoughts are no sooner out of my mouth when she sighs and hangs her head.

"'Tis alright, My Love. We don't need t' get any closer t' that madness."

"Arseholes!" she says.

I can't argue with how she feels after foreigners took over her childhood home and playing fields and drove her family away, forever. Yet I'm glad she easily accepts and likes my American friend who's now *our* friend.

"I know, I know," I stutter, "but let's make the most o' this lovely day. At least it seems they're after clearin' our waters o' the Germans. As bad as 'tis been fer you an' yer mudder, brudder, an' yer poor fadder, we might not even be here if it weren't fer them *foolish* Yanks."

"I know yer right," she says. "Sorry, b'y. Let's go t' Sandy Beach an' have a feed."

I lift the left oar and dig the right-handed one into the calm water. In seconds, the dory is facing the cliffs of home. I let the other oar drop back into the water and lean hard into both paddles—hauling harder than I ever have in my life. The sea's surface remains as smooth as untouched lard in a giant tub, as My Love's stare catches me off guard.

"I love you," she says.

My heart shoves blood through my body and my legs used for pushing off the bottom of the boat to add more strength to my row instantly tumble into weakness.

"Why did ya stop rowin'?" she asks. "I'm sorry. I shouldn't have…."

"No, no, no," I interrupt her. "I'm sorry. I just…I don't know. If ya knew how long I'd been waitin' t' hear that come out of yer mouth…"

"So…." she never removes her gaze from my blurry eyes. "Are those…"

"Nah, 'tis just the wind," I lie.

"What wind?" she says, laughing.

"Alright, alright, ya got me. Jesus, girl, ya half frightened the life outta me is all."

"I'm sorry," she begins.

I interrupt her with a kiss. Both oar handles dig into my ribs as I lean into her, but I couldn't care less about a little bit of pain—as long as it is caused by her.

"Hang on," I say, before sitting back and hauling the oars in and across the seats on either side of the boat.

I drag the sleeve of my Sunday shirt across my eyes, no longer able to hide my tears of joy. I lean forward again and take her hands in mine.

"Must seem awfully strange how I've been callin' ya *My Love* fer ages, but never said it."

"Never bothered me, sure. I would o' said it long ago but I was afraid I'd scare ya off."

"Not likely," I laugh, still sniffling like a spoiled youngster.

Twisting the ring, a little big for her tiny finger, I cough before looking into her eyes. They're still glowing of the sky's blue but are also multi-coloured with moving clouds. A gust of wind stirs the surface of the sea. When the scend caused by the sudden gust of wind rolls beneath the dory, I quickly but softly grab hold of her face. I kiss her. She kisses me back, more enthusiastically than ever. I know people are supposed to wait until they're properly married before they have too much pleasure, but all I can think about is tonight, up in the fresh hay of the barn, the horse's winter blanket clean and covering us.

"Let's get in out of it," I say. "Alright?"

"'Kay," she says. "Safer in closer to shore in case the wind comes again, an' besides there's likely more fun t' be had on that hidden beach. I don't see anyone else in there. 'Tis a wonder—such a nice day an' all."

"Not that easy t' get to from the top," I'm pleased to say.

Her smirk reveals *a streak of badness*, as Mother used to say, and my knees are nowhere to be found again—I look to make sure they're still there. Without delay, I grab the oars and row until the dory is cutting through the calm-again water like she's under sail.

Other than us, the beach is empty. It is cut off on both sides by sharp cliffs reaching hard and confidently into the sea. We quickly gather bits of driftwood, and My Love has a fire lit in no time. From her mother's basket, she unwraps sliced baloney, laying it into the cast-iron pan I keep in the boat. I raise my head and stare at the basket for a sign of a shortbread biscuit, but she catches me.

"Yer some impatient, b'y," she laughs.

"Ya have no idea," I say.

"Maybe I do," she says, grinning again.

I grab a fork and turn the baloney over before removing the pan from the flames. My Love pours steeped tea into two mugs. My right eye squints from the glare of sunlight off the ring. It also gives me a swift kick back into the real reason we're here.

"Bun?" she asks.

"In a minute."

I stand up, stretch, and look at our surroundings. The roots of tuckamore trees protrude firmly from the light-brown ground above while crows caw to one another from tree to tree.

"The b'loney," My Love says.

"Oh, to be sure," I agree. "Ya needn't worry; they smelled that long before it was put in the pan."

"I 'spose the gulls will soon be here, too," she laughs.

"Well, before they do come an' drive us off our heads…"

"Yes?" she says, patiently—her eyes glowing with excitement.

I reach for her. She comes to me with ease. Holding hands, we lower ourselves to the rounded boulders of the beach.

"Alright," I say with more confidence than I've ever known, "hold out yer hands."

I hold her hands and look into her eyes. A lifetime of waiting has ended and now's my chance *not* to screw it up. *Don't fook it up, okay*, I hear my father's voice; he's laughing.

Wha's so funny?" she asks of my foolish grin.

"Oh, nothin', girl." Just rememberin' somet'ing Father used t' say that made us laugh."

"I knows that feelin," she says, pretending to have found happiness in the immense angst cast upon her by the death of her own father.

"Sorry, girl!" I say, smiling.

"'Tis alright," she says, finding her real smile again.

"So," I say, stalling in my fright, "now that we're not in the boat an' not out in deep water where I don't have t' worry 'bout fallin' overboard wit' the weakness…"

"Or gettin' sunk by a bomb," she reminds me.

"Yes, that, too," I stutter.

I stare off, half afraid she'll say *no* and then what a long ride it will be back around The Point to the beach. *Then* what?

"Wha's wrong?" she asks.

"Nothin', me dear. Nothin' at all. In fact, it seems like the first time in me life somethin' feels right, an' it's all 'cause o' you."

"Yer some sweet, ya are," she says.

She really means it. The blue of the sky above the hill behind me reflecting in her eyes distracts me yet again.

"Yer pretty sweet, yerself," I say, the confidence having returned to my new self. "Do ya mind?" I ask, catching hold of her ring.

"'Course not," she says.

I twist the ring gently and pull it towards me slowly. It comes off with relative ease. I roll the ring between the thumb and index finger of my right hand and admire Great Grandmother's initials, *B.C.*.

"Bethany Clancy," she says. "What a lovely name. 'Magine if we had our own little *Bethany*."

"Ya really means that?"

"Why wouldn't I? Why wouldn't *we*?"

"Yes, yes," I say, happier than ever.

The inside of the ring holds the sun's gleam. My Love takes a deep breath to help stir me from my current trance. Without apologizing for my tardiness, I take her left hand and turn it up. She gasps again.

"I really, really, really love YOU," I say, calmly.

"Oh!" she exclaims. "I really, really, really love YOU."

"If yer satisfied, I'd be very happy if ya'd consider bein' me wife," I say. "An' maybe, please God, someday, we can have youngones t' call our own—our own Bethany?"

"An' little brothers an' sisters fer her t' play with," she says. "Yes, Jesus, sorry, I mean *yes*; I'd be so contented t' be yer wife."

She holds out her left hand and points to the finger the ring should go on.

"Just in case," she laughs. "I know. She told me."

"Wha'?" I ask, surprised.

"I went t' see Nan before I come down here," she says, laughing quietly, without taking away from this moment—*our* moment.

My trembling left hand tries its best to hold her waiting hand while I place the ring over the tip of the finger which will hold evidence that she'll be mine for all time. Hot tears from her eyes drip onto the ring. I fight to hold back my own tears of joy.

"You've always made me very content," I say, "even before we met. The first time I ever lay eyes on ya, you were all I ever wanted. An' now yer mine at last."

"At last," she says. "I've been swept away."

The ring goes smoothly over her finger, and I think of what Nan said about losing the ring.

"I really do love ya," I say. "I promise t' always do me best t' make ya happy."

"Just knowin' yer in me life is happiness enough," she says, reaching in, and pulling me closer to her.

She squeezes her head into my shoulder, then slowly moves her face, dry now, up to mine until our lips meet. Again, the whole world disappears with her kiss. Even the bawls of the birds covering the trees above us seem to vanish during the length of our show of affection. A brisk gust of wind, followed by another seconds later, breaks up our moments of true peace. Love. Her. *Finally*.

"Have our tea an' get goin', will we?" I suggest.

"'Kay," she says, smiling. "I'm not hungry anymore, though. Oh my, I can't wait t' tell Mother."

"Ha! Me neither," I say. "…for you to tell her, I mean…must be the nerves."

We laugh at the obvious, as we gather our belongings.

"Here!" I shout to the noisy birds before flinging the hot baloney halfway up the bank.

"I'll put the pan and kettle back in the boat," My Love says.

"'Praps you'll get a biscuit when we gets back to the beach."

"I almost forgot about them," I say. "Ya never knows; me appetite might come back by then."

I row out into the growing waves. We're well clear of the craggy hillside before I turn the boat towards our beach. We look in at the entrance to the Googly Hole and make a couple of remarks about the times we've spent upon the grassy slopes above.

I stare at My Love, the wind in her hair, the kindness in her eyes, the wisdom beneath all she is. She sees something good in me, too, and looks intently into my soul. Instantly, our latest special moment is shaken to pieces by the sea.

We're just past The Point. A big wave lifts the dory. The right oar is hauled in under the boat by the force of the current. I struggle to get it out. I manage that much and fit the oar back between the thole pins.

"Ya got her!" My Love shouts over the sudden racket of wind and wave.

"Ya alright?" I shout back.

"I'm alright," she says, "a bit nervous, but I'll be alright when we gets in. I love you."

"We'll be fine, My Love," I say, fighting the sea and the rocks with the oar. "I love you, too."

I battle to straighten our path again. The rising wind and the disturbed sea have carried the dory very close to the sharp rocks. If the boat does strike the rocks, it won't damage anything, maybe a bit of paint, but that's no odds—the boat can take it. I use the right oar to shove us a few feet away from the serrated rocks.

When we drift out from the cliff, a rare, rogue wave comes barreling around The Point. I grab hold of the gunwales and am about to warn My Love to do the same. Saltwater fills my mouth, drowning my words. The oars are still there, bobbing, and shifting back and forth between the thole pins. I shake the salty spray from my face and look to make sure My Love is okay.

She is nowhere to be seen.

Aftermath

"My Love!" I scream. "Where are you? Where are you? Jesus, please, answer me. I'll throw ya the rope. Hang on! No, God! No! Please God, no!"

Even though the sea is only half angry now, there's still no sign of her. I wonder if she'd struck her head when she was thrown from the boat. I use the oars to take the boat back towards The Point. I let the dory drift in against the cliffs, haul in the oars and scour the sea from both sides and ends of the boat. No discolouration of the water can be seen which gives me hope she never hit head and she isn't bleeding. Perhaps she was carried towards the shore and is clinging to a slimy rock and waiting for me to notice her. She doesn't have the strength to call my name. I turn and look at every spot along the shoreline, but I don't see her. Maybe that's where I should have first taken the boat to look for her, instead of out into deeper water. I've never had someone get washed out of a small boat before, so I didn't know where to look first.

I'm dizzy. Everything around me is spinning—the rocks, the sea, the boat, the oars, the sky, and the growing number of people in their Sunday best on the beach.

I curse two shags meticulously cleaning their breasts upon the sharp rocks not far from the boat. Not a wing nor a cry for our peril do they offer. Instead, the birds remain unphased by the tragedy in their midst, continuing to pick at their feathers. An oar beats me in the guts, knocking me over backwards. A lead jigger lodges into my back.

"Fuck ya!" I yelp.

By the time I get up to rid the barbed hook from the flesh at the bottom of my back, I notice the boat has drifted quite a bit—long past wherever it was she'd fallen out. The swiftness of the powerful, erratic wave allowed her no time to utter a word, let alone sound for help; and the volume of the water raking the rocks, along with the racket of the shrill wind, muted any attempts she might have made to announce her hurried heave into the sea. There's still no sign of her.

"Jesus Christ, no!" My voice comes back at me from the sloped valley. "Why did ya have t' throw water in me eyes when I was about t' tell her t' hang on? Ya bastard! Help! Help me! She's gone into the water! Help! Jesus, someone help!"

It's like she never existed—a beautiful dream-turned-nightmare at the height of what began as the calmest Sunday afternoon ever.

Her quilt, the one her mother had sewn for her, is still on the seat where sat her beautiful self—kept in place by the weight of the water soaking it. The print of My Love remains in the floral-patterned quilt. I want to pick it up, cuddle it, cry more and smell it—anything for a trace of her, the only girl I'll ever love. I will bring it back to her mother sometime. Right now, I do what I must—keep looking.

I continue to row like a madman, screaming her name. The wind has returned, twisting the tempering sea into a moody imbecile which doesn't consider calming so I can properly look. If it weren't for the wind in my ears, I might be able to hear her calling me to save her.

Whitecaps casing the sea's surface cloud my vision, as I lean over the boat and stare into the deep greenness. Bits of kelp mess with my mind, floating in my face, offering false hope.

"Oh, thanks be t' Jesus, there ya are," I say in my panic.

I grab for her black knitted sweater.

"Goddamn it!"

I haul up a ghost net, set free by the relentless tide barreling in and out of the bay every six or seven hours. Father always said ghost nets would be the end of the fishery, but now I know, surely, they're the end of me.

The commanding scend of the sea keeps my dory moving. I struggle to row back to wherever we were when she disappeared. I haul in the oars and put them to one side. I grab the grapnel I'd intentionally put behind My Love earlier and fling it into the water. Rope in hand, I follow.

"Jesus!" I say of the shock from the cold.

My arms lose their strength within a minute of floundering in the water, as I keep hold of the extra rope always tied to the risings of the dory. I hold my breath and try to let my body sink. I open my eyes, but I can't see five feet in front of me. I kick my feet to get back to the surface and bump my head. I'm under the dory and flustered and scared. Now, I'm waiting for My Love to save *me*. My head breaches the surface again and I let out a mouthful of saltwater. The dory is being carried away on the tide. I use the strength I have left to drag myself along the rope. The sea lops over me, robbing me again of air, and I realize the sure peril My Love has been in since she ended up in the water. Into the air again, my breath spews saltwater. I reach the dory and grab the gunwales by the thole pins on the starboard side. I use my weight to tip the boat and lean in over enough until I reach the bottom of one of the seats. I pull my arms and kick my legs until the boat is a third full of water. Finally, I'm on the floor of the boat. The growing momentum of the sea's send causes the dory to shift violently, as the water sloshes from side to side and stem to stern. I get to my knees, get my bearings, and grab Father's wooden bailer from its place—its handle tucked securely behind the risings. I cling to the gunwale of the port side and bail as quickly as possible. The cold has set into my bones, and I can hardly utter her name through the shivering. I hear her and turn my head towards The Point.

"Goddamn gull! Batter!" I try to scream.

With most of the water out of the boat, I grasp the rope of the grapnel and start hauling the rusty, clawed anchor from the seabed. When its ring is visible, I grab the grapnel and haul it aboard. I place it back in the same place I'd taken it from. Why was I so greedy? If she'd been in the bow, she'd have had a better chance of staying in the boat. I've never felt more useless.

"I'll find you," I finally manage to get enough strength to shout. "I'll find you, My Love. I will."

If I'd been working down on The Base, instead of still raising cows and sheep and fishing, I might have had to work today, and this wouldn't have happened. I'd have been thinking of her all day and then whistled my way back home, scrubbed myself at the kitchen sink, scoffed tea and leftover fishcakes into me for supper and headed straight up the hill to see her.

I grab the oars and head back towards The Point. The closer I get, the less control I have of the dory. I try to turn the boat around, but it keeps getting hit broadside by the waves. I'm not worried about getting turned over; dories are made to handle much of what the sea can dish out. But this is the worst storm I've ever been in—the sun is out, the wind gone again as quick as that and with it the love of my life.

The sea—responsible for stealing the lives of thousands of people in Newfoundland—scowls over another sudden disruption by the wind.

There's still no sign of My Love.

Can she see me, I wonder?

Beached

With no recollection of how I got here, I'm sitting on the beach. I'm looking at the dory, safely out of the reach of the sea. I'm squeezing my head, as my tongue screeches for answers: how did I get here? Where is My Love? If she's not alongside me, then where is she?

I hear a woman's voice and thank God. I turn to see My Love, but it's just someone else.

"The b'ys rowed out an' towed ya in," she says. "Ya looked like ya needed help."

"Why?" I try to shout. "Why? Why didn't they leave me alone? She's gone! My Love, she's gone, into the water. I don't know what…"

"'Tis alright," the kind voice says, "the b'ys went straight back out t' look fer her. We all heard ya in here, so we knew what was goin' on. They'll find her, don't worry."

"But *I* need t' go out an' find her," I say, panting. "What the hell is *he* doin' here?" I ask, seeing the priest strutting over the rocks towards us.

"Ya knows the priest have t' be in the middle of it all," she says, quietly.

"If he was a diver or a doctor, he might be o' some use t' us," I bark. "Anyway, help me up, will ya? I have t' get back out there."

"Let's go!"

I'm relieved to hear My Brother's voice. He extends one of

his massive hands to me and I grab hold of it with both of mine. He hauls me to my feet, but everything is still spinning.

"Stay here an' wait fer the doctor," My Brother says.

"Not likely," I say.

He laughs and leads me to the dory. Still holding my hands, he guides me over the gunwales and onto a seat. This time, I untie the grapnel from the risings and fling it onto the beach, then sit in the stern of the boat so I can lean over to have a better look for My Love.

People mill around us. I hear their voices, but they sound too far away for me to understand what they're saying. The cry of a lone gull dancing on the sharp, black rocks of The Point shakes me from the numbness of my mind. I wonder if it's the same bird that called earlier, making me think it was My Love. Or perhaps the gull was trying to tell me where My Love was. Where she *is*. I get up and see My Love's quilt, still on the seat where she sat. My knuckles turn white from wringing the dory's gunwales.

"What the hell are ya after doin' to her?" screams a man's voice.

It's a cousin of My Love's. Before I get a chance to look up, he's grabs me and hauls me out of the boat. He throws me to the ground. I touch the back of my head, then hold my hand in front of my face. There's blood.

"Arsehole!" I say, half quietly. "Were you in the boat wit' us? I don't remember ya there, if ya were."

More than half the town must be standing around, murmuring, pointing, and praying.

"Where is she, ya idiot?" the cousin asks.

He's trying to get at me, but My Brother has one hand on his chest and the angry man can't get far.

"Shag you!" I yell. "I looked, I did, I swear. Let him go."

My next words are cut off by my own sobs, followed by great cries. My Brother does as I ask, and the cousin lunges at me. He grabs me and flings me at the dory.

"'Twas fine," I say, "a bit windy, but not bad. But a wave, a goddamn big wave lifted the boat. I poked an oar into the rocks t' keep us off. An' when I…"

"That's enough," My Brother warns the understandably angry man. "Get yer boat! You'll be o' more use to yer cousin out there."

The cousin tosses his head in involuntary resignation and storms off.

"Let's get our boats ready an' head out," a man says.

"I'll get mine now," another says.

"Me, too," says another.

"Anyone wit' a motor or set o' oars, get in yer boats," My Brother shouts.

Back on the water, many smaller boats seem to be following us, as if we know where the sea has taken My Love. My head is still pounding from the collision with the beach rock.

In what seems like minutes, the hours of evening evaporate into dusk. The silence of the many searchers howls of their vanishing optimism and hopeless enthusiasm. I want to go up the hill, to see My Love's mother, tell her I'm sure her daughter must be safe on one of the beaches dotting the coast. But My Love's cousin warned me not to go near My Love's mother—the woman wants nothing to do with me. So, I go home, instead.

My Brother, his wife and their newborn baby are at my place, waiting for me. The kettle is boiled, and the baby is asleep on

My Brother's old feather mattress. The silence is heavy on the head, the neck, and the whole body. But there's nothing to say and we know it. I slather butter over a thick slice of date and walnut cake made by My Brother's wife.

"We'll head out again at dawn," My Brother says. "Get some sleep!"

I toss my head, and slurp tea from my mug.

"The baby's awake now, hungry," the child's mother says.

"The cake is good," I manage to show a little gratitude.

"Glad ya likes it, me dear," My Brother's wife says. "'Tis the least we can do. Don't give up. She'd never give up on you."

I nod my head and try in vain to hold back tears of disbelief and indignity.

Three days later, the search is called off and My Love's name is added to the never-ending list of missing or drowned. I understand everyone, myself included, must continue to fish six days a week, and many have already given up fishing on Monday *and* Tuesday of this week to look for My Love. A handful of boats even spent half of yesterday, Wednesday, helping with the search.

Again, it's just me and the sea.

A Week Later

This time last week me and My Love were at Nan's and caught in a whirlwind of love and hope. The ring, literally, seemed to bring all aspects of our relationship full circle.

I've finally mustered the courage to tell Nan the awful news—not that she hasn't already heard, I'm sure, but she's never sure of what's real and what's not. I'm not so sure, myself, anymore.

When she asks of My Love's whereabouts, my first reaction is to make up a fib and say she's helping her mother with chores or down on the flakes with other women. But her expression tells me she already knows and is waiting for my account of the details of that awful day.

"Oh, Nan!" I cry. "'Twas dreadful. One second, she was there an' the next she was gone."

"Someone was by an' told me," Nan says, staring out the window. "I don't understand it. Sure, ye were no distance from shore, I heared."

"Nan, I can't get into all of it now because I have t' go back lookin' fer her."

"I knows that's why ya haven't been by the past week," she says, "an' I understands. Now, go find her! Go! Get!"

"Sorry 'bout the ring, Nan."

"No odds 'bout the ring," she says, smiling. "It made it to a hand deservin' of it an' Mammy'd be very pleased wit' that."

"If…I mean, *when* I find her, Nan," I say, sobbing, "I promise t' return the ring."

"That's what ya won't," Nan says, upset. "Yer Love will be buried wit' that ring on her finger. Now, not anudder word about it."

"Alright, Nan," I say, leaning down to give her a little kiss on the cheek, "it'll stay on her. I'll be back."

As the weeks wear on, each day and night spent in the dory looking for a trace of My Love feels more despairing. Lying in bed has become my favourite time of the day or night. It's then I get to think back on how lucky I'd been and how sweet she was. Guilt tugs at my memories, but nothing or no one will ever steal her from my thoughts, from my heart. I'd jump into the sea and drown a million times if I could, if I thought it would give up My Love. Then, she'd have a chance to live a life of her own.

I'm liable to look for a job on The Base—my American friend says he can help find me one there. But then, I'd never be able to concentrate because I know I'll always have to look for My Love.

I appreciate the photograph of My Love which our American friend dropped off today. I doubt I'll ever read the sympathy card it was tucked into, though. Too sad.

In the photograph, My Love is kind, devilish, confident, relaxed, excited, and happy. I wonder how things would be different if our friend hadn't found us on the beach that day? I wouldn't have this picture of her, and right now it's all I have. I will carry it in the pocket of my oilskins when I'm rowing the dory, and perhaps it will attract her to me. I will hold it and kiss it in the dawn and dusk of each day the sea allows my presence.

I will show the fish, the birds, strangers, and people who spend a lot of time on the water and around the beach. When I walk past the old men occupying the doorways of their old stages, their offers of beer are their way of saying they're sorry for bawling out uncouth comments about My Love. I decline their beer but stick around long enough for them to know what they said is the least of my worries and it's not their fault the sea stole her from me.

"Me fadder was lost out fishin' when I was a youngfella," says an old man.

"Mine, too," adds another.

"Don't be talkin'," another old fellow says, "when I was 10, I was out wit' me fadder, t'ree older brudders an' our sister was along as cook. It got right stormy an' fadder sent me below t' keep me sister comp'ny. My son, we were beat around the bottom o' that schooner like we were little dry sticks. When the sea seemed t' be settled enough, I opened the hatch an' went up t' see if fadder an' me brudders needed a hand. Not a sign o' eider o' them on deck. We never laid eyes on 'em again."

"Go on!" I say, pretending to be interested.

"Yes, my son," the old man goes, "the Argyle or the Glencoe, one o' the coastal ships, anyhow, found us adrift an' towed us back t' land."

"Sorry fer yeer troubles," I say, honestly this time, to all three storytellers.

Fall came and went. Winter allows little opportunity to row safely—the wind, the slob ice, the spray freezing onto the oars and all over the dory, making her twice as heavy to move and three times as hard to row. I have more time home in the house now, by myself, which means I have more time to think about how very special My Love was, *is* to me.

No one could ever have been as beautiful as the Girl from up the Hill. I was too big a fool to deserve the likes of her. I remember feeling funny when I saw her, and I was frightened to death she'd see me looking at her. But she *did* see me, and I *didn't* die—at least not outright. I was summoned to my death the moment I first laid eyes on her, and my mind has settled on nothing but her since. She was murder and I an eager corpse awaiting a lovely slaying. I followed her around in my head like a lost dog, waiting and wanting to be eliminated from a life of nothingness, by her—and *only* by her. I secretly, shamelessly, and boldly consented only she was worthy of robbing me of air.

A person alone can have heart galore, dreams to dream and ones to follow, if he or she ever found the nerve; but someone without a heart is as good as dead. Some people seem that way and they seem content. But I don't have that in me, anyway—confidence. When I first saw her, something strange caused me to believe that one day she'd love me—the extra breath that followed her laughter at my instinctive foolish behavior and attempts to be witty, and later—the way her eyes jumped out of her head when we kissed, her dimples, ever-deep when her smile was all for me, and the way her hand would sweat as we walked and talked or just sat on the grass and watched the moonlight streaming across the bay. The constellations sparkled for us. How she'd stare off and sigh whenever I sang the song I made for her. She loved me. And for that I need never love another to feel such inimitable warmth in my blood—even if, right now, it's a horror-filled blanket begrudgingly draped over my weary bones. My eyes have dried a little. Now and again, they might even shine. For all those reasons, sometimes I even smile—but never in public. True love can never be swept away.

I wonder if she'd stayed, if the wind hadn't shot in from the bay, if I could have gotten past my nine-foot oar—the one I'd used to help push the dory from the ragged cliffs always showing their vicious teeth on the face of The Point—could I have reached her in time and kept her from disappearing into the sea?

Guilt

Guilt is an awful thing.

When the priest says My Love's death and disappearance is God's will, I feel like punching him in the face. He'll show up when I'm busiest which is always. I *have* to stay busy. Every rip of a log or a board with the bucksaw or handsaw defines moments requiring my full concentration. That way, there are no seconds to give to my misery. But when the priest shows up, I'm expected to halt my distractions and focus on his common efforts at consoling me when he wouldn't have the slightest notion of what it is like to have had a beautiful young woman looking into his eyes and whose touch magically made the troubles of this old world disappear.

I'll god ya, I feel like saying. I wonder because we're not in the church and he's getting on *my* nerves, would it alright for me to give him a good clout across the side of his head because he's already struck me? My Brother says he'll gladly hit him for me, but we both know poor Mother would roll over in her grave and our cemetery has enough horror attached to it, already.

"Yes, Fadder," I repeat. "I know, Fadder. Yes, Fadder."

"You must leave your misgivings and the tragedy in God's hands," he says, as the fury in me builds and my face is almost as red as his.

I want to ask him why he was at the beach the day My Love vanished because he certainly didn't get aboard a boat when men were filling them and grabbing boat hooks and gaffs to join in the search. I'd also like to ask him *if* he is taking the place of

Jesus on earth, as he says he is, and *if* Jesus could walk on water, then *why* didn't he, the priest, mosey out over the harbour and pluck My Love from the salty devil of a sea. But I say nothing, waiting for him to leave me be.

The shade of burgundy on *his* face is from the bottles of liquor he devours alone in his community-built house. He assumes no one can smell it because his mouth is always full of a drop of homemade soup or a fresh bun, dripping with butter, fresh from someone's oven. His hot, sickening breath turns my guts, as he robotically recites a litany of prayers.

"Then who's fuckin' fault is it?" I finally scream.

"Young man!" he says, appalled, "you will not talk to someone above you in such a manner! I order you to say 10 Hail Mary's, 20 Our Father's, and four novenas. That, and an apology this instant!"

"Sorry, Fadder!"

"I forgive you," he says, "considering all you continue to go through. Jesus will see you through this."

You'll be seen through the Jesus door, if you soon don't leave, I want to say.

Instead of throwing him out of the house, I inch my way towards the door of the porch and comment on the niceness of the day.

"Good day to be at the wood," I say.

He finally gets enough sense to finish his tea and leave.

"I'll be back to see you again," he says.

My skin crawls.

Everyone knows I'm an idiot and had no business out in a boat, let alone taking a prize such as her along. And she must have been just as bad to be with me in the first place. But it was summer, and I was the best she could get, they all suppose. She could have had a thousand Americans, but she didn't want to end up like most of the girls around home, marrying the first fellow she went with. She was better than that. She was better than the goddamn ocean that took her for no reason. Better than the meadows of soft grass, the lovely rock walls made two or three hundred years ago, the fascinating mounds of the graveyard where French soldiers are said to be buried, better than Castle Hill with no castle, better than the ancient black oil paint of cannon radiating along the banks of the ocean in the sun at low tide. Better than any of that. Better than me. Better than this town where people will talk about you until the day you die and then say how nice you were. *He never harmed a soul, well, except for her—the one he seemed happiest with.*

Father

The longest winter it had been. In early November the snow came and now, April month, our bones still retain traces of winter's distinctive bitterness. Its consequent gloom exhausts our already-clouded minds: massive slabs of ice three feet thick are lodged against the wharf and with every reserve of its dwindling strength, the ice clings in vain to the cribs beneath the walkway to the stage—even below the stage itself. The sun's growing strength will pry the ice away from our fishing premises, leaving the frozen water absent from our eyesight and clear of our oars for a few months—a reality which warms our bones, if only in our imaginations, and one which will scrape away the poisonous film of depression from too many months of another repetition of winter's unsympathetic sogginess.

Even though it's liable to snow this evening or tonight, I decide to give the dories a fresh lick of paint. I love oil paint—the smell—I suppose because it reminds me of when Father and Mother were alive at Christmastime. Every Christmas they painted the wooden kitchen table and chairs, the doors and their frames, and anything else that needed touching up for the guaranteed, endless onslaught of company dropping in for a drink, a bite to eat and a yarn.

I lightly push a wire brush over the planks of the boats. Old paint scales fly on the wind. I pick up a can of paint, half full, and give it a few shakes before prying the lid off with a flat-top screwdriver. I grab a skinny piece of driftwood from the beach, remove the thin, semi-hard film of paint on the surface, then stir until the oil and paint inside the can are as one. Using Father's home-made maul and his corking steel, I've re-caulked every seam with oakum. I only have enough yellow paint to touch up two of the dories completely. I trim them in green, same as always. Then, with a decent brush, I slather the remaining yellow dory buff on the seats and gunwales of the third dory—my favourite boat. For this boat, inside and out, I use a gallon and a half of red oil paint my American friend gave me from The Base—left over from a job he had to do and was then told to throw the paint in the dump. I drag the brush from stem to stern until each of the three dories look as good as the day they were first made.

Sawdust from planks a fellow is replacing on his skiff catch a ride on the wind to my newly painted boats, sticking immediately—black flies, grains of sand and other dirt do the same. I begin to start dragging the brush through the unwanted debris ruining my new paint job, but quickly decide there's no sense: no one can see that stuff unless their eyes are glued to it—as if there'll ever be time for gawking at a paintjob.

From the walkway of our stage, my eyes search the water below. I expect to see small schools of connors or a lone, greedy sculpin. But it's too early yet. Crabs, fresh on the scene and still sluggish from the half-icy temperature of the water, take their time crawling from rock to rock. A curlew yaps—its long legs breaking the lop which falls constantly upon the time-worn, interchangeable rounded pebbles of the shoreline. The distressed cry of the thin bird yells for something, but for what I'm not sure. I want to cry with it.

At night, as I sit against wood piled by me and My Brother last fall, I search the water and sky for a sign of Father. Heavy with remorse and its best friend, predictable depression, I feel extra heavy—one with the wharf beneath my boots and tired body. No sign of my dead father on the shore—nor in the sky or the water—so I mope back up the road to the house. It's easier to miss Father because he was such a mystery—barely speaking, yet seemingly knowing how everything worked, mind-wise and mechanically—and you had to admire the way he didn't give a *fiddler's fook*, as he used to say, about what anyone else thought, said or did: unless they deliberately did something not nice to him or one of his own—which didn't happen often, but when it did, *look out*, Mother used to say.

Once, when me and My Brother were very young, playing in a meadow while Father and our uncle drove fence posts into the ground, a local nuisance strutting by decided he'd torment us youngsters. He pushed My Brother to the ground, then turned on me. I thought my life was over. Then I saw the look of menace on his grimy face change to one of unadulterated fear. He turned his body in an opposite direction and took off running, with Father chasing after him—the ax used to drive posts into the ground still in my quiet father's hand. Me and My Brother laughed nervously, as we wondered what Father was going to do with that big ax once he caught the tyrant. Luckily for the persecutor, youth was on his side; the hill became steep, and Father gave up the chase. He walked back down the slope, tossing his head, and cursing quietly before going right back to what he'd been doing before the attack on his boys. Our uncle never questioned the incident; it wasn't uncommon, and the pair carried on with their hard work. Time isn't something to be wasted, and the bored, useless idiot had wasted enough of theirs.

When we got home, we hoped Father would tell the tale to Mother while she cooked our supper of boiled beans and saltbeef. But no, not a word about it. Or about anything for that matter. If it had been the other way around—if Mother had done the like or attempted to do the like—everyone in Freshwater and beyond would know about it, especially the aspiring offender's parents. Father said how useless it would be to try and tell an arsehole's parents what their *little darlings* were up to because they, the parents, were likely arseholes, too, and what would be the sense of wasting time on a bunch of arseholes?

"Mudder'd be chasin' him yet an' God knows what she'd have done to 'im," My Brother laughed.

"He'd at least have shit in his pants," quipped Uncle Din.

Our collective laughter confirmed our agreement of Uncle Din's theory.

There was a mystery about Father which provoked more thought about him. Even as he lay dying on the kitchen daybed, he hardly uttered a word—only to ask for a drop of water from the barrel in the porch or *even better*, he'd gasp, *from the brook*. When Mother's time came to die on the same daybed, we couldn't find a way to shut her up—demanding this and that and ordering us to fix this and fix that, *'fraid the house'll fall apart* and *if yeer fadder was still here, he'd have that fixed long ago.*

There was no pleasing her. But Nan said that's what she was always like—even as a youngster—and it was easier to go along with her than to argue against her constant list of demands.

"Precocious," Nan said of her daughter, "an' well aware of it, too."

Not that Mother wasn't a good person and full of love—maybe she carried too much love and not enough understanding of the magnitude of thoughtlessness in the world in general. She was always quoting someone who had said or written profound words. She'd quote the Irish poet, Yeats—something about indifference, how people show neither love nor hate toward others. I believe it said *indifference is the essence of inhumanity*. It made sense and she knew it. It helped shape who we were and who we'd become.

Here on the stagehead, even though the fog is thick as pea soup, I sense the sun is up there working hard to cut through the haze. Vague traces of its heat whisper, gently touching the back of my neck and a side of my face now and then. The cancer that had taken my father will be laughed at by the sun, should it win and fully make its way to my face—meaning I'll momentarily forget about the misery and trauma of watching him suffer and die.

When the sun's warmth does reach me, tears for Father dry onto my reddened-by-the-wind face. I even get to remove my knitted stocking cap from my ears for a few minutes.

I took the framed photograph of Father which had always stood on the mantle in our parlour. I made a little shelf on a wall in the stage to hold the picture. Now I can look at his face when I talk to him there. I imagine his voice—soft, barely clear—saying things only he could say in his quiet, yet firm manner. No doubt he'd been raised sternly, as we'd been. Yet, respect loomed large for Father in our family. Words I imagine him saying encourage me to keep looking for My Love.

We had a sister, but she died long ago. No one ever spoke of her. Pneumonia killed her, someone said. I barely remember her. I was five or six when she died. *She was handsome*, Mom said. In the same breath, Mom said she'd never wish for any of her children to marry and move away forever with their youngsters—the way many couples from here have been doing for decades. Most of them moved to cities and towns along the Eastern Seaboard of the United States. Mother would get sad talking with relatives of these people when she'd hear how they only received letters and a picture of their children and grandchildren every few years. Not that she was glad her daughter had died, but somehow, she was relieved she didn't have to hold the mental burden so many mothers here carried.

As soothing as the rain pounding the felt of our roof may be, it does little to ease the ache in my back and arms. The back pains are old: the same ones I recall as a child trying to sit up on the kitchen floor or out in the meadow while Father sawed logs or piled hay. I always wanted to stay, but I'd have to get up for the pain to subside.

It kills me I can't be out in the boat looking for My Love this day, but what's the sense? And the extra wind this time of year, as bad as the fall, makes it useless to even think about going. Another few swallows of moonshine and my mind will settle into some version of contentment—be it real or made-up. *But what else is the drink fer, sure?* My Brother always said.

Here I am, still caught up in My Love's fight for the loss of Argentia, and she still drifting, what's left of her, I suppose, in the dirty bastard of a sea. Because of the drink, the sound of rain begins to calm my nerves. I take another gulp. Then another. My guts cringe at the drink's grossness, the bitterness, the goodness, the awfulness, the relief, the extra pain it eventually sends to my mind. But I love it and I wouldn't wish it gone for the world. Enough has been taken already.

"Loves yer drink," My Brother says, sucking the bottom of his own glass dry.

"I can see why Uncle Din's been drunk all his life," I say.

"'Tis a wonderful thing," My Brother says, laughing. "Sure, what would we do wit'out the Yanks?"

"What did Uncle Din do before they came here?" I ask, rhetorically.

"Made his own drink," laughs My Brother. "Same as everyone always done. I won't stop makin' me own, but 'tis just as cheap t' get a bottle off The Base now, sure."

"'Tis," I agree. "An' 'tis nice t' go t' bed sometimes wit'out fear o' bein' woke up by the glass bottles full o' fermentin' ingredients explodin' beneath a heavy quilt behind the stove, too."

We laugh at our memories of exploding bottles.

When Mother was alive, I spent night and day fretting about her loneliness over Father being gone—of me never knowing how to occupy her time, what to say, what to do, what to bring her: too many fish, not enough fish. Too salty. Too fresh. Waiting for the salt beef to come back from Nova Scotia. Praying for one of them fridges the rich crowd have, but we would never own, or so we thought.

"Poor old Mudder," My Brother says. "Hard as she worked, she never knew or understood the half o' what Fadder did fer her. 'No odds 'bout it all now,' she used t' say."

The next morning is a calm one. I'll be back on the water in no time. From the dory, I prod the water with the scull oar, in the hopes it will strike her—give me a sign she isn't all that far down. But the old fellows say she'd be long out Placentia Bay the way the currents work, and I should have better sense. That and the ugly, contrary squid looking up at me with their big, round eyes—thousands of them stirred up by my oars, squishing and squelching and squirting their inky dirt and saltwater in every direction. They remind me of running into another fellow as crazy and as angry as myself on the road—the hate screaming from his eyes, how he'd like to tell me I'd no business being where I was, or anywhere for that matter—how he'd just as soon smack the mouth off me than look at me, and he knowing I felt the same way about him. About everyone. Barely keeping it together—those squid. If they had their way, they'd be the only living things in the ocean. The changing of their colours and their rapid movements in all directions make it impossible to see anything else, let alone My Love twirling in the undertow. The old men's words remind me what a fool I am for daring to reach her with a thirteen-foot stick in two-hundred feet of water. "Yer only born wit' so much sense," I heard Father's tender, but meaningful voice once again whispering through the din of water splashing.

"Goddamn squid," I shout. "Goddamn everything!"

As quickly as the sun had risen, the sky clouds over. Rain begins. As it pounds the old roof, I remember with great clarity Father and my uncles fixing or replacing the roof—they all loaded drunk and Mother scowling at them from the clothesline and muttering curses under her breath to her sister—the two of them sneaking drinks themselves and partially sheltered by flapping, drying sheets. The men couldn't hear or couldn't have cared less to know what the women were saying, as long as there was food on the table, and they had a path to the kitchen daybed for a sit-down or a nap when the booze completely overtook their senses and when their bodies yelled for rest. It seemed they were at the roof most of that summer and Mother was at her wit's end. But the roof got finished. Maybe not fixed, but finished, as far as any ordinary eye could discern. Looks, however, never stopped the leaks and it leaked whenever the rain was hard and when the wind blew up from the shore—especially when shoved by the unforgiving northeasterlies of fall, winter, and our illusive spring.

All this rain and all those thoughts and memories. Now the rain remains and there's no one here but me to care if it leaks or not. Mother and Father up on the hill, side by side: the most peace either of them ever had—dead. It has bugged me a lifetime, especially during Sunday Mass, when the priest and other hypocrites repeat *Give your life to God, Let God take your cares away, just pray to God and all else will work for you, for yours, Hand it over to God and rest my child*, and other nonsense of the same. It poisoned me then and it poisons me now.

If we'd spent the bit of time we have on this earth thinking more and figuring out solutions to our real problems (like whales tearing up our nets and dogfish and seals eating the cod and the lazy, ignorant men who steal lobsters from your traps)—if we'd done some of that instead of listening to a priest who'd never dirtied his paws for a hard day's work in his life, we might have gotten somewhere. But this life and every other life before me in this place knows nothing of comfort, rest, and peace. *Rest in Peace*, my arse. Headstones should say *About Time he or she got a Break*.

Where is My Love? Surely not resting in peace just because she no longer breathes salt air. And as far as we know, no one ever breathed saltwater. If God cared or if there is a god looking out for us, wouldn't He have plucked her from the water that day? Why would it be considered *God's will* to have her lost and drowned? Gone. Forever. How long have I been looking for her? Waiting for her? All I can figure is He thrives on the misery He creates for His *children*. And that leads me to question if our so-called *god* is really the devil. What a tangle.

I walk around enshrouded in an invisible cloak of misery for all to talk about behind my back. But I'll never give up. One day, I know, I'll find her—around the coast during a jaunt into one of the many hidden coves, hooked in smashed lobster pots and discarded cod traps set free by the ice and currents of savage winters. I'll find her. I will.

Eyesore

Letting the fire go out in the stove, Nan watches the last trails of smoke from her chimney blow over her rosebushes—just outside her front kitchen window. The wind and the ocean, most always the best of friends, are a pair of enemies few wish to encounter. But folks living in Newfoundland often have no choice but to accept their assured interruptions. It's all Nan hears and feels these days and nights. The old house rattles a little, continuing its tune of death.

"'Praps 'tis me auld bones," she says, laughing to herself.

The very thought of the house being empty and alone one day, when she dies, drives her. And one day again the beams, where her pot and pan and the oil lamp hang, will crack and another day, the once solid milled wood will break off altogether. Such a calamity will send glass from the windows she cleans every morning out into her lovely front garden with the little patch of wild strawberries often orphaned and left smaller than they could be by the covetous September Mists. But likely, she knows, no one will be near enough to even notice or care. *What odds*, they'll say, *about an old house that should have been hauled down years ago.*

"They'd grow up yer arse if ya slept too long," the Crooked Auld Bastard would say of the September Mists.

"The Crooked Auld Bastard," she says, laughing and grudgingly blessing herself the same time—rolling her eyes to Heaven.

She says an extra prayer, thankful *they* have him up *there* and he's no longer *here*. Truly, by now, with the likes of Himself around, the Lord *really* knows what suffering is.

When she's gone from this life, the crowd going by the front gate will say what an eyesore the old house is, not to mention the mangy rosebushes after taking over the garden all hands once adored and how awful it is for the old house to be left in such an unpleasant state. Or perhaps no one else ever noticed the lovely rosebushes and their grand scent.

What am I getting' on wit' anyhow, she wonders, when 'tis soon time to be goin' t' bed?

Again, she tries to laugh off the conspicuous straying of her lonely mind.

In his chair, Himself is sitting up straight as a newly forged nail, and cursing on everything he can think of.

"Goddamn gover'mint! Goddamn fish!"

The high-pitched whirr from the stovepipe is worse than ever now, as the breeze slaps tree branches against the clapboard and the windows. Shadows of the rosebushes on the old house get bigger and smaller as they sway in all directions to the out-of-sync rhythms of the wind. Nan has a mind to go to bed out of it once and for all.

After flicking a drop of holy water in the sign of the cross into the parlour where her grandfather died, she watches Himself nod off in his chair, arms dangling—his big mitts almost scraping the canvas.

"I 'spose he's not dead," she mumbles under her breath, careful not to wake him, in case he's only asleep and not dead at all.

"Crooked 'nough when yer wide awake, let alone half asleep," she mutters, laughing to herself while scuffing by him in her worn slippers on the rutted planked floor gouged by the almost flattened rockers of her chair.

"'Special'y now," she says, looking at me, the only other occupant of the rectangular kitchen, "wit' the Yanks here an' they wit' their jeeps an' big Jesus trucks tearin' up the works."

"I know, Nan, girl," I say, even though I haven't a clue what she's getting on with. "No one cares 'bout anyt'ing but themselves since *they* got here."

"An' they t'inks I don't know what's goin' on, ya know," she says, matter-of-factly. "I knows me mind 'tisn't what it used t' be, ya know. I *knows* I says t'ings I shouldn't be wastin' me bre't' on an' takin' away yer time. An' I knows yer heart will never be the same. I wish I could bring her back fer ya."

"'Tis alright, Nan," I say. "No one minds that, an' what odds if they did. 'Tis none o' anyone's business if they got not'ing better t' do wit' their time than t' talk 'bout someone else. Lord knows they talks 'nough 'bout me."

"Sure, why would they say anyt'ing 'bout you?" she asks, as if her mind has never been gone. "Not like ya flung her outta the boat on purpose."

"'Tis not wort' talkin' 'bout, Nan," I lie. "Don't worry 'bout it. Like I said, they're gonna find somet'ing t' say about ya anyway."

As I get up to leave, she asks where I'm going.

"Oh, yeah," she laughs. "'Anyone wit' a bed now should be in it. That's right, isn't it?"

"'Tis, Nan. 'Tis," I say, forcing a laugh. "'Night!"

"Mind yerself goin' 'round the corner o' the house," she says from her slow climb up the old rickety steps. "'Tis hard t' see at night."

"Maybe one day," I say, "they'll have them big lights on the tall poles 'longside the road an' we'll be helped along a bit by them, I s'pose."

"I doubt it," she says. "Now go home out of it, an' mind yerself on the step an' goin' out through the garden gate. The latch is often hard t' lift this time o' year, I finds. Must be the frost."

"I will. 'Night, Nan. See ya t'morrow."

The gate to her big garden was never there—not since she's been living here, anyway. It's that kind of talk which tells me she's nowhere near Freshwater and, in her mind, is back in Placentia or down in Argentia. Or both.

Still, she's well aware of my plight and the worse plight of My Love.

On the Beach Again

How I hate evenings, the way they invade my strong faith—the reoccurring belief I will find My Love this day. Darkness robs air from my lungs and kelp-covered rocks from my sight. Down I go again: elbows beaten off me, lying on the broad of my back, my hands slimy with green guck and bleeding from broken glass carpeting the beach. Much of the glass are remnants of green glass floats, made in Japan from used sake bottles, ones which floated in the sea for a hundred years or more. Clever bunch, the Japanese—probably too smart for their own good, and certainly for ours. For the past 10 or 15 years everyone uses what they call the *gill* net, invented by the Japanese. Its mesh is too small and when they're run over and ripped apart by trawlers and schooners, they're set free to float and tumble forever, snagging everything in their path. Again, I'm reminded of Father saying how ghost nets *and* trawlers will be the death of the fishery.

The sinking light of dusk offers no assistance in getting me back to my feet, or at least to a rock fit for sitting. The moon taunts me now and then from behind the listlessly moving clouds of black and dark blues. The wind is from the northeast. It pinches and slaps me with cool gusts from over the Googly Hole and down across the meadow of uncut hay. My old coat doesn't stay together. The zipper broke not long after the winter started, in late October. I should be home, but I'm no good there. I feel guilty in the heat of the kitchen knowing she's out there in the freezing water of the sea. How can I justify leaving here? I can't. I turn my head toward the inner banks, where I've lit many fires and where I'll light many more. No sense tonight, though, with the growing wind.

Staring into the black of night, white caps dance and flicker wildly on the sea's surface and, now and then, I see her—My Love. I'm freezing again. The water soaking my pants and the bottom of my shirt is so cold it burns. My screams bounce off the hateful sky flicking drops of rain to mock my miserable existence. No one hears. Maybe everyone hears. No one answers. *She* doesn't answer. But she will, someday. I know she will. As I drag my feet into the night, they curl inside my wet rubbers. I stop and sit upon another big rock, struggle to remove my boots and wring the water from my socks. I then dump the water and bits of kelp out of my boots. Both my heels are moving blisters of skin made soggy by the sea.

When I get home, My Brother is there, passed out on the daybed. Once out of my wet clothes and into a sweater and my other pair of pants, I give him a shake. There are plenty of sweaters here in the house; Mom never stopped knitting. I give My Brother another shake and make sure he's on his side—afraid he'll throw up and choke.

The rain has stopped. It's about three-thirty in the morning. After a mug of tea and four or five thick slices of molasses raison bread toasted on the bent clothes hanger, I have a nap.

After another mug of tea, I leave to head back down to the beach. I stop on the step and light a smoke. The valley is beautiful in the moonlight, and I see her so clearly, as if it was yesterday—The Prettiest Girl in Freshwater—strolling through the tall grass in her loose cotton dress. The orange flowers and bits of green grass of the dress's pattern help blend her into the splendid show of summer surrounding her; yet she shines like the rotating light at night on Point Verde Head—her loveliness capable of navigating through the thickest of fog. She fumbles playfully with a stick of timothy hay, pulling the stalk from the pile of soft seeds until her palm is full. Then, as she blows them to the wind, her lips pout. My heart pounds. As she sticks the stalk between her teeth, I wish I was that stalk. I would settle for being one of the seeds she'd held for a moment and blown away with her sweet breath. Freedom by a kiss. I suck on the cigarette like it is a Peppermint Nob. Thank God for Peppermint Nobs. I must be keeping the Purity company in business since she…since she went.

The slight hand of the moon's light reaching across the bay waves me down—back for another thousand looks for My Love. I have nine or ten Peppermint Nobs and mountains of memories to mull over while I suck the candy until they're as small as I feel—the nothingness I've been graced with, full of. Daylight brings promise and I manage to present a fake happy face when two youngones who should be in school say hello with big, bright smiles—grins only children who've seen little of this miserable world could possess. The moment they pass, on their way toward the meadow heading for the Dead Man's Cave, my forged smirk is hauled hard to the ground and swiftly crumpled by fault: I had no right to smile. I *have* no right to smile.

The knocking of an engine gets louder, casting me headlong into the most awake state of the day's dawning so far. I'm already cursing the evening-to-come, knowing it will be here before I know it. For a second or two, I look to see if it's her coming back from one of her jaunts to Placentia. But it's just one of the many fishing boats fortunate enough to return to this harbour before night covers the land and sea, altogether.

Today I'll climb both hills—Castle Hill and Crevecoeur. Maybe I'll go farther. A buddy up the road has a magnifying glass, but that's only good up close. I need a telescopic lens, like real sea captains use.

My eyes caress the coves and breakers, sunkers and caves, as I tread foolishly along the steep, rocky inclines between the wood-topped coves. I fall through a pile of shrubs and straight over a cliff into a pile of tiny beach rocks. My lower arm bones feel like they've been shoved up past my elbows. But nothing is hurt too badly; she's watching over me. I get up and stretch while taking in the view. It is beautiful—a different colour sand than on our beach—beige, almost. Surely, people lived here years ago. It's perfect. If we'd seen this together and she'd lived, I bet we would have built a small home here, above in the trees. From the little brook alongside our home, we'd get our water for boiling, drinking, cooking, cleaning, and bathing.

I am tired. I fall asleep beneath the roof beams of a fallen down barn in the meadow where the bones of dead French people lay. If I freeze, I will die, and me and My Love will be together. If I wake, I will keep looking for her. Her body. Bury her: tell her mother how sorry I am, *but at least we, you*, I'd say to her mother, *can say a proper good-bye to her now.* Then, when her mother finally leaves, I'd lie on her grave and sing *Peggy Gordon* and all the other lovely Irish ballads she adored.

Flood

The next evening is as calm as the one before. Left behind by the deserting sun are hues of yellows and whites softly painting the sky. A pleasant pink cast upon the water runs all the way to the beach of smooth, dark sand and loose rocks.

Last night's tide brought lovely driftwood, just the right size for Nan's stove. The soles of her second-hand, patent leather shoes sent home from her older sister in Brooklyn are on the floor alongside the stove—still full of wet sand and bits of kelp.

"Down to the beach, Nan?" I ask the obvious.

"Yes, b'y," she moans, "had t' get outta here fer a spell. Nice down there; 'twas me first time since I come here t' Freshwater. Make no wonder yer always down there."

"It is a nice spot, yeah," I say, reluctantly while bursting to tell her the truth—she's been there more than once.

"I 'spose yer missus loves it there, too, do she?" she asks, forgetting My Love is gone.

"She do, Nan, yeah."

"Some auld stuff comes in wit' the sea, don't it?" she says.

I die a thousand more deaths, thinking of the very thing—the One—the only one I want to come ashore.

"Yes," she goes on, "the stuff I counted tucked amongst the kelp line markin' the last high tide came an' went before me eyes: a rubber boot, whores' eggs, mussels, shells o' crabs long eat by seabirds, the colours o' the rocks, bits o' rope, an' oars so warn down they must be in the water a hun'red years."

"Go on," I say, acting surprised.

"Yes, b'y," she says. "I even picked up a broken oar handle an' carried it home, luh."

Showing her find, she says she likes the bits of old-fashioned paint still clinging to the wood once held firmly in the stout grasp of the massive hands of a dory man. She lays it on the windowsill and wonders if it was discarded purposely after years of use or lost with one of the thousands of men who've perished in Placentia Bay.

These simple things separate Nan's days: their imagery occupies each lonely night. The odd time there are dead birds, saucy dogfish dead or dying and drying up in the sun—even whales, always accompanied by hordes of people climbing all over the poor creatures with knives carving out large chunks of blubber and meat. That bothers her. She never had the heart to do the like of that: cut up an animal barely dead. *The poor thing likely got too close to the beach when chasing a meal of caplin and cod and got caught unawares on the sloped seabed.* That's what some say about the poor creatures. The beach allows her safety of the mind outside the safety of her garden, and it is hard not to care when it's all you have to look at, she figures.

"T'ank God," she sighs, "we were never hungry enough t' have t' climb aboard a dead whale fer a bite t' feed our crowd when they were here."

"An awful lot o' dead whales washin' ashore," I say, trying to steer her clear of her often-undesirable past.

"Oh?" she says, confused.

I want to tell her the truth—how the Americans use the gigantic fish for target practice or sport, but that would only upset and confuse her more. She dislikes the Americans enough, as it is.

The yellows of the passing sun sift through Nan's rosebushes and into the kitchen, almost reaching corners of the room where shadows will spend the night. The usual light evening breeze entering beneath the raised window stirs the flame of her hanging oil lamp, allowing exaggerated movement to the creeping shadows now and then.

The day's sun left its mark on the back of her neck, as she moseyed around the garden. She'd been letting on she was doing things she was once able to do, as if there were people nearby to notice. No more growing vegetables: she buys them from a fellow who comes door to door every so often. The warm sting of the sun on the nape of her neck blends just enough with the cooling wind, sending a satisfying shiver down her tired back. She hurts all over: her poor knees, and *that blessed right hip*. Her shoulders feel like they'll soon fall off her body.

Gazing in through the front hall and out the pantry window, the serenity created by the sun over the far end of Castle Hill leaves her with a comforting radiance. Her pains briefly disappear. She just *is*, and for these precious moments, it's better than anything. She loves when this happens—when something unexpected takes her mind from all things. It's what she considers to be in the presence of God. But fight all she like, and she can never make it happen when she wants. A real mystery it is—just as it's a miracle when it's there. Beyond words. Beyond thoughts even. It just *is*. And she just *is*. A rare, slow-moving upsurge of peacefulness washes over her.

The embellished rectangles of both kitchen windows glow sharply in the kettle's polished, round face. Voices of the wind go in and out every window, rattling panes.

"Put on the kettle," he bawls at her.

Put it on yerself, she wants to say back. She turns her head towards his chair to see no one scowling back at her. Relief forces a big, slow breath inward, down her lungs, and slowly back out through her nostrils. The headache he'd just caused dissipates with each deep, unhurried breath to follow.

From her chair Nan can barely make out the roses through the porch window; but, to her, they're as beautiful in the faded light as they'd been all day in the sun's sparkle. The fog, having moved off as quickly as it had arrived, allows light to display a pair of silver maples in the side garden under a gibbous moon. The trees carry on, dancing to the rhythm of the wind.

"I must get a start on paintin' me shed," I tell Nan before leaving.

I kiss her on the cheek, and she smiles.

Soon after I close the porch door, she sits on the daybed and falls gently to one side. In less than a minute, she's asleep and back in her grandfather's house in Placentia.

A silhouette in the corner of the kitchen—the old bridle from Paddy 'Reilly's horse in Little Placentia—hangs on a nail drove into the wall near the stove. She remembers this old house, too, belonged to Little Placentia one time, floated here with barrels, and rolled up the beach on big logs with the help of big horses and big, strapping men.

Her grandfather's cane hangs where he last put it—a reminder that these four chairs, and the long table Himself got off a stranded ship will be here long after she's gone.

The balls of her feet sting, as she rocks in Mammy's chair. Gulls cry while make 'n' break engines push home damp boats and drained men from another day of little or no fish. It's the middle of July month and the caplin haven't showed their skinny faces yet. Although someone said they saw whales galore yesterday. *That was probably lies*, she thinks—reminiscent of such bitterness often conceived seemingly out of nowhere, same as her Mammy before her.

She has a little nod, until she hears the stomping of boots in the porch.

"Oh my!" she says "an' me here in a state. Awful hour o' the night fer comp'ny."

But it isn't dark. She must have slept in the rocker all night. She jumps up, grabs the kettle from the stove and hurries outside to the rain barrel. At the stove, she can't get the boughs to light.

"What a fright ya give me," she says to her grandfather, as he hangs in through the side kitchen window.

"Come on, girl!" he shouts.

Placentia has flooded again, she knows, and the old man won't take a spell until every soul is safe and sound.

"Hold on!" she shouts. "I'll make us tea."

"Alright," he says and climbs in through the raised-up window. "Get outta the way, girl! The stove's not even in."

"Must be the green boughs," she says, unmoved by his inconsiderate ways. "Who else is in the boat?"

"No one. Only a couple o' cats I took from yer trees, an' yer rain barrel. No good t' ya now! But ya can burn the salt outta the staves an' use it fer somet'ing. We'll get tea someplace else," he says. "Come on."

Her grandfather goes out the window first and will take her hand, as often before, and guide her into the dory with relative ease—no matter the might of the wind. But when she leans out under the raised window, he's not there. Nor the dory. Nor any water. It's dark and the moon is lovely, shining above the graveyard hill.

A tom cat yowls pitifully from beneath the house for a mate, waking Nan.

"That was a queer one," she says of her dream. "I must go t' bed out of it."

She leans in across the kitchen table and sees the black line—the new road ripped through Freshwater. With the back of her hand, she makes a motion to stir Himself from his chair. She stops when she realizes he's not there.

Dragging one leg after the other going up the narrow steps of the steep stairs, she wonders if tonight she'll really die in her sleep and be spared another day and long night of watching her mind wander further away. She frets over dying and the possibility of running into Himself again and having to listen to him grumble. She clings onto the night, her brittle fingernails clawing at the flannelette sheet riddled with knobs and holes. She fights sleep as long as possible to avoid meeting the Crooked Auld Bastard there—in her dreams. She goes back downstairs.

She closes the drapes she forgot to close earlier and feels solid, almost powerful—as stout as she knows she can feel given the vast number of summers she has seen. In daylight when the drapes are open, she sees past the meadow, past her world of confusion, where strangers traverse the busy road. She tries to envision the valley of Freshwater, quiet, just a handful of families—the path-turned-messy-road once busy with horses and sometimes carts and bobsleds attached. Now loud trucks, jeeps and other vehicles shred any additional hope of silent nights like the ones she knew so well, so long ago. Quiet times they were, indeed, except on Saturday nights when the men were drunk and fighting. *That still goes on*, I've told her, *only much worse now that the Americans are here catching hold of the eyes of most of the older girls and young women.*

Nan gets dizzy and staggers back to the daybed. She grabs one of Mammy's quilts and cuddles it like a baby. Soon, she's sound asleep again.

Himself falls in the door, roaring the top of his lungs the chorus of *Toora Loora Loora, the Irish lullaby*, telling her how much he loves her.

"Mind now!" she snaps at him, never taking her eyes off the burning log she chooses to nudge with the iron poker instead of looking at his hateful mug.

"I've a mind t' give ya a good clout wit' this hot iron," she says under her breath—her hatred as strong as the stench of booze on his revolting breath.

"Whadgeya say?" he says, the tones of desire fading like his slurred speech.

She's not scared. She knows he'll try to get her to the bedroom at any cost, and his need to fight will soon drown in sleep when he passes out from the heat of the chimney during his slow crawl up the stairs. She'll leave him up there, on the floor, wishing the stairs were wider so he might fall. And when the ranger comes tomorrow, she'll tell him it was bound to happen sooner or later when a man gets on like that—drunk all the time. *Serves him right.* She'll probably leave out that part, though, afraid the ranger will think she had a hand in it herself. *Good thing they can't read me mind*, she thinks. But then, though, she'll have to look at the Crooked Auld Bastard dead for three days in the parlour in his suit of clothes. The thought of using good candles and all the food wasted on the likes of him with times so hard and everything so scarce rattles her. She cringes at the thought of the stories guaranteed to be told by visitors, all the wonderful things Himself did in his *too-short-of-a-life, the poor soul.* They'll all ask how in the name of God will she ever get along without him, he was that good to her. She'll pretend it was an awful thing he died so horribly, but will likely say, on the last night, *anyone with a bed now should be home in it.*

But no, the stairs are narrow and Himself is wedged amongst

the top two steps and half wrapped around the rail, with little chance of him going anywhere but to sleep this night.

A barking dog rattles Nan from sleep and her delusional thoughts.

"Goddamn it!" she says, getting up off the daybed and closing the drapes.

Wishing

It's morning again. Standing and leaning across the small kitchen table, Nan's heart breaks at the sight of rose petals lying on the grass. And it was only like yesterday they'd first bloomed for the new summer. The rosebushes, slowly stripped of their fragrant flowers, sway in the gathering wind.

Nan wishes it was her birthday and a neighbour from Argentia or Marquise would make a special trip to visit her—maybe even bring her a cake.

"Partridgeberry's me favourite," she says, beaming with happiness in the hopes of someone else showing up.

But I know the people here in Freshwater are in more turmoil than they can bear—living in slapped-together sheds and getting driven from one house to another because wrong lot numbers for parcels of land have been drawn. Someone's birthday is the last thing on their minds, I imagine. Nan's real friends from Argentia are all dead and there's nobody from her generation left to remind her of her birthday, anyhow.

"I'm 'fraid t' go pickin' berries alone, ya know," she says. "'Fraid o' the moose. I 'spose the Youngfella from in the Lane went t' Boston or New York, like everybody else, or t' T'ronto, wherever it is they goes t' find work these days."

"Sure, I gives ya lots o' berries, Nan," I say, laughing.

She ignores my comment, altogether.

What she's really referring to stems from scraps of remembrances from her grandfather's mention of the Youngfella from in the Lane. She didn't know the young man well, if at all—but I leave her be.

A long silence follows Nan's patchy ramblings, but I don't mind the stillness; I know she's happy I'm here. She'd be the first to say if she wasn't content and that's how I like people to be. *No arsin' around*, as Father used to say. I try to focus on the good Nan can have in her life now, but I'm always lured to the past by the endless number of stories she has told me over the years. As if she knows what I'm thinking, she starts again.

"The nice man from the Cape Shore must've died 'cause he hasn't been 'round all summer," she says, staring out the window. "He usually stops in fer a mug-up an' a bit o' news a couple o' times ev'ry year."

Again, from her stories told before her mind went, I recall Mr. Morrissey was her grandfather's friend: much too old for her. Perhaps it was Nan's Mammy who'd said all those nice things about the visitor?

"Maybe he's the best kind an' is just too busy yet t' come in t' see ya," I say.

"He used t' make me laugh some; a lovely man, he was."

"Sounds like a good fella, alright," I say, enthusiastically, as if we haven't had the same conversation a million times.

"Yes," she goes on, "even Himself was a bit relaxed when his auld friend stopped by. I never t'ought I'd lay eyes on him again after Himself died, but he never missed a summer in, my God, must be twenty years since the Crooked Auld Bastard finally died, is it? Never laid eyes on him this year, though, Mr. Morrissey. He must be dead, is he?"

Or maybe, I think, Mr. Morrissey visited them at Argentia while waiting around to have his fish weighed and graded by the merchant there. But I nod and smile, as if the whole scene had taken place in Placentia proper.

Weeping in her chair, Nan thinks of those days of floating around the meadow and admiring the lovely flower beds me and My Love helped her plant—the peace and warmth of that luxury is over for another long year of frost, cold, wind, snow, sleet, and hard rain. She speaks of the special feeling a big breath of roses in the salt air leaves in her chest—almost as full as if she'd just finished Christmas dinner once enjoyed with family galore.

"I can already feel the cauld clingin' to the back o' me neck," she complains, tossing her head at the unpredictable weather.

"But, Nan," I remind her, "the winter is just goin' away an' spring an' summer have yet t' show their faces. 'Twill warm up yet; don't be frettin' now."

"Oh?" she says, stretching her neck forward, her little nose almost touching the single-paned window.

"Gonna head back o'er to the house now, Nan," I say, "an' light the stove t' keep the chill outta me bones t'night. 'Sposed t' be nice t'morrow, so…."

I catch myself from repeating my daily business of losing my own mind and searching for My Love.

"'Night, Nan," I say, hauling my knitted cap over my head and turning my coat collar to keep the dank wind off my neck.

"Yerself an' the missus will be by t'morrow, will ya?"

"Yeah," I lie again, closing the porch door behind me.

From her chair, Nan hopes to warm her legs, but the rising gale steals most of the heat up through the chimney. *Nothing's the same anymore*, she thinks. *Not even the weather*. She gets up and drags the chair in front of the stove. She grabs the lifter and slides the front damper across the top of the stove, unphased by the possibility of flankers flying out and burning the floor's canvas. The extra heat is nice on her face, and the pain leaves her feet and legs almost right away.

She wants to go outside. Go for a walk. Maybe she'll meet the nice man, Mr. Morrissey from the Cape Shore, and they'll stroll along the beach rocks under the bright moon lighting up the harbour. She smiles, imagining the charming Mr. Morrissey telling her about life on the Cape Shore, the many great tales of ghosts and faeries and even the devil himself. He lived alone, Mr. Morrissey, and was never *tangled up with* a woman, he was always proud to say. And the most pleasant face she'd ever laid eyes upon. She'll hope someone will see them out walking together—give them all something else to talk about.

"Go t' bed out of it, girl!" the Crooked Auld Bastard says from his chair, banging his pipe hard on the table.

The son of a bitch, she thinks, an' he not even here, takin' me from me dream. 'Til death due us part, me arse. I'll never get clear o' 'im.

She opens her eyes to grab another piece of wood for the stove and remembers the cold outside this morning—how she had to go back out to the smelly porch after the low tide and lug enough wood into the kitchen so she wouldn't have to stir anymore this day.

The sound of a stray sheep, full of twigs and God-knows-what-else, brings her to the kitchen window. She laughs at the animal, as she watches it beat its backside off the clapboard of the house. In the fall of the year, her grandfather would give her two pence for every sheep she could round up and bring back.

"Oh, my," Nan says, taking a breath, "the state I'd be in when I'd get back—but never wit'out a sheep, an' often they'd be three times the size o' me. But 'twas some spurt o' fun, say what ya like."

It was one of the rare times she remembers the Crooked Auld Bastard lifting the end of his lips enough to show he had a bit of spirit left—when he'd listen to Nan's memories of gathering sheep.

"I'd get two pence fer a sheep," she says. "No trouble t' stay warm at that racket."

She laughs under her breath.

Maybe the dirty sheep alongside the house is a sign from Above to stay determined and to not give in to the cold. The wind is liable to change tomorrow, and she might even get out in the yard for a spell when the sun is high. Maybe she'll even go out and try to catch the sheep, now that the pain has gone from her legs. But where would she bring it with no one left to give her a few coppers for her troubles? At least she'd be warm, even if she just chased it for a while. Between the cold and the knowing she doesn't have a chance of getting near the sheep, she finds new comfort in her kitchen, once again, and enjoys the strong heat from the stove. If Himself was here, she knows, the sheep would be skinned and in the pot. And then he'd make her clean up the mess. Thoughts of the stink, alone, turns her stomach.

"Jesus! Don't be talkin'," she says to no one.

"Will ya scrape that goddamn ceilin' before the paint falls into the pot," Himself roars at her.

"I wish you'd fall into the pot," she'd like to say to him.

Chopper

The next evening is as calm as the one before. Typical hues of yellows and whites have been left behind by the deserting sun. A pleasant, familiar pink cast upon the water runs all the way to the beach of smooth sand and loose rocks. The dory she'd fallen from beckons me, as always, to drag it across the sand and into the water. The boat's bright red, as opposed to traditional dory buff yellow has long since a laughingstock for the town's idiots. The dory glistens in the setting sun. No trouble to see her on the water; that's for sure. My American friends love the red and yellow dory so much, they're constantly offering me money for it. But no amount of money could replace that boat, especially since it was the last place My Love had been.

So, that's what I decide to do. Sure, what have I got to lose? If I die or disappear, no one will care—perhaps My Brother, but he wouldn't be surprised. In a way, he'd be happy for me because all I ever said was, *I couldn't care less if I got lost in the dory, as long as I'm looking for My Love.*

The dory floats on just a few inches of water, so I shove her out and hobble over the gunwales, holding onto the bow seat to steady myself. I sit in my usual place and steady my feet against the two-by-four on the floor for helping me push my feet and legs to haul harder on the oars. I take one oar and use both arms to push it off the seabed, sending the dory on a skew—out into deeper water. With both oars between their thole pins, my right hand and arm strain to turn the boat toward the open sea. I then drop the other oar into the water, and in no time, I'm making good headway on the water as smooth as oil tonight.

The Americans from Argentia appear in a helicopter over the Googly Hole hill and it gives me a start—the searchlight is blinding, but it also gives me a better look into the water, not that the wind from the flying machine doesn't disturb the water. They're familiar with my habits—like rowing at all hours of the night—and they no longer bother waking the town with their foolish megaphone, asking what I'm up to and don't I know the enemy could be just feet below me? On land, I've told them *what odds* about the enemy and how looking for My Love is more important than anything they or the Germans are paid to do. They say I'd make a good soldier, but I can't imagine a war any greater than the one I'll probably always be in. They've long since given up stopping by in person to politely argue with me and they allow me to go about my business, no matter the hour. I could be after causing them to crash with a couple of shots from my double-barreled shot gun, but I wouldn't waste shells. Once, soldiers of an American flight crew laughed and said they could split me *and* my dory in two with the 50-calibre machine guns mounted to the sides of their aircraft, but they wouldn't waste bullets on me, either. At least we have *that* in common—the humour.

When I bring up the atrocity of them killing whales for sport, they always have a comeback.

"That's different," one soldier said over a beer on The Base together. "It's target practice, and plus fishermen are always complaining about whales getting caught in their fishing traps, ruining gear they cannot afford and how can you argue with that?"

In a way, they are right, but to break the food chain we depend upon is wrong—everyone knows that, especially the older generations.

Anyway, the *chopper*—that's what the Americans call their helicopters—takes off and I'm glad for the calmness once again granted by Mother Nature this night. With the moon full and the sky nearly cloudless, I don't need their bright lights. The stars twinkle paths in any direction I please to take, once the scend of the sea caused by the flying machine's propellers has passed and the surface is again calm.

Surely, tonight, I'll find her and have her back to our beach and her grave half dug by the time the morning's light shows its face. But no such luck finds me, or her, this night. After four hours of rowing, forward and backward, combing the edges of the cliffs and staring into the coves and little beaches otherwise impossible to reach on foot from the steep land above, I give up and go back to the beach. Once I land the dory, I feel refreshed again. I light a fire before heading back up the road. Perhaps a passing fishing boat has picked her up, and they'll see the fire and bring her ashore. Love will be ours again. An hour later, sleep begins to strike, and I walk home.

Following a fitful sleep, I wake at 5:30 in the morning. After tea, I head back down to the beach. Last night's tide brought lovely driftwood, just the right size for a fire. I'd traded my old flint and stone to an American for a Zippo lighter—The *Cat's Ass*, they said it was—but I don't see any resemblance to the arse of a cat and certainly have never seen fire blow out of a cat's rear end, let alone the way the flame crawls so lovely out of this shiny thing. The smell of lighter fluid is heavenly.

At dusk, I watch the growing fire and look around the beach partly lit up from the glow. I think of My Love and all the things she'd collected and used. She would count the items tucked amongst the kelp line marking the last high tide which came and went before our eyes—a rubber boot, mussels, the shells of crabs—their insides long eaten by seabirds—variations of colours of rocks big and small, bits of rope, and broken, worn-down oars. She loved it all and always found a place or purpose for her treasures found.

I get up from the fireside and find myself continuing her search for all things tossed up by the ocean. My heart throbs, almost as much as the first time I saw her—that day lugging her family's belongings through the muddy lane now called the Main Road and taking the turn past Kelly's Meadow to tackle the slippery, mucky slope of the hill where their new house was supposed to be finished. It wasn't, and they squeezed into an old, abandoned hunting shack off one of the many ancient paths on top of the hill. Her father didn't look the strongest then—I guess he was dying of whatever ailment would eventually take him—and the poor mother was all in from lugging a flat-topped trunk (full of their clothes and photographs, I imagined). It was torture watching these displaced souls and we with so much work to do ourselves. But all I wanted was to run and help them. Some families did that, but My Brother said the Americans, more like *our* government, advised against helping them, as it would "impede" progress of the entire movement and growing operations at Argentia. The only thing *impeded*, once I learned what the word meant, was my ability to function like I was half normal every time I laid eyes on My Love. During that big, awful move, I caught her looking at me once, but she was too proud or embarrassed to ask for help. Of course, I helped her anyway. What did I have to lose? If I'd only known. Her family, and all the uprooted families of Argentia and Marquise, made out alright and they eventually settled into their homes, big and small. And, best of all, in time she cared for me, and that was all I'd ever dreamt of.

Evening is passing into night again. My heart vibrates and pulsates so heavily, I feel I will faint any second. A skin-toned leg shines in the moon's bright light, as I amble away from the fire. Partially covered in kelp and other dirt found on a beach, I gulp my way towards her leg. No sign of her pretty skirt, nor her knitted sweater. The closer I get, the more I know it is her. Finally. Hot tears sting my cheeks, as I wipe my eyes with the sleeve of my coat. Caught between elation and hurt, I walk even slower—not the way I'd imagined I would for so long once I've found her—the curve of her back looks as strong as ever, and I'm embarrassed for her: for her backside to be partially lit by the moon. At the same time, I'm glad no one is out at this hour to see the spectacle that is My Love: even though she will likely be lifeless, but at least I can cover her with the blanket stowed in the dory's cuddy.

Once again, I fall to my sore knees and cry as quietly as my crushed, yet hesitantly relieved heart will allow. My eyes sting and burn, and my breath finds another place to hide. I am just several feet away and none of the features I'd noticed from afar have changed. It is definitely *her*. Bad feelings, or wrong thoughts came to me, as I wonder if her face is still as soft as it had been the first time that I held it in my hands before I kissed her—will it feel the same—the way skin becomes soft in a warm summer's rain, moistened by the fog which girls and women always complain ruins their hair, wasting time getting ready for courting or just going out for a stroll? But, yes, that is wrong—yet the heart remains strong and fights away those feelings; it's nearly impossible, even despite the circumstances. How I love My Love and long for her to be alive again.

"Please turn o'er an' show me 'tis really you," I cry.

No movement occurs.

If she were alive and with me, I imagine the things she'd say upon seeing such a spectacle—what she might suggest we do. Would we get a message to the constable who lives all the way up the bay, or would we wait until morning to invite others to make the momentous decision as a community?

Through blurred vision, I crawl towards her body. Her rear end is closest to me. I get up and run back to the dory lashed to a tarred post—I don't care about the boat at this point, if the tide takes it or beats it up—and grab from the cuddy the damp, heavy quilt Mother made years ago.

Approaching her body again, this time with the quilt, I fall face and eyes into the kelp and quilt and say the Our Father and ask God for His forgiveness yet again—the old, decent folks of the town always said I had to trust whatever happens to be accepted as God's will and I should never have the gall to question His ways. Out loud, I say how sorry I am for doubting His all-knowing ways. The miserable priest even crosses my mind and I almost decide to accept him. From the quilt, now soggier than ever with tears and the wet and slime of the kelp, I lunge forward and cast the coverlet over the bottom half of her beautiful, lifeless body. The tips of my fingers overshoot the blanket and the cold, hard flesh of her body startles me even more. I've half a mind to run up the road and get My Brother out of bed to come help me. The cold of her skin slices my soul, as I try to roll away in a means where I won't disturb her any further. I use my knees to drag myself backward and up, but I slip on the greasy kelp and land right across My Love's back. This time my face hits her spine, causing her head to rise. Big, bright eyes frighten me, piercing my already-sluiced soul and once again I roll over and away from the body.

"Damn you, God! You bastard!" I yell, kicking at the rocks and sand.

It's one of those life-size dolls—the kind they sometimes give away as prizes at garden parties and this one made its way to me: to torture me. I pick it up. The heavy quilt falls to the kelp. I run and fling the cursed piece of plastic towards the water now rising. I think of grabbing it again, the doll, and jumping on it and throwing it as far as I can into the sea, but the moving dory interrupts my thoughts and needless actions. The dory needs to be hauled farther up and lashed better so it will be of use to my search again tomorrow.

The next day I want to scream to My Brother what had happened, or more like what *never* happened. I want to tell Nan, too, but what's the sense? At her house, Nan goes off on a spiel about how she used to find stuff on the beach, and that useless prate does my mind no good. Yet I must listen to her every word and pretend to believe it whether it is real or not. These simple things separate Nan's days and the imagery she conjures occupies each of her lonely nights. It's only right I give her every second of attention I can afford, even if I don't want to.

I'm ready to die.

Winter or Spring

A print of a painting of Jesus on the wall behind the stove catches Nan's attention. She wonders why the Lord is covered in a reddish robe and the curly-headed, winged youngones reaching for his hands are in their bare skin. No one in the picture is standing on land and she imagines Himself in heaven, floating around tormenting the souls out of everyone. For everyone else's sake, she prays to God that Himself has a robe or a pair of pants covering his shame. She snaps back to stoking the fire's embers before adding more wood.

"The stove wants a lick o' paint, too," she says.

I agree with her this time, as I try to get up and head back down to the beach. I wish Nan constantly understood the agony I'm in. But it's a waste of time and I don't bother getting into it.

"I'll paint the stove sooner than later."

"What are ya talkin' 'bout, me son?"

"Nevermind, Nan," I say. "There are new buds on yer rosebushes, Nan, girl."

I smile, trying again to cheer her up and to help her realize nature will be in full bloom in its own sweet time. She gives me a dirty look and tosses her head, continuing to look out the window at an ocean not there.

"They'll soon be in, I 'spose," she frets over her young husband at sea in search of cod. "Look at the whitecaps! Sacred heart!"

"They're used t' that, Nan, girl," I say. "They'll be in an' tied up to the wharf in no time."

"That's good," she says, sighing a little less, though still gazing out the window.

The rosebushes and September Mists continue to lean in the ruthless wind.

Looking out the kitchen window at the muddy main road of Freshwater, I wish for darkness so I can get to the beach without anyone seeing me, or worse again, asking me questions: ones to which they know I have no answers. Poor Nan is still talking, not knowing *her head from her arse,* as Uncle Din says. She thinks she's still in her imaginary house on Placentia beach or at her old Argentia home and I must pretend I'm right there with her.

As I watch her thoughts get swept further into her troubled mind, I quietly rise from Himself's worn, wooden chair. I notice the grooves in the chair from decades of sitting to eat, drink, smoke and play cards.

The setting sun has changed the mood of the day, and the branches of the old trees of the meadow around the house have gone back to sleep—hardly a whisper of wind now, as quickly as that—perfect conditions to head back down the road.

In twilight, I shove the dory out, hop aboard and row serenely over the calm sea. Perhaps *this* will be the night I bring My Love home.

Cannon Balls

For the second day and night in a row, the weather has been beyond miserable. I hurry across the half-rotten planks bridging the madly flowing brook and head to Nan's—the crossing myself and My Brother cut, shaved flat with our axes, and placed there securely: too many years ago to remember exactly when. Every couple of years, we replace rotten logs.

It hurts my heart and my head, as always, that there's no sense in getting aboard the dory and combing the waters for My Love this evening. But I've had enough mishaps, either on the wet, slippery beach or rowing through rough seas, to know the difference by now. God knows, it took me long enough to get a bit of sense—if I ever had any. I've broken my ribs over and over, cracked my elbows, twisted ankles, threw out my back, along with dozens of more injuries caused by nothing but my stubbornness and stupidity.

Now, running and lunging across the trench scooped out the length of the road running through Freshwater, I flap my arms backwards, like a duck trying to slow itself while landing upon the water. I barely make it across the rapid flow of muddy rainwater racing through the dyke, downhill, towards the beach. I curse the rain, knowing it will cast mud far into our harbour—making it impossible to see anything beneath the surface.

Hurrying up Nan's well-worn path, I want to scream again, but don't want to frighten what's left of the poor old soul. Knowing I'll soon be a bit dry in the heat of her kitchen, I turn to face the new, mucky road which not that long ago was a well-beaten path our people used for generations—either hauling wood on sleighs with dogs, goats or horses, or one stick at a time on our their shoulders when a certain, desirable tree presented itself while out snaring rabbits or hunting grouse, or moose since they were brought here for the last time in 1911 and finally took hold of their new wilderness—our woods. That was before my time, but Father talked lots of the big animals. When he had a few drinks in, he had no shortage of the prate. He loved to share his humble, but now wonderful-to-recall memories of growing up in Freshwater.

Among his stories, he'd tell us about the Railway Coastal Boats, the *traders*, anchoring in the harbour and the dozens of trips he'd make in a dory back and forth from the beach to the steel-hulled vessel collecting supplies for older folks—especially widows, as men always seem to die long before their wives—without smaller boats to row or motor. He always joked, although it's probably what killed him, how the bread, buns and toutons Mother made tasted like kerosene—*not'ing a bit o' molasses couldn't cover up*, he'd laugh, as he ate fiercely before heading back to sea in his Western boat with his crew of seven or to the woods alone with his ax and bucksaw to chop and saw next year's loads of firewood—until we were old enough to properly chop, saw and haul wood, ourselves. Of course, little did we know until we got wind of it that most items, including flour and kerosene, *were* stored side by side in the holds of the traders. That information explained what Mother called Father's *sauce* about her baking. *Ya brazen divil*, she'd say to him across the table, as he winked at us while we tried our best not to titter. We dipped our bread and butter into the molasses poured sparingly onto our plates, and *said nutting an' sawed wood*, as we were taught.

How I miss them both, our parents, and what I wouldn't do to be at the table again, the four of us. They'd torment each other over bread and kerosene. I wish Mother was around today, so I could tell her what we've since learned about the way supplies *are* stored in the holds of supply ships. Nan had been saying it for years, but no one paid much mind to her ramblings. But she, too, is right, and they *still* store our meagre necessities the same way they always have.

"We'd probably turn our noses up at it now, bread that *don't* taste like kerosene," Nan says, "if they ever stopped keepin' the two t'gedder in the trader."

Still staring through the wind-blown rain and mist at the barely visible line which is the new road, I remember those somber nights and fretful next days when they were hauling bodies and remains from Argentia's three graveyards. It seems like yesterday. To know the depth of many of the tracks and ruts in the road were made so because of the weight of dead people and dead people parts can be disturbing. But that storm of madness and emotions cleared away with a warmer climate and drier grounds during that awful spring of '42 as summer pushed the nasty weather aside for a couple of months of less-dirtier climate—especially when I first laid eyes upon My Love.

I'll never forget that spring. There she was, perfectly intact, strong as a bull, determined not to be
dragged into the depths of despair as her parents seemed to be after being drove from their home and hometown—their house torched by strangers and nothing they or anyone from here could do about it. All was left smoldering for them to see and smell while they straggled away with their sparse wares.

As the Girl from up the Hill was going to their new house, she paused to take in the lovely scenery of the meadows sloping gracefully to the sea, the flatness of Placentia proper across the way, and the straight-across-the-valley view of Castle Hill. Yes, she noticed all those impressive sights, so she told me by and by. Burnt homes and dug-up bodies aside, she eventually accepted the abrupt change to their lives. Of course, when her father died soon after the big move to Freshwater, she cursed the Americans. Perhaps that's why she never considered batting an eye at them, and why she settled for me. Either way, I was contented with her decision—no disrespect to her dead father.

Once we were *an item*, as Mother called it, me and My Love often found cannon balls of all sizes and had contests to see whose ball could roll farthest off the rocks and into the ocean. You'd get extra points if your ball did the Dead Man's Dive—making that smooth, sucking sound as it entered the water. If she'd found a twenty-four-pound ball, I'd be the fool and offer to lug it to the top of the hill for her. I couldn't have cared less about cannon or cannon balls—some were still used as part of the ballast in Father's schooner. All I ever saw was *her*, and she resembled nothing I'd ever compared to things used for war and killing. I was more than happy to throw out my back for her, as long as she was happy, too.

In the 1960s, Resettlement came. Members of each forcefully abandoned island in Placentia Bay were lured by Government's lies and jobs that would never be. They settled in their own little corners of this area and remained cliques—fighting with those from other islands and with us, too, the locals, over where they could and couldn't fish. Now that several years have passed since that dreadful scheme concocted by Premier Smallwood, fist fights upon the beaches are much less frequent and resentments, once capable of lasting years, are put aside in no time for the sake of getting along and getting things done.

My Love—to see her now, lugging sacks of bedclothes, chairs, and other items in her strong arms over that muddy road to her family's new parcel of land, seems like yesterday. It was the racket of a big green truck which first caught my attention. I was in the meadow swinging the ax to cleave wood at the time. She was hopping from the back of the dirty vehicle when I first caught sight of her—when she first grabbed hold of my heart without her knowing, without even seeing me. They were dropped off at the bottom of the hill, to save the Americans time; each family had to unload their possessions on the muddy road and make several trips up and down the hill, to and from the plot of land where their new home was promised to be. The emotional, even spiritual burden, so I later learned, was heavier than all their belongings combined. It was a true test of who they were and are as a people.

A bitter chill passes through my spine like a ghost and I'm fiercely fired back into this moment. It's raining again, harder this time, and I reluctantly leave the memories of the first time I laid eyes upon My Love.

Electric Lights

I open the storm door of Nan's home, then the inside one. I stomp my boots on her hooked mat, so she'll know I'm here.

"That you?" she sings out.

"Yeah!"

"Come in, b'y, outta the dirt!"

I remove my wet cap and clasp it tightly in my cold hands.

"Sit down," she says, as the flickering lamp casts strange shadows across her face. "Hang yer cap on that nail behind the stove. Take down yer gran'fadder's shirt an' sling it o'er the back o' the chair there, now, luh."

I pretend to remove the shirt that isn't there, hang my cap as instructed upon the nail driven into the wall and then feign tossing the invisible shirt onto the daybed. Three chairs, as ever, are accessible around her small wooden table placed against the window and the too-long, once-white drapes. The fourth chair is alongside the stove and used to hold splits and shavings for lighting the fire on winter and spring mornings or cool summer evenings—the kindling is always laid neatly in an old wooden tea crate we *forgot* to return to the crowd on the trader years ago. It was the least me and My Brother could do, *considering the way they mistreat our food ingredients*, we figured. Nan never knew the difference, and if she did notice the Newfoundland Railway and Coastal Boats' stamp on the sides of the crate, she never let on. Her expression always seems to indicate she's tucked away someplace far from this world. Who can blame her?

The drip from the bib of my drying cap onto the canvas

floor gets on my nerves. I go to the porch and bring in the mop to place beneath the water wrung from the cap by the intense heat of the stove. I want to ask Nan how she never forgets to light the stove, or to cook and eat, but I don't bother. She does what she needs to do to survive. It's the outside world she wants nothing to do with, and that makes sense, too.

While standing the handle of the mop against the casing of the door frame going into the little hall below the stairs, I glance at her—almost for her approval, not wanting to upset the way she's comfortable existing here alone and with habits suiting her, the way we all have small-but-necessary-to-us customs while in our own spaces. She tosses her head playfully—a smile in her eyes I know she has only for me—*her favourite*, so everyone has always said. For a split second, she looks about half her age. Until I sit across from her again: then she looks about a hundred.

"How long've we been here in Placentia?" she asks. "Shockin' what they're after doin' t' us in Lil' Placentia an' Marquise!"

"A long time, now, Nan," I'd say, not bothering to tell her she's in Freshwater and not Placentia.

"Nan?" she asks, almost mad.

"Ya reminded me of me own nan," I lie, pretending to be Himself, the Crooked Auld Bastard.

"A lotta good ya are t' me!" she snarls. "If ya were here mindin' youngwans, sewin' veg'ables, washin' clothes, cookin' an' cleanin', *ya'd* look like yer gran'mudder, too! Turns me guts, auld men. Go out! Supper's not gonna be done fer anudder two hours yet. Make yerself useful, b'y!"

Searching quickly for a way to bring her back from her life with a man she clearly despised, I take a deep breath. The soothing smell of her soup will do it.

Having fished my whole life and knowing I'll be at it until I die, I want to pick up for her dead husband—tell her how there's no time to be home helping her and the children because by the time we get to the fishing grounds, catch fish if we're lucky, get back to the stage, fork the fish out of the bottom of the dirty boat and aboard the wharf, head, split, gut, salt and stack the fish, sure we're scarcely able to drag our legs up the road for a mug of tea and a biscuit before passing out on the daybed for two, three hours if we're lucky. Homemade poultices of bread and cloth temporarily soothe the waterpups on our satched hands—and they red-raw from the friction of ropes and nets. Then, we have to drag our arses back down to the stage and haul on our damp, cold oil clothes and row out to the schooner again—if a storm hasn't pushed and dragged her chains and ropes attached to grapnels and anchors meant to fasten her to the seabed—hoist the dory with the derrick and block and tackle back aboard the schooner, stack it on top of the other dories on the schooner's deck and lash them together, the same for the barrels and tubs of trawl lines and bait we've yet to chop up, hoist the proper sails, break our backs turning the handle of the windlass used to drag the biggest anchor back in place at the ship's bow, haul up the grapnels from her stern, fill the port, starboard and mains'il lanterns with oil, climb the mains'il with the clear light and tie it in place, and a dozen other things besides.

But I turn my focus back to her lovely drop of soup, and not only because I'm dying for a drop—because she needs to know it's *me* here with her and not Himself.

I'm extra grateful she doesn't bring up the toil necessary for an older girl or woman of any age to mind the flakes where fish need to be spread for drying in the sun and wind or from where they need to be hastily collected from sudden downpours of rain and protected in precise, round piles under layers of tree rinds.

I'm liable to get the remnants of her soup bowl in my face if I bother to bring up a woman's work. So, I keep my mouth shut. As Uncle Din used to say about all the times that he'd gone home drunk to his wife and youngsters, "I'd like t' be killed!"

In the shadow of the tall, kerosene lantern I notice different sizes of smallish bones she has picked out of the turkey soup with her boney fingers or spit from her mouth—over her gums scarce of teeth and past her contrary lips. Soup is a meal she can count on for three or four days since electricity has been long hooked up here. She looks at the rounded fridge like it's some alien object and asks about it.

"Sure, how do that work, anyhow?" she asks. "Makes not the one bitta sense, that don't. I 'spose Himself put that there. Takin' up the little bitta room we have is all that's at now. Wait till he gets home! The Crooked Auld Bastard! Some sicka him!"

I'm about to tell her that Grandfather is long dead, and that the fridge is where she keeps her food from going bad—the way root cellars used to. But that would have only become another source of confusion for her.

"Hear the lighthouse horn on Fox Island?" she asks, "or is it from Lat'ny?"

I pretend to hear the horn and count the seconds between each blast until we agree upon Lat'ny—the lighthouse point off Little Placentia named for a Spanish vessel wrecked there ages ago (the name, *Lat'ny*, of course, our ancestors' version of the proper pronunciation, spelled *Latine*)—even though there are times she knows that lighthouse was burnt and bulldozed to make way for the runway covering a good portion of Argentia. The same can be said for the lighthouse on Fox Island, with whatever the Americans have set up there.

She remembers what she calls dreams of *Project 500*—what

the Americans named the digging up of the three graveyards in Argentia—and how she finds it hard to sleep knowing Himself, whatever state his body was in, was amongst the freight of dead but not gone passing a hundred feet in front of her kitchen window at night. As much as she's glad he's gone, she still says the rosary for him over-right her tea and molasses bun, even though she never wishes to have him back.

"I'd keep the blinds drawn," she says of that time, "in case he'd look in an' know I was here. Last t'ing I needed was him fallin' in the door. No, not fer any reason would I wish him back. Sure, some nights, when I can't sleep, I comes downstairs t' add a bit o' wood to the stove t' hasten the boilin' of the kettle…an' there he is, sittin' to the table, mud from head t' foot, bitchin' an' complainin' about his supper not yet done."

"Sorry ya have t' go through that, Nan."

"Don't be talkin'," she says. "Sure, I'd say to 'im, 'I t'ought they buried you!'"

"Never buried me deep 'nough!" he'd say, forcin' a laugh.

"Ya can say that again," I'd say under me breath.

"Whadjasay?" he'd bark.

"'Not'ing, b'y,' I'd say, 'Go back t' wherever ya come from, will ya?'"

"I'm some sicka ya!" he'd shout.

"'Go on, wherever yer go'in!'" I'd shout back. "'All yer do'in is dirtin' me floor an' ruinin' me good tableclot'.'"

"'Women,' he'd say, as the door slammed behind him.

"There were times," Nan laughs, "when the storm door would catch the wind, crash into him, an' send him sideways o'er the rail o' the step. That was wort' a nickel."

When that happened, a great satisfaction overtook Nan and

her desire to pour tea diminished as quickly as Himself had left in a huff. When she'd noticed her tablecloth still clean and no muddy boot tracks across her well-kept canvas, she'd whistle as she'd turn the key to dampen the wick of the lantern.

Again, trying to bring Nan into the present, my nose finds the aroma of her soup. I search the tablecloth beneath her for another topic to discuss.

"N'er bitta fat from the saltbeef left in yer bowl or on the table, Nan," I blurt out with a fake laugh.

"'Twould be a mortal sin t' spit that out, sure" she says, laughing for real.

The smell of soup kept hot in an aluminum boiler on the stove never fails to make the old house feel like a home. It feels as if I'd grown up here—or at least, spent a lot of time here, as if it were Nan's and Pop's home all along. I suppose that's what I would've called him, *Pop*. I remember Mother, a native of Little Placentia, saying how her father, Pop, died when she was a teenager. That was a few years before I was born. Perhaps he would have been *poppy* to me. I wonder if he was half as bad as Nan makes him out to be.

I look around the long, narrow kitchen, breathe the smell of soup and notice the holes we'd drilled with the brace and bit and put through the knob and tube wiring. Nan saved a little bit on kerosene and candles and, for the first time, had the comfort of electric lights. She couldn't get over how they turned on and off by pulling on a string or chain. And she no longer had to leave the radio turned off to save battery power for the news. She couldn't get over that, altogether. How she mocked us when we first tried to tell her about the coming of electricity. A good many had had it in Argentia since the 1930s, but she and Grandfather never bothered.

"Ye must t'ink I'm clean off me head, do ya?" she'd say,

wishing us away with a downward sweep of one of her hands, and tossing her head to make sure she knew how off our heads we really were.

"But, Nan..."

"I b'lieve ye're worse than them *foolish Yanks*," she'd always finish with.

When she finally agreed to let us run the wiring through the ceiling and around the walls, she couldn't believe it. I was surprised she never complained about the exposed wires interrupting the tidiness of the place. Every spring, she painted the ceilings and exposed timbers, wires, and all. Anything in the way of her brush got painted—not to mention the drops which fell and splattered to the floor below; the mess was nothing a gas-soaked rag couldn't take away. She especially loved the switch at the bottom *and* the top of the stairs—having spent most of her life carrying in her shaky hands a candle or a kerosene lantern, with just one hand on the rail to help keep her steady in the dullness of night.

We even put a light in the pantry, so the rats would get a good fright when darkness instantly disappeared, and they'd been caught trying to nudge the cast iron shoe last used to keep the wooden lid on the flour barrel. Nan had an old fox trap she said her grandfather used in the hills of Marquise and later around their chicken coop at night in Little Placentia.

"If I had a fish fer ev'ry time I baited an' set that, I'd need never salt anudder fish again," she's said of the trap.

Nan told me to keep the trap alongside the wall because rats and mice stay close to walls. While setting the trap, I'd try and picture my great, great grandfather on his knees, tying the chain of the trap to a low-lying tree branch or near where the hens roosted at dark. He'd bait and set the little steel trap, then excitedly check the traps the next day. Fox pelts, Nan often told me, afforded them a good many of the commodities which helped them survive in what could be a very stark place—the Little Placentia peninsula, open mostly all around, except for Marquise Neck, and where the cold wind had no trouble finding your tired, aching bones most of the year.

On good days, Nan remarks how lovely it is here in Freshwater.

"The French named this place, too, ya know," she says, proud of her knowledge. "La Fontaine. Now 'tis just plain, ole Fresh*Water*. I likes the sound o' La Fontaine."

"Me, too," I say. "The Fountain."

What's left of it, I think to myself, wondering if what the men working for the Americans say is true—that they unload truckloads of metal drums marked *Hazardous Materials* and then store them in our woods, as long as the dirt is out of sight.

Swan Song

Nan's humming of a lovely Irish ballad drags me back the moment, and I feel a need to apologize—until I look at her; she's nowhere near me in her mind. Her smile is real. The hummed tune soon envelops pleasant words. Oddly, it doesn't send me into a downward spiral. Had I been given prior notice, it would have, I'm certain.

There ya were, wit' the heather all 'round yer sky-blue eyes

An', I, the young maiden, taken by such grand surprise

Yer smile, it soon cast me fears away

Ya then asked if wit' you forever I'd stay

How I wanted t' say I love you, through my lonesome sighs

By the end of the last line, I've been thrown headfirst into depression, thinking only of My Love *and* the opportunities I may have had over the years to find new love. But I never wanted it. Don't want it. Don't want another. Never will.

But I don't have the guts nor the heart to distract Nan, to get her to stop. *Yer killin' me*, I want to scream. But there's great comfort, too, in the beautiful yearning her soft voice delivers.

If I wasn't looking at her, I'd swear she was but sixteen. When I look away from her, it's as though she's been waiting for me to stop thinking so loudly. She continues:

Ya see, fair man, I once had a sweetheart

He promised me love till the end

An' sadly, although, his life was short lived

T' love another, I could never pretend

Is Nan singing this for me? Has she made it up? No! She couldn't have. Sure, she can't remember yesterday, let alone such details we've never discussed. Yet, of all the Irish ballads I've heard or learned, I've never heard that tune before or since. But I suppose that shouldn't surprise me, the way the Irish are able to make songs up night and day.

During the last lovely verse sung, Nan gets up from the table and strolls past me. It's as if she's onstage in a big, fancy play. Her nimble fingers caress the paint-flaked doorframe, as if it were a co-star, the nice man who needs her love, but her heart—being bound to a man long dead—has neither space nor interest for new love. It's the most confidence I've ever witnessed radiate from her old self. I wonder if this was her personality when she was young. I'll never know.

Still humming, she flicks the light switch on and off, showing the dust and dirt at the bottom of the stairs.

"'Tis a miracle, sure," she beams over the invention of electricity.

She sits to the table again, as if she just hasn't given a brilliant performance.

"'Tis so," I agree.

Even though there was electricity in Argentia and Marquise since the '30s, it must have been close to 1950 before we had it here in Freshwater. Perhaps later. The Americans were clever—far more advanced in the ways of technology than us—but they could never figure out why they had to keep replacing the ceramic insulators for the wires attached to the poles spread throughout our always-changing town. Fishermen, clever in ways all their own, realized insulators were the real thing for attaching to frapes—the clothesline-like mechanism set up to keep a boat on collar. So, no matter how much twisting and turning the ropes do under the strain of wind and sea, they'll never get tangled. The same insulators are still used on dories and skiffs for allowing fishing lines and trap floats to be hauled from the water, especially with a string of cod on trawl hooks. The insulators, acting as rollers, are secured between metal stands, and attached to a boat's gunwales. This method also saves on wear and tear of a boat's edges—much the same as most men and boys here take the long metal or plastic covers from ground wires attached to light poles and nail them to the gunwales of their boats and to the runners of their bobsleds.

Within a minute, Nan's face takes on a scowl fit to scare the rats away. The nice man from the song is nowhere to be found, and the lights are long gone down upon the big stage.

"The 'lectricity can kiss me arse, now!" she says, quietly through her teeth, as if she's in the presence of someone older who might give her a good clout her for her saucy mouth.

Momentarily, I struggle to adjust to the fact she's away with the faeries again, and likely about to have a racket—hopefully not with me.

"I'm no-how again t'night," she says, closing the blinds. "Pray t' Jesus no one shows up here this hour o' the night. 'Tis the last t'ing I needs."

"Do ya want me t' go, Nan?" I ask.

"No! No, b'y," she laughs, "yer the best kind. I'm just not in the mood t' have t' talk t' anyone else, that's all."

"Okay," I say. "Another drop o' tea, Nan?"

She doesn't answer—just stares off.

"I can't get o'er the lack o' colour," she says, "an' the look on Mary's face, Mammy's friend, ya know…when they lugged her from the front room of her house an' carried her o'er the meadows to the Mass at the graveyard t'day. At least the wind ca'med down fer the burial."

"That's good," I say, casually yet awkwardly as ever.

"Yes, b'y," Nan goes on, "she died a hard deat', Mary did, 'ccardin' t' Mammy. After the graveyard, we had tea an' a few biscuits at Mammy's. Mary's husband invited us o'er t' their house, but Mammy said she'd sooner be dead than be handy t' him, 'specially now wit' Mary dead an' gone. I don't know what made Mammy say that. I always found him the best kind."

The pouring of boiled water from the kettle and into my mug distracts her, as I'd hoped it would. Perhaps we can talk about something else. Perhaps I can slyly drag her mind into this moment and tell her how many years have passed since My Love was taken and, although I don't hear much said about me anymore, I'm sure the newer generations of youngones pass stories and lies along to the next person, same as their parents and grandparents before them had. But there's no need of *draggin' up old stuff*, as Father always said.

Again, I wonder if I can bring Nan into the moment; will she wonder where My Love is? Or will she recall my sweetheart was captured by the sea?

"Bet'any," she says. "How old's she now? Prob"ly looks like her mudder, do she?"

Tears fly from my eyes, and I turn away from Nan. I take my hankie from my pocket and blow my nose. I use my sleeve to dry some of the tears.

"We never got t' have a baby, Nan, remember? My Love was taken by the goddamn sea when we were just eighteen. We never got t' have our Bethany, sorry."

"No child, no," she says. "I fergets stuff, see, b'y. I'm truly sorry. That must make ya awfully upset."

"'Tis best kind, Nan."

I don't bother questioning Nan's thoughts or words. I get up, take my still-damp-cap from the nail in the wall next to the stove, haul on my coat and reach across the table. With both my hands over Nan's clasped in a ball of prayers and too many thoughts piercing her tired eyes, I give her a big smile.

"See ya, t'morrow, Nan."

She smiles meekly, tosses her head, and wears a look of uncertainly, as if she's not quite sure who I am. I don't question. I go to the end of the low-ceilinged kitchen, open the door to the porch and reach down for my boots.

"Move the splits' box, an' sit down an' put on yer boots," she says.

"I will, Nan. Lock yer door now when I goes."

"I will. 'Night, now! Mind the water crossin' the brook."

"Yeah!" I say, dying to go back in to try to keep her in the moment, so I can have someone listen to *me* for a change.

But I close the big door and latch the storm door. I make my way over the concrete steps and onto the mucky path towards the garbage-filled ditch and the road. I mope down over the meadow, trudge grumpily across the bridged brook, and head up the other side of the meadow to home.

Ugly Days and Nights

I loved her. To this moment I still do. I always will. She went away and I'm bleeding still.

I am old. It happened so long ago—when I finally got to love her the way I'd always dreamt of. Then she was swept away. My body has changed, and circles, wrinkles and darkness surround what used to sparkle with hope—my eyes—mere holes behind uneven slits of loose skin, formed by a lifetime of fear, pain and uncertainty. I've always been scared: Of something. Of everything. Of nothing. Afraid of gaining. Of losing. But the heart, beating fast or slow, still reminds me of her and plunges all I'd conjured as memories of her, real or imagined, deep into my soul which Mother always said was certainly an old one, as odd as I was.

In my dreams, My Love manages to find me. I wake every day lonely for her. Always, at the knowing it was a dream and not real, my sight is dimmed by tears. The moment I realize I'm about to wake up, I slip, grasping for those flickers of the mind I cherish most—just seeing her face, her smile, her eyes. I long for what might have been, hadn't she been robbed from me. Eventually, the tears dry, and haziness is replaced with visual clarity—enough to see another ugly day.

Every night I dream of her—not once a week or once a year like some people say they dream about a loved one dead. Every night. It never fails. And I'm glad of it—the dreaming. It's what I look forward to the most every day when darkness steals my ability to properly search for a trace of her, or especially those nights following a day of high wind and rain or a gale with snow.

Many times, in those dreams she's a different girl—always beautiful, though, and smitten with me—more so than in real life, or so my insecurities once had me persuaded.

I welcome those fantasies with unlimited imagination and strut about my fully awake mind while my body sleeps—cocky, but not raucous like the rooster. But cocky, nonetheless. It is all laughter. No crying over lost loved ones, nor complaining about the weather. Real fun. She holds my hand, the ring warmly reminding me of her devotion to me. We walk and dance and skip and laugh and she *really* loves me. No questions. We are what we are, and if you don't like it, then… I was forty-four before that certainty occurred to me—twenty-six years after it happened. I've never looked for, nor loved another since. Why would I? Mother always said if you were lucky enough to find one person to truly love you, *really* love you, then you'd be better off than most—*a lot of the crowd around here marry because they feel they have little choice*, she'd say. *Better to be married than be called an old maid, spinster, or bachelor.*

My Love always preferred I go on home or, at least, sit on the big rock by the entrance to the graveyard—kind of hidden in the shelter of trees. This gave her time she needed and deserved to be alone with her father not long passed. She'd put things on his grave—things she'd buy at the Trading Company in Placentia. I knew that because the bag she carried up the Back Path was always less full after her usual stop into the graveyard. When she'd lean in to kiss me, her blue eyes showed the sky above and a path halfway to her heart. But just halfway. There was no getting in there—to her heart—or at least that's how it seemed at first.

It was the trauma of losing Argentia, I knew, but would never speak of it—unless *she* brought it up. Me and My Brother couldn't believe the stories she'd told, about what went on there; and there was little doubt why she always wore those sad eyes, as lovely as they were. Not even the machinery used to destroy Argentia and Marquise could remove those mysterious barriers around My Love's heart. But it was certainly worth the trying. Yes, the trying, alone—to get a step closer to her real self, maybe even a small piece of her soul, was worth every moment of effort I'd ever put into my attempt at making her mine for the rest of our lives.

I often wondered was she *really* as beautiful as I had her made out to be? But those doubts never lasted more than a split second and I'd immediately feel ashamed they'd entered my mind in the first place. Of course, she was that beautiful—that beautiful and more.

I long for death, to see if I can find her. Maybe those dreams are telling me that's the way things are going to go when I'm done with this place—earth.

If she'd lived, we'd be married and have a houseful of youngones—some like me and the better-looking ones the spit of her.

Lessons

I'm a *sad old man*. That's what they call me around here. They think I don't hear their sneers and snickers, but I do, and I couldn't care less. One day they'll have their own troubled minds and broken hearts to fret over, and they might think back on me and feel bad they were so ignorant.

When I was a boy, I threw rocks at old men I thought were simple-minded, only to later learn they'd survived shipwrecks amongst hundreds of drowned bodies—some of the dead their closest friends who'd boarded the same ships with them. Talk about hard lessons, and ones you'll never have a chance to mend. To ask the Lord's forgiveness is all I can do. That's what Catholics do—ask for forgiveness. But I'm more pagan than Catholic because I blamed God for taking the only girl I ever loved, and why would I, in my youth, ask Him for forgiveness for things I never had sense nor years enough behind me to know better and He after doing that to *me*?

I've since returned to God, but I don't feel the safety I once felt in looking outside myself for guidance, the way we all tried to when we were young. If I could ever say I know something, it's this: if I *ever* had a heart to take, she took it the moment I first laid eyes on her. And if it is possible to lose control of your heart, to somehow gain it back and be senseless enough to let it slip away again, then that happened, too.

The first time I saw her, her beauty knocked me down. How on earth did I ever get the gall to amble up to her later in life? And how bad was it that she said yes, she'd love to go for a walk with me to the beach? Or down to the club for a beer, with the priest looking on, half drunk and envious of one or the other? Why didn't she go after My Brother, the better-looking, more-popular fellow? Of course, no one from here was ever considered popular after the Americans arrived.

I always knew she was too good for me, that one day she'd break my heart. Leave. But it didn't matter. Nothing ever mattered but her. She was the prettiest girl in the world and there'd never be another for me. I suppose there might have been more handsome girls elsewhere, but I never ventured past the end of Dunville—even after the good road was put through all the way to Whitbourne where the highway can take you from one end of Newfoundland to the other.

Years after she'd been swept into the sea on that lovely Sunday afternoon, I still manage to make it to the beach and scuff along the bit of sand left there, over the tips of rocks I played on as a child, to sit upon the grass of the meadows on both sides of the beach and pray—pray for her return, pray to stand over fresh earth covering a plot where she's finally at peace and adorned with flowers from the lush hills where we once lay together—hugging, kissing, and rolling onto our backs, laughing at life's simplicities, and guessing aloud how many stars were shining and twinkling behind the unending mantle of fog above Freshwater, our town, and she no longer part of the sea and all its nastiness. That's what I will always pray for.

I spent years on every inch of the hills surrounding Freshwater and other communities of our area close to the open sea. Oh, all the times I'd sworn I'd finally seen her in the sea, and then jumping face and eyes into the rough trees below my feet and tumbling over jagged rocks, beating up my face and the rest of my body, getting to my sore feet and legs again and bolting like lightning over the rocky path until I reached the bits of meadow left above Freshwater Beach—only to see nothing once I made it atop those points of land. Then, in a state of massive panic, sure I'd miscalculated her position, I'd fumble back over the same roots and rocks and try to find the very place I'd been sitting, standing, and squatting to see where I'd been sure I'd seen her—only to be disappointed, over, and over, and over again.

Discouraged, I'd go home and drink away my tears until daylight inspired the strength to go back to Castle Hill and begin my search anew. As much as I'd cursed the Americans for throwing My Love into the collective spiral of bad thoughts and sadness over ripping her hometown from its existence, and her from her place of peace, at such times I praised the friendly invaders for their endless supply of cheap booze.

But *she*, My Love, went forever. Somewhere tangled in the bottom of that harbour—the one I always imagined drained. No water. Just floundering whales and old nets, and bits of dories, punts, skiffs and splintered schooners, trawl tubs and barrel hoops, boat hooks and gaffs, jiggers, ships' wheels, darkened brass compasses and barometers, anchors and grapnels galore and broken oars, cannon balls, and cannon, too: empty of that salty devil, the water. With the help of the wary sun, the leftovers of the drained sea have turned white with salt, making it more difficult to spy My Love.

In my dreams at night, I see something moving beneath the sludge of the drained seabed. I slip and slide my way to it in my rubber boots. When I reach it, my knees and lower legs are torn, sore and bloody from old grapnels lost or left behind by their ropes worn and wasted by steady heavy currents and indiscriminate storms. I fall upon my sore knees and dig into the earth with my bare hands. Sure enough, it is her—My Love—rotten with dirt from the sea, but not too bad, or so it seems. Then I realize she's not moving or is unable to move. Until one of her eyes opens and blinks.

"Jesus Christ!" I scream, "Yer still alive!"

I dig around her until she can help me free her. She climbs on my back. I reach behind and entwine my arms around her slimy legs. Her shoes, skirt and woolen sweater are gone, long eaten away by fish, tide, and time. Together, we traverse the problematic ocean floor until we're up on the rocks of the beach.

With no memory of how we got here, I reach over the solid planked walls of one of the stalls in our barn and pour warm water from a dipper over her naked body. She says she's freezing but is happy to be getting clean and especially happy to be out of the sea. I pass the horse's winter blanket, clean now that it's summer, and My Love wraps herself in it while I run back and forth to the barrel stove Father made years ago.

Through shivering lips, she thanks me, and I tell her to save her words and energy for when she's all better. I have so much to say to her, and I can't imagine what she'll tell me.

I keep splits to the stove's fire to hasten the heating of the water in the iron boiler with the black wire handle.

"I'll be right back," I tell her.

I run out through the side door of the barn. I try to determine the source of a loud, strange sound. Down at the beach, the seawater has returned with great force. Boats and people are smashed against the rocks. Our schooner is on her beam ends, as the sea churns in anger. Our stage is nowhere to be seen. I shake my head, turn, and run back to the barn.

When I open the door, the horse shakes its blanket from its back, and the damp garment slaps me across the face.

"The whole harbour," I say to My Love, "is awash—almost like that tidal wave they had across the bay one time."

"In '29," she says.

"Yes, '29, that's right," I say. "Sure, they'll always be talkin' 'bout that," I add.

She doesn't answer.

"The warm water will be ready again soon," I say, but again no response comes. "Are ya alright?" I ask.

Still no response.

Creeping along the stalls, I hesitate before standing in front of the one she's in—in case she's after falling asleep from exhaustion.

"I suppose ya never heard me," I say, "but the water will soon be warm enough again fer me t' pour o'er ya."

No answer. At the risk of her getting mad at me, I kneel to look under the stall door. I turn my head, open one eye (as if that will make me seem any better), and peer upon hay and nothing else. I jump up, open the stall door and cry at the emptiness she has once again left for me.

That's usually where *that* nightmare ends.

When I shake off the webs of those wicked dreams weaved in my sleep, I go to the window or open the door and look toward the sea. Always, I am partly disappointed, partly relieved that the water is still in the harbour—yet, like her, the moon's path lighting its surface is never any less beautiful.

I've been walking this beach for years, back and forth, up and down, from where the slipway used to be to where the brook flows from Larkin's Pond into the sea, to the smooth rocks below the meadow leading to the Deadman's Cave—waiting for her body to come ashore. It happened down on First Beach before—a body coming ashore, years later. Another reason to instill a bit of hope, I suppose. Then again, it has happened many times since.

"As long as there's a sea," Father once said, "there'll be

drowned bodies t' help fill it."

You'd just never imagine yourself to be associated with such a saying.

Unimaginable

The moment I enter my home, loneliness cloaks me like a rain-drenched blanket. I soon get over my crookedness about poor Nan and her inability to have a sensible chat. Part of me wishes My Brother was still here and not married with youngones and living up the hill behind me. Another part of me welcomes the emptiness. This life I've chosen, or was meant to live, craves for spaces empty of people and the rarity of silence few seem to know how to appreciate. It allows me more time to imagine where the tides may have taken My Love.

What if she'd been picked up by a passing steamer and she didn't know who she was and was dropped off across the bay, somewhere, or worse again, in a place far, far away? No wonder I could never find a trace of her. Somehow, there's pathetic relief in that dream, but it is one of the many reoccurring visions I've had, asleep and awake, in all the years since she was stolen from this world which we sometimes think we know but surely never will.

I boil the kettle, then decide I've had enough tea this night. I slide the kettle off the damper above the fire, so the bubbling water inside the copper container isn't rattling my nerves, especially when a drop or two flies out of the spout and sizzles into nothingness on the stovetop.

I sit to our old table and have half a mind to start up the gas-powered washing machine, the way me and My Brother used to do on the beer for a laugh years ago. I might be able to afford a new, electric one, but the gas one still works and why would I waste the little bit of money I've managed to put under the mattress? Mother's voice tells me to get a bit of sense, and I quickly forget about that foolishness—not to mention the waste of gas it would be to start that noisy machine tonight.

The life, heart and soul of Mother lays scattered about the house in a thousand pieces, with all the appropriate verses of the bible forever vibrating in the ever-shifting beams. Through the tentest walls, I still hear the murmurs of Mother's and Father's dreams, secrets (so they thought), agitations, fears and whatever else they used to talk themselves asleep about.

"Go t' sleep outta it, ye!" I say, just to make sure no one is in the house to say anything back.

In my dreams, I'm at sea. Cold, stinging saltwater races across my lips, over my tongue and down my throat. As I lean over the gunwales to haul her in, a sharp pain shoots from the ribs on my right side.

"Ya, alright?" I ask, catching hold of her sweater.

I'm careful not to put my hands anywhere I shouldn't without her permission; this is certainly not the time for the like of that.

"Christ! I thought ya were gone!" I say. "I never see anyone get washed out of a dory like that before…that quick. Ya poor thing! Are ya alright? Here, put this blanket 'round ya an' I'll get us in outta this before ya catches yer death."

"At least the sun has strength," she manages to say, half laughing and half shivering.

"Do ya think you'll be alright t' hop aboard the horse," I ask, "so I can get ya up o'er the hill in a hurry, to yer mother's woodstove an' heat?"

"Yes, b'y," she says. "I'll be fine. I'm an Argentia woman, remember?"

Rowing ruthlessly, I never miss a beat in our conversation. I couldn't afford to miss a trick with the wit of her coming at me a hundred miles an hour.

"Yer not an Argentia woman any longer," I shouldn't have said.

"'Ndeed I am," she says, "an' I always will be, thanks very much. Ya better mind yer mout', me son," she says, then bursts out laughing.

I'm relieved she isn't mad. I really shouldn't have said that, especially after what the poor people of Argentia and Marquise are going through and might never get over.

When we get to her home, her mother is in the doorway.

"My God," she gasps, "how'd ya get so wet, my child?"

With one corner of her mother's lips pressed firmly together in disgust, and utter blame shooting from her glassy eyes in my direction, I reluctantly follow both women in through the narrow back porch of the house. Rounding the turn, her hands tightly gripping her daughter's shoulders, she gives me a hard look. I'm so relieved to have saved My Love from the water; I really don't care what her mother thinks of me at this moment.

"Go on up in yer room," her mother says, half shoving My Love, as if the poor girl never had sense enough to change out of her wet clothes on her own accord.

"Where's her other shoe?" the mother asks, sternly.

"I, I, I don't know," I stammer. "Neither of us noticed it missin' once she was back in the boat."

"Wha? Sweet Jesus!" she screams, "Back in the boat! Whaddaya mean, *back in the boat*?"

"I'm not sure what happened, or how it happened."

I'm so relieved those words came off the tongue of My Love, as I waited an eternity before I could come up with any explanation to help calm her rightfully upset mother.

There she stands, My Love, more beautiful than ever, dry as a bone in her other Sunday dress—the one she never had a chance to wear properly before she.... Then, after running one of her hands along her mother's shoulder, she grabs the back of a wooden-spindled kitchen chair and slides it across the floor towards the stove.

The mother's head hasn't let up shaking from side to side since we entered the house. Even with the unpleasant coolness coming off her mother, the heat in the room still hugged us both—me and My Love. Her mother has never looked at me this way, nor talked to me in such a belittling fashion, as she's plainly doing.

My Love casts her head forward, bending her slender body at the waist. With a wide brush, she combs her wet, newly washed hair from the back towards the front at first. She is careful not to let its lovely length contact the floor. Although it is new, the floor was and always will be full of sawdust, bits of bark and rotten tree rinds ground almost to a soil on account of the wood stove—no matter how often it's swept each day and night.

It's a wonder her mother doesn't drive me out of the house with the stove poker the way I'm entranced in her daughter's loveliness. With each stroke of the brush's bristles through her yellowish hair, my heart races and I can't think about anything but getting out of this house—somewhere, anywhere but here, and alone with My Love. As I wonder about being alone with her again and whether she'll have a fight on her hands with her mother, my mare out in the yard whinnies for me to hurry up—she's been in a strange place long enough.

Although I try to hide it, I feel sad, hurt, and My Love's mother must sense it.

"So, how'd ya manage t' fall outta the boat, girl?" she asks, looking at her daughter who is seemingly unphased by the ordeal.

Then the mother looks to me, raises her eyebrows, and keeps her head and chin raised, as if she'll stay like it until I deliver my version of events. Because she's never treated me with any form of disrespect before this moment, at least not to my face, I resist the urge to crack a joke about the wretched face she's wearing.

Once again, My Love enters the would-be conversation between me and her mother. This time, My Love's pretty face is tilted to the side facing the wood stove, and she continues brushing her hair as it dries in the stifling heat. *If I was home, I'd be in my drawers, sitting to the table or hove off on the daybed—my aching bones enjoying the heat.* That's what I'm thinking, until my foolish thoughts are seized by the lovely scent of Sunlight soap meandering throughout the kitchen's warmth.

"'Twas a rogue wave," I finally manage to say. "She was half sittin', half leanin' against the dory's gunnels, the way she always does when we goes out on Sundays, lettin' the water glide past her hands."

My Love senses I'm about to mention the ring, but I'm stopped by the stern flaring of her beautiful eyes.

"Sure, we were nowhere from the shore, were we?" My Love recalls.

"Maybe a hun'red feet, that's about it," I say, looking apologetically. "Maybe a good bit less. The wind, it…"

"B'y, 'tis not like ya threw me outta the boat," My Love interrupts my prattling. "Don't be so foolish, b'y!"

"What happened? What Happened?" The anxious mother wants to know.

"Ya know how the water sometimes crashes against those jagged rocks stickin' out from the bottom o' the Googly Hole

Meadow?" I say.

"Yes," the mother says, "sure that's only when 'tis stormy, though! My Jesus, ye have more sense than t' go out in a dory in poor weather, haven't ye?"

"Look out the window, Mother!" My Love says. "'Tis a lovely day still, an' it was when we went out fer our Sunday spin in the dory. Now, let him finish, will ya?"

"I 'spose 'tis my fault," I say, looking at My Love.

"What are ya gettin' on wit', b'y?" she asks.

"I was distracted by something," I said with a look My Love understood—a look to be followed by an in-depth explanation next time we're alone. "If I'd kept the stern or the bow o' the boat facin' the send o' the sea, we'd have hardly known we were on the water."

"My Jesus," the mother gasps, "yer never goin' out in a boat wit' him again!"

"Mother!" My Love says.

"How else do ya expect me t' act?" the mother asks.

"I know," I say. "I was taken off guard, first time in my life on the sea, an' I let the boat turn side-on to the waves. An' ev'ry now an' then, a bigger-than-usual wave makes its way 'round The Point. By the time I righted the boat wit' the oars, I noticed she was no longer aboard. I never panicked—just hauled in the oars an' crawled along the gunnels. By that time, the sea was smooth as oil again an' she was wadin' in the water just about ten or twelve feet from me."

"So," My Love chimes in, "he threw me the extra rope he keeps tied to the risin's an' I towed myself along it until he caught me under the arms an' hauled me back in the boat."

"Mmmm," the mother sounds in disgust.

The impatience My Love carries and the possible bad behaviour capable of following it is written all over her lovely face. I'm more nervous than ever. At this moment, she is clearly her mother's daughter. My Love coughs then looks away—out the window, as if there was anything to see but the sky still the colour of her eyes, and the drifting clouds—how I wish I was aboard one of those clouds instead here beneath the wrath of an angry woman ready to rip my head off.

Ignorant of the fact her vexed mother is only a few feet from where I sit, a wildfire suddenly fills my body and I jump from my place of discomfort. My quick movements give the mother a good start and I notice her flinch in her spot at the table. I walk towards My Love, extend my right hand, and wait for her to take it. When she takes it, I'm surprised her touch is so clammy and cold. I gently move that hand from my right hand to my left. With the fingers of my right hand, I stroke her hair. Like her hands, even though she's been sitting by the heat of the stove, her hair, too, is wet. I push the wet mass from her forehead. The smell of soap is absent—only the stench of moldy seaweed and rotting fish fills the air.

"Ah-hum!" her father barks from the entrance to the bottom of their hall and the small front room.

I seem to be the only one to notice him. I nudge My Love, but she doesn't remove her gaze from the sky through the window glass.

"Whatta ya after doin' to me little girl?" he demands to know.

I'm wondering if my mind has left me completely, and I say nothing. I don't know what to do. Run? And why isn't My Love stepping in and helping me answer *his* question, the way she did with the mother? I look to the mother. She screams.

"Answer him!" she screams louder. "Answer us! Whattaya

after doin' to our little girl? Ya useless bastard!"

When she's done asking me the same question, over and over, she stares at My Love and screeches so loud the thin glass of both kitchen windows explodes and crashes all over the room. I cover my head with my arms and my hands. When I raise my head, there's no sign of the father and I figure he's hurt and has fallen where he stood. I can't see him past My Love at the stove. She's still staring ahead, out the window through broken glass and she seems, otherwise, untouched by the flying glass or the commotion caused by her mother.

Although I'd rather give all my attention to My Love, I figure I might as well have it out with the mother—let her tell me what she thinks of me, and I'll try my best to convince her what happened on the sea was an accident.

"Look at her!" I yell. "She's the best kind, yer little girl, sat to the stove, as content as can be. Alive. Jesus! What else do ya want me t' say?"

I turn my head to the table where the mother is slouched over; a rectangular shard of glass is sticking out of the back of her neck. The rosary she wears around her neck has been cut in two and it lays in a pile of rubbed-worn, bloody, beaded saints at her feet. Resting on the table, her arms keep her steady—like she has had too much to eat or drink. Part of me is glad she's unable to blame me for ruining her Sunday best because I have no clue how to clean stains of any kind from an attractive, flowery dress reserved for Sundays and funerals.

My Love still hasn't budged. I step towards her. Her small nose highlights her profile and, once again, I'm struck down by her exquisite beauty—even though she's sweating from the growing heat of the stove. Her hair is matted to her forehead more so than it was a minute ago.

"I didn't," I begin, "I mean, I never said a bad word to her, even after she screamed at me. An' yer father! Jesus! I thought he was dead. Ya said he died. Christ, I *remember* when he died because I was at his *funeral.* Have I lost me mind? Can ya at least say *something,* so I don't feel like such a goddamn fool?"

I lift my hands to her delicate face. It, too, is clammy and bitterly cold. Leaving my left hand cupping her strong jaw, I stroke her unkempt hair with my right. It's as though a brush had never touched it. Strands of hair stick to my hand and fall effortlessly from her scalp. I flick my hand to get rid of the hair, but now the hair is kelp—seaweed. I manage to flick the oily, greenish-brown sea plant to the floor, and I turn My Love's head toward mine. Expecting to be relieved by the cobalt eyes which lured me to her so many years ago, I gasp at the sight before me. Where her eyes had been are big, dark holes: the same as you'd see while squinting into a crisp winter's clear night sky—only one without a moon or stars. These empty spaces hold no answers, only horror.

Running to find help, I race around the corner of the house. My horse, still neighing, only louder now, has turned from brown to blonde. Its mane is drenched. I try to stroke the big animal's blaze, but I'm swiftly shoved away with its head and nose. I lift my hands to feel the rain, but there is none. The leaving sun bends the day towards dusk in a sky bluer than My Love's eyes—or how they used to be. Surely, the doctor over in Placentia can make her all better again.

I untether the horse and we speed off down the road, take the sharp right by a small food store, then the hard left leading down the always-muddy Back Path. It's the quickest way to reach Placentia. I'll get to the beach and get someone to motor me across the harbour so I can fetch the doctor.

I lash the horse's leather bridle strap to the post of a flake above the beach and run to the first man I see. He doesn't say a word, only gestures with his head for me to hop aboard, as if he's been informed of my coming. With gigantic hands, he easily turns over his six-horse-power Acadia engine and off we go in his long trapskiff. I let my right arm hang over the boat's gunwales. My fingers are relieved by the sting of cool summer saltwater. A pain shoots across my wet hand and up my arm to my shoulder. My body lunges sideways with the weight of something caught hold of my hand. I look down into the water, through the waves cast aside by the boat bouncing off the sea. I see her—My Love.

She reaches for me, and I grab her carefully beneath her arms. Safely in the boat, she lets out a sigh of relief. I smile.

"Christ! I thought ya were gone!" I say. "I never see anyone get washed out of a dory like that before. Ya poor thing! Are ya okay? Here, put this blanket 'round ya an' I'll get us in outta this before ya catches yer death."

"At least the sun has strength," she says, half laughing and half shivering.

From that nightmare, I awake to a lonely house. My heart pounds and my legs are weak as my feet touch the cold floor. It sends a hurtful, cutting sensation to my knees—much like the bite of the sea I continue to feel in my sleep. I leave my chilly bedroom and walk onto the canvas of a cooler kitchen. The mat Mother hooked still lies in front of her rocker. I skip onto it for a moment to help take away the chilliness.

On my sore knees in front of the open stove, I layer twigs, Old Man's Beard, a sliver of birch bark and top the works with small sticks of driftwood. I flick open the top of the Zippo and strike the metal wheel with my thumb. I hold the flame beneath the concoction of kindling. Almost instantly I am overcome with a sorrowful, yet somehow-contented sense of nostalgia.

The smells of the burning wood, bark and moss invoke a

lifetime of memories. The smell of lighter fluid reminds me of my American friend, and *he* reminds me of My Love.

I'm almost happy to be alive—at least glad to be out of that reoccurring dream.

Stare at the Wind

As she's about to bring her lips to mine, I'm slapped across the face by a gust of wind. My daydream is drowned. The sea heaves salty spray into my mouth, as I take a big breath before hauling hard on the oars. My nose is stuffy from a lifetime upon the sea. I spit seawater from my long face. I wipe my pursed mouth with the cotton cuff of my rubber coat. The soggy material is miserable to the touch. I curse to the top of my lungs—blaspheming the same god I'd prayed to a million times to have the Girl from up the Hill, the same spirit I'd thanked a million times when she finally allowed me into her life.

I wish to Jesus I'd been washed into the water with her. But no, I have to live so I can walk, stand, sit, lie, nod in and out of sleep, bawl like a baby, laugh like a lunatic, haul on my hair (what's left of it), punch myself in the face while drunk and complain of the headache later, and get thin as a rail because I won't eat half the food My Brother's wife cooks and brings to me.

Of the gulls I've become best friends. I've even named a few of them, recognizing them by their cries, markings, movements, behavior, colours, injuries, or scars.

Staring into the wind is hard, trying to concentrate on the water, looking for a sign of My Love. Generations of gulls, seemingly ever lost and sad, screech and bawl above and around me, for me, throughout each long year.

I miss her so much. I always will.

Eventually, her mother forgave me, although the look of disappointment has never left her face. When she goes out of her way to speak with me, I try to say sensible things. But I have nothing to say. I'm never mentally present in her physical company.

As she talks or cries, sometimes both, I crawl the bottom of the ocean, avoiding ugly sculpins, flatfish, maiden rays, make 'n' break engines, shafts, props, connors, oar locks, smelt, pollock, haddock, and cod of all sizes with their gaping mouths always ready to swallow whatever they see—the image of their torn, ugly lips etched in my being, having taken them off lead jiggers and trawl hooks since I was a child. *Are ya alright?* her mother asks—more of a reminder for me to snap out of my trance and to listen to her: it's the least I can do, than true concern for me. And who can fault her? She has lost the only person she had left in her immediate family. Whenever she starts talking again, I resume my search of the seabed for My Love—her precious daughter. Fighting to keep the weightlessness of my body upon the ocean floor, I wade my way through millions of crooked crabs, harmless starfish, useless jellyfish, saucy squid and conches, and those black things with four antennas—*sacks for sharks' eggs*, an old fellow once told me. Forged, iron spikes from schooner masts and spars tear into my flesh, anchors galore jab me in the sides and back, ghost nets catch my boots, grapnels snag my feet and legs, holding me back while brazen dogfish and vicious wolfish snap at and tear my paler-than-ever Irish skin. Whales of every size frighten the life out of me until I'm dragged back into the monotoned remembrances and vivid wails of My lost Love's reluctantly forgiving mother.

I don't deserve her mother's pardon; I know that—especially knowing I'll never absolve myself. Telling her I'm sorry is more to hasten our meetings, drive her away, back up the hill to her own misery, and to leave me with mine.

When she speaks softly and calmly calls me by name, I feel even worse. Why didn't ye do somet'ing else—a picnic in the grass o' the field above the Googly Hole, or in the meadows o' Castle Hill. Anyt'ing but a row in a dory. Oh my! Sure, that's only meant fer fishin' from. Oh my!

I don't know what to do.

Bakeapples

After banging the main door shut, I latch the storm door into the eyehook screwed into the white clapboard of the house. Aware of the familiar scuffing of my boots and my perpetual morning cough, the cooped-up chickens are set off their heads. A flurry of hen squawks and bawls fills the air. Even the rooster has added enthusiasm in his strut. I open the little door to their outside run, and they nearly trample each other to get out for the handful of breadcrumbs from my table and mashed-up stale biscuits from Nan.

I open the roosting boxes and half fill a yellow, plastic bowl with eggs—some clean, but most of them covered in dirt which I'll wash and scrape off when I get back from Nan's. When I return, the hens can run around the yard pecking for worms, snails, spiders, and anything else daring enough to move while I cleave firewood. Right now, the hens and rooster are fine in the wire-covered, wood-framed run.

I put my hands out in front of me, as I go through the droke of alders, then scuff down over the half-slippery path to the brook.

When I get to Nan's, I can tell by the look on her face glaring out through the window that she's back someplace long before my time. I've half a mind to leave her there with Mammy, her grandfather or Himself, but she sees me and beckons me in with a tap of her boney fingers on the side kitchen window of the old house.

"She's gettin' on wit' her auld nonsense again," she says to me as soon as I enter the kitchen.

"What's wrong now?" I ask, unsure if I should say anything.

"Ya knows how I give up goin' t' Mass after all the youngones died?"

"Yeah!"

"Well, she's callin' me a pagan again, an' sayin' she wishes Mary was here—someone fer her t' talk to, 'cause I'm not worthy o' talkin' to fer not goin' t' Mass. Just because she lost youngones of her own an' managed t' hold on to her faith, don't mean I have to. An' I'm not! She can kiss me arse now, I've a mind t' say t' her."

During the mandatory mug-up, little is said between us. Every now and then she casts me a dirty look and mutters something saucy while pretending to look at something going on outside.

"*You* should say somet'ing t' her!" she finally speaks.

"Me?" I say.

"Yes, you! Do ya see anyone else here?"

"What would I say t' her, sure?" I ask, hoping Nan's state of mind will flicker back to the present, and maybe we can talk about the poor weather or the lack of fish—anything but this.

"She likes ya! Why, I don't know, but she do. Says she needs someone t' confide in an' she couldn't be bothered wit' me 'cause I'm nutting but a pagan, a heathen. Says I don't understand the ways o' the Cat"lic Church an' where did she go wrong after spendin' her life tryin' t show me the ways o' the Lord?"

Nan then asks questions—ones I've no way of answering.

"But Mammy said a pagan like me got no business knowin' the business of a good Cat'olic. Sure, what else am I 'sposed t' do? Go t' Mass so everywan can talk 'bout how I was never t'

Mass in ages? Not likely. I'm hardly goin' tellin' the priest I'm sorry the Good Lord stole most o' me youngones an' left me nobody. Go on out in the yard, somewhere, then, if ye're not gonna help! Go on! Go on! Get!"

I look away to conceal the tears pooling in my eyes, as Nan resumes her stare out through the old window upon the old meadow—its once-pristine beauty shredded by the sod, mud and rocks removed forever for the ditches alongside the road. I leave the house, as instructed, without a word. What's the point in staying? I'll come back tomorrow, and she will ask me why I wasn't by last night. I'll just say I had too many fish to clean and salt.

Once off her step and onto the grass, the tears roll across my cheeks and their heat soon becomes a cutting cold in the end-of-winter air.

I wonder whether my tears are for Nan's sad state or for the want of finding My Love, or the fact I'm not out there searching for her night and day. I wonder if Nan would be better off out tumbling, drowned in the sea, rather than sitting like a lump to the kitchen table and peering out a window which reveals to her anything but what's there.

As I mope through the dead, yellowish grass of last year and the fledgling flecks of this year's new growth, I imagine My Love alongside me, holding my hand. I'm instantly bashful, as she pulls me closer to her and lays her beautiful, sparkling hair on one of my tired shoulders. Her left hand caresses my arm, the one she's holding, as she dreams aloud. *Imagine if, one day, we could own this place or a place like it here in Freshwater…an' we could look out the windows an' watch our youngones swing from them big trees up on the hill an' roll on their sides down the Grassy Meadow. I'd keep bread poultices upon their cuts an' scrapes while you piles hay fer the horse, cow an' sheep—when yer not out fishin', of course. Then, when the youngsters are able, they'd help me an' keep me comp'ny on the flakes an' we'd be all the better off fer it when 'tis time t' lug our fish to the merchant.*

When I turn my head to look into My Love's eyes, I'm distracted by a tapping sound. I look back towards the old house and see Nan, her face more wrinklie than ever pressed against the glass pane. One of her long boney fingers half savagely beckons me back. By then, My Love has vanished from my arm, from my sight, and I feel like picking up the nearest rock and throwing it as hard as I can at Nan's mug in the window—put her out of her misery.

Again, I'm emotionally torn—did My Love appear because she's calling me from the sea? If I run down the road now and go out in the dory, will I finally find her?

Instantly, I'm filled with shame. Imagine, wanting to throw a rock at my only living grandparent. I fret over returning to her kitchen to be blamed for not stepping between her and her dead mother's fight over who's a pagan and who isn't. But I go back, anyway.

When I enter the kitchen, Nan smiles her gummy smile and beckons me to sit to her table.

"The kettle's just b'iled," she says, smiling.

"Alright," I say, unsure if I want to waste more time here this day.

"An' I made yer favourite, bakeapple jam," she beams.

"Where'd ya get bakeapples this time o' year?" I ask.

"Where do ya t'ink I got 'em, from you, last year. Jesus, b'y, yer not losin' yer mind are ya?"

Nan was right. I did give her bakeapples last year—ones from the marshes of Argentia, too, even though we're not allowed down there. When an American soldier pulled up in a green jeep alongside me and My Brother, we were told we weren't permitted to be there, or anywhere near Argentia, for any reason.

"Pickin' bakeapples, b'y, frig off!" My Brother said saucily to the soldier.

"Pardon me?" asked the armed stranger. "You might think you're funny, but I certainly don't. Now, move it along before I arrest you both and take you in to the authorities and you can explain your imaginary apples there!"

"You sap!" My Brother snapped. "They're berries, ya arsehole, an' they're called *bake*apples. Jesus Christ! Pretty goddamn bad we can't come here where we've been comin' all our lives t' pick a few berries."

"I'll assume you cannot read," the American replied, "so I'll read the sign for you!"

"Yes, b'y, can't read," My Brother said, his face almost purple with rage. "I'll read ya!"

"Are you threatening me, sir?" asked the soldier.

My Brother got up in the soldier's face.

"Put down yer big gun an' yer bullet belt, an' we'll see how tough ya are *then*!" My Brother said, calmly.

"Jesus, b'y," I said, whacking My Brother across his shoulders. "Give it up, b'y, before we gets shot!"

The soldier, seemingly unphased by My Brother's anger and threat, coughed and looked up at a sign not far from where we stood.

"'Trespassers will be Prosecuted' the sign says," the soldier read aloud.

"Did anyone prosecute yeer crowd fer burnin' an' bulldozin' homes an' everyt'ing else down here? Did they? Whatta ya t'ink we are, a bunch o' friggin' dummies? I assume *you* cannot read.

Me gran'mudder could knock *you* down. Go on an' let us pick a few bakeapples, I mean *berries.* If *anyone's* trespassin' here, 'tis *you*!"

I chose to leave My Brother alone because he was right. We *weren't* doing anything wrong and how could strangers expect us to *not* pick bakeapples or any kind of berry—things we've been doing and food we've been living off all our lives? The American, somehow, must have realized truth in My Brother's solid, accurate words and turned away.

When the jeep sped off, My Brother fell to his knees and rested his head on the bog. I thought he was having a nervous breakdown, until I realized he was laughing to kill himself. That caused me to laugh along with him. I, too, dropped to my knees and breathed a deep sigh, as if we'd won a war of our own. It wasn't our first such encounter with the Americans and it would hardly be our last—especially if they were planning to stay for ninety-nine years.

"Sweet Jesus," My Brother finally spoke. "I thought we'd be shot."

"Then why'd ya bother arguin' wit' 'im?" I asked.

"'Cause somet'ing tells me them poor bastards are more afraid than we are. Part o' me wanted t' pat 'im on the back fer catchin' the Germans in U-boats, an' fer catchin' that German fella out the road—the one posin' as a Yank—wit' the radio wire hidden in his chimney…but when he insulted us 'bout not bein' able t' read, I decided t' see how brave he really is."

"An' what if he wasn't afraid an' he did shoot us?" I asked.

"Then, I guess we wouldn't get a bakeapple t'day," he said.

We laughed, as I climbed the chain-link fence. I landed on the soft ground. My Brother was still laughing, as he rolled beneath the galvanized mesh I was straining to lift for him.

"By da Jesus," he said, "Nan better eat ev'ry last one o' these, after what we've been through this day."

"Ya need never worry 'bout Nan turnin' down a bakeapple," I said, laughing.

My Love

When My Love left, she took my heart, and I bled all over this town for years.

Although I could never say so, I was glad Hitler's forces were sent our way and twice as glad the Americans had come and driven My Love and her family to our once-quiet town. To have known the likes of her existed, and to have her as my own, if only for a while, was worth the heartache I'll take to my grave.

I was too young back then to grasp the intensity of the hurt she'd felt for her mother and father—having to walk away from the land which once held their home, and to know their relatives and friends were being dug up from what was meant to be their place of eternal rest and dragged, shoveled, and slung into pits in our graveyard. I was too hot-blooded, like an old hound dog, to really care about their plight because all I saw and wanted was her—their daughter. I'd felt a mild pang of guilt in my guts, as she turned away, teary-eyed, after talking of her Argentia lost and all I could think of was watching her from behind without her catching me. But I was a teenager. All of this and more I would later have chances to tell her. And I did.

She pretended to take none of my ramblings to heart, and she did her best to be the best friend she could be—not the kind of great friend My Brother is to me, but very special, nonetheless. Some invisible cloak of a condemned existence always veiled her—something I couldn't pinpoint or attempt to grasp. Perhaps it reflected her parents' feelings. She was secretive—an unintentional mystique surrounded her most of the time.

Regardless, all the while I planned to somehow conquer her love. How I craved it. I also felt, deep down, if I was ever granted such a glorious occasion, I would never truly break through that shadowy cloak. The only thing I did know was that robe of ill fate wasn't nearly thick enough to conceal from my eyes what I saw as the most beautiful creature God had ever set down upon this meadowed land. And *that* was good enough for the likes of me. *Too good*, My Brother would say.

Blue Eyes

I was eighteen when she was swept away. We were the same age. The very year I can't recall, but I suppose it was two or three years after the Americans arrived. That was in '41 and it was well into '42 before many ever saw the foundations of their homes mixed, poured, and set. Some were beat around from dog to devil and never got to settle into their new homes until 1945 or '46.

It was during the spring of '42 when they started hauling truckloads of bodies and body parts from Argentia's graveyards. Or so they said. No one really knew because it was done under the cover of darkness. With the hurry the Americans were in, with residents not even allowed to take a window or a door because Hitler was coming, it's doubtful all dead bodies and certainly not every body *part* made it out of the deep bogs of Argentia.

I haven't heard the name "Marquise" hardly since—only The Southside, or *McAndrew*, what they say for short for the army basȩ, Fort McAndrew. The roar of big guns firing for rehearsal, the taking-off of fighter jets, the air-raid siren, and a host of other invasions of the ears, if you were lucky enough to have any hearing left, became as common as the salty wind in our ears, or the sounds of waves washing the beach and their scend leisurely grinding the rocks of our coastline.

The Second World War wasn't long ended before the Americans entered what they called The Cold War—a war of words between the United States and the Soviet Union. And even though it was called a war of *words*, millions of deaths occurred as the result of proxy wars fought between the US and the Soviet Union. The Russians were *definitely* coming for us, so the Americans kept the air-raid siren blaring everyday as a reminder of our impending, certain doom.

Down on The Base, Elvis Presley, Bob Hope and Frank Sinatra were just a few of the many entertainers who stole rare moments of wretchedness from me with their well-rehearsed, off-the-cuff humour and pleasing singing voices.

I'd become friends with lots of Americans who, themselves, had become part of our landscape—renting or even owning houses and apartments in Freshwater. For the most part, they were friendly, generous, and appreciative. Many married local girls, as My Brother had predicted all those years ago.

Most of our friends and family are dead, up on the hill, alongside Mother and Father, Uncle Din, and Nan, what was left of her—all shimmied into the overcrowded ground.

My American friends would show up with a bottle of whiskey or rum and cigarettes and tickets to whatever spectacle the USO shows had to display. I always said *no* at first, but drinks at my kitchen table easily lured me into their vehicles and down over the steep hill to Marquise or Argentia where famous singers and actors galore were flown in to entertain US troops, and us—the locals who needed special permission to be *sponsored* onto land once their own and open to all residents of the area for fishing, hunting, and berry-picking.

When Sinatra held that long, skinny microphone and made his way to tables, as far as the mic's cable would allow, the women, married or not, stared at him like he was the best piece of saltbeef in the world. They tore at their bee-hive hairdos and jumped up and down in their seats. They screeched and bawled. I wanted to wail, too. But not for him.

I try to think that love's not around

Still, it's uncomfortably near

My old heart ain't gaining any ground

Because my angel eyes ain't here

We didn't say words like *ain't*, but the Americans had been around so long, we knew what it meant and a ton of other words, too—some not fit to repeat and others deemed acceptable for the changing times hushed in with each passing decade. If I had been a woman just inches away from *Blue Eyes* Sinatra, it would have made no difference.

"Pretty moving, isn't he?" my American friend shouted through the din.

I nodded just to get him out of my face, so I could stay hidden in my mind with memories and images of my own *Angel Eyes*—My Love.

"No trouble t' find a nice gal for yourself here tonight, friend," the American said.

"Whattaya mean?" I asked like a youngster.

"Jesus, man," he went on, "the way old Frankie's got 'em all worked up, they'd go off with a dog if they were asked. Not enough men t' go around, can't you see?"

But all I saw was My Love and *her* blue eyes. Everyone would laugh if My Love had been next to the man they called "Blue Eyes" because, in comparison, her eyes would make his look like those of a dead fish.

"Blue eyes, my arse," I said low enough, thinking my friend couldn't hear.

"It's not his eyes they're after," laughed my friend, ignorant of my bleeding heart and my wrecked soul.

I knew it was the booze talking for him, so I left it alone. It's not like he, and many others, didn't know my story—how I'd spent the past number of decades walking and crawling the beaches and hills, and rowing and staring into the sea and the wind in vain for a trace of My Love's body.

But news, good or bad, becomes old very quickly, as it is always replaced by other events, be it a tragedy or something deemed worthy of celebrating. So, in the presence of Sinatra, I understood my friend's unintentional obliviousness to my tedious despair. Not that I didn't blush when an attractive American woman asked me to dance to one of Sinatra's smooth ballads. She must have thought me soft in the head to decline her charitable advance.

I was afraid of feeling fascinated by another—the way I'll always feel about My Love. I was afraid of others thinking I was finally letting go of my permanent, well-known purpose of finding My Love and to live contently without another because *she* was the only one for me. And the more I drank, the stronger those feelings rang true; whereas the opposite seemed real about everyone else who drank. One of my goats could have been sitting next to me and some drunken man would have tried his damnedest to take it home, if only for the night.

Sinatra was something else. When he sat upon a thickly cushioned, red leather bar stool, surrounded by serious-looking men in sharp suits, I wanted to walk up to him and ask how he seems to move through life with such ease when fellows like me can barely scrape my way out of my own head. I wanted to cry to him about My Love. Perhaps he'd sing a song about her. But I knew he wasn't interested, as he signed autographs and pointed to certain women while his henchmen approached those and other women in the dimly-lit room with tiny slips of paper—invitations, I'd been told, to have a drink with him in his room after the show.

Throughout my twenties, thirties and forties, American

friends came and went, as they were sent to other US bases around the world. We kept in touch by writing letters which were always a treat to receive from the post mistress two or three times a year.

By the time I was in my sixties, my declining strength slowed my body's ability to search for My Love the way I had for more than forty years. Not that I still didn't attempt every time the sun shone, and when the wind was sensible.

From late 1955 to the spring of 1975, Argentia was a taking-off point for US soldiers on their way to the jungles of Vietnam, Laos, and Cambodia. Girlfriends of those soldiers waited in vain for letters never received—nor did they ever hear from their lovers again. According to newspapers of the day, many soldiers never made it out of the jungles. Tears gushing down the reddened faces of young women in Freshwater weren't much less powerful than the torrents of water viciously overflowing the brook from Larkin's Pond after a heavy rain. With the fall of Saigon in April 1975, the Vietnam War was finally over, but the toll of its horridness and subsequent sadness would linger in hearts and minds forever. In private, I cried over their losses, too, but really, I was just sobbing for My Love because everything, good and bad, reminded me of her. Just *her*.

Some Americans decided Newfoundland was the best place on earth to live and they happily settled down with local girls who became their wives and later the mothers of their children—followed, of course, by grandchildren.

When I turned seventy, to paint a dory I'd built was hard on my back and my knees. A well-made, hard-rowed dory could last twenty years, easily, sometimes longer. They laughed at me for still drinking kerosene and molasses for my ailments, but it got me through, and God knows I was long over worrying about what anyone might have said or thought of me. I always thought back to Uncle Din and Father—*Fook 'em all*, they used to say, and that phrase brought a smile to my creased face every time I got a strange look, or a slur thrown my way.

The old house where I'd spent so much of my youth occupying Nan's time between trips upon the sea or along the beach in search of My Love was a crumbling shell of rotten wood—its untouched meadows of hay around it a haven for felt blown from the roof of that house and another old one down by the road built soon after Nan moved to Freshwater from Argentia. In the far end of Nan's meadow, a once-red stable leaned away from the wind always blowing up from the beach. The young crowd set that on fire one night, and the next day it was hurtful to see. I was glad Nan wasn't there to see another structure up in flames, as she wouldn't have been all that far away, physically, or mentally. The burning of her home in Argentia began the end of her sanity—another such fire would have killed her, altogether.

By the time I turned ninety, nearly seventy-two years had passed since My Love was taken from this life and into the dreary sea. People I'd known my lifetime, the few who remained in the town and were still clinging to life, had grandchildren; some even had great grandchildren. I had no one—no Bethany, nor grandchildren to call me *poppy*.

By 2015, there was scarcely an American left in the Placentia area. The Base at Argentia had closed in '94 and the prosperity it once bestowed upon the pocketbooks of locals had been squandered away in one fashion or another. It marked the end of a lot of things once considered decent or worthwhile: things once viewed as entertaining. The announcement of the Americans pulling out spelled the death of the lucrative economy they'd created in Newfoundland.

With Smallwood's 'Confederation' with Canada in '49,

Ottawa was given free reign to dip its greasy, greedy hands into our colony's fish-filled pockets—a death sentence for what once fiercely defined Newfoundland and Newfoundlanders. What our government called the "Resettlement" program or *Centralization*—a scam luring families from their traditional ways of living on hundreds of islands dotting the bays of Newfoundland in the '50s and '60s—bore similarities to what had happened to the former residents of Argentia and Marquise: the uprooted folks received a pittance for trading the very essence of their existence for government lies and age-old political rhetoric.

Also like the people of Argentia and Marquise in the early 1940s, some from the resettled islands in the '50s and '60s traded their conventional ways of life for jobs on land—as there was always a spot to be filled at Argentia. Yet, many, unable to read or write and not the least bit interested in anything except fishing and boatbuilding stayed true to themselves and their forefathers, and continued sailing the sea for food.

Oh, the changes I've seen. Yet, my heart saw nothing but My Love. I was content still living in the home I was peacefully reared in, and the few dollars I got for my doryloads of fish were more than I needed to exist.

When the fishery closed in '92, I held back tears of my own as those of seasoned fishermen soaked their rugged faces for the loss of their livelihood. By then, I was getting a cheque from the government for being sixty-five years old, and with the bit of wood I sold, I wanted to tell those former fishermen I couldn't care less. But I knew what the fishery meant to all who embraced it. As I still combed the beaches, I now had over-turned boats to sit upon—not to mention more company than ever: men not allowed to fish, only to complain about not being allowed to fish. No more did anyone ask why I was there.

I was relieved when My Love's mother died. No more did I have to dream of ways to console her, or to have that conversation we'd had for years—her talking through tears while I crawled the ocean floor in search of her beloved daughter. I believe the mother died in the early '80s. She was an old lady who bore a similar sadness, like the one I've lugged in my heart. I'm sure she was more than glad to get out of this unpredictable world. I envisioned her smiling alongside her husband, her son who finally crumbled at the feet of TB when he was twelve or thirteen, and My Love, all so long gone.

Yet I still held onto the hope I would find enough of her daughter to lay alongside her. The best I could manage, was to go back to the mother's fresh grave and bury the quilt My Love had sat upon that awful day. I'd hoped the old blanket would link the family back together—maybe keep them warm whenever a nor'easter sweeps through the gates of Heaven.

Twinkling Star

I loved her. To this moment I still do. I always will.

In my ninety-sixth year, I lay on the same daybed my father died on. Mother died on the same kitchen bed. Now, I am dying, too. Finally.

I hold and stare at the photograph our American friend took of My Love on our last day together. Seventy-eight years have passed like the wave which stole her.

This is the closest I've ever felt like I might manage to find My Love—when I take my last breath. I long for it—to relive our short glimpse of true love, as we did on Sandy Beach, just us and the boisterous birds. From there, we'd make it safely back to our beach where we'd kiss and hug and dance when the dory was hauled ashore, and what odds about the old men and their covetous cackling. We'd run to her mother's door, burst in and I'd sit nervously while My Love delivers the good news—we're to be married and one day she'd have a grandchild to care for, to love.

Our story, according to My Brother's grandchildren, has long been legend around here. On foggy nights, which are most nights in Freshwater, My Love has been seen hovering above the sea. Her ghost is often seen on Saturday nights by crowds of young people drinking booze. My Love has often been seen back-on in her knitted sweater and long skirt sitting on the ragged rocks of The Point, her eyes never turning to meet the cries of the drunk and suspicious. Some say they've seen her move, but most agree it is just the fog.

There must have been twenty youngsters and adults here over the past seventy-eight years with My Love's ring—a thing which has long taken on a life of its own. The youngsters have had contests to see who can find it, and God knows there have been plenty of rings found; but they've never found the one Nan gave My Love on that Saturday night all those years ago.

"Jesus Christ, yer not still alive," My Brother roars in my ear.

"Unfortunately," I say, seriously.

Then all hands burst out laughing at the expected foolishness between us old men.

"Alive? Sure the divil's after havin' *you* a dozen times—too bad t' keep, I 'spose," I say, winking at the horde of people filling the small kitchen.

My Brother's wife joined the over-crowded graveyard up on the hill years ago—cancer, they said, from PCBs found in Larkin's Pond, now called The *Drinkin' Pond.* The man-made chemicals from capacitors and transformers used on powerlines on poles running alongside the old railway track leaked into the water supply.

My Brother will be ninety-nine his birthday, and there are sixty-year-olds going around in worse shape. In his fifties, he started jogging and hasn't stopped since. Most of the area's widows find him irresistible with his full head of hair, slim figure always precisely slipped into his Sunday best, and feet able to tear the hardwood off the Community Centre floor down the road every Saturday night when a band is going full tilt. The smile never left his handsome face and he's well known for passing walkers half his age on the lovely boardwalk they made years ago spanning the length of Placentia Beach. Nan's grandfather would have been pleased with the way they built up the beach and then made a lovely place for people to walk and admire our charming surroundings. Dories are scarce as hens' teeth now, let alone boats tied to people's doorsteps for a quick departure, if necessary.

"Ah, fook off, b'y, ya crooked auld bastard," My Brother says, without cracking a smile.

"Poppy!" one of his grandchildren scolds him.

All hands are quickly relieved of the phony tension when we both smile before tittering and laughing like youngsters.

"Ya could be o'er in the home in Placentia, ya know," he says, knowing what my answer is to such a remark.

"Ya knows what *you* can do now," I say.

The young crowd laughs, as they sit or stand around the kitchen. They're a good bunch of youngones. I know they're here because they *want* to be. And My Brother doesn't use guilt to get them to visit. They recognize the importance of knowing older relatives—all they ever had to do was ask a question and we'd do our best to answer—the best way to learn, they know.

After a lifetime of looking for My Love, what was once a hardening heart in my chest has long since turned to an emotionless stone when it comes to remembering her.

By the time I was in my thirties, I'd been fishing those same waters long enough to understand and to never underestimate the unyielding, commanding undertow of the sea. I'd long stopped asking myself what if I'd rowed back towards Sandy Beach instead of cutting across the water in front of our beach—would I have found her then?

A few years after My Love's mother died, someone from her family brought the basket to my door and left it there on the ground—the same basket My Love held by her side that last day on the beach, the one I'd hoped contained shortbread biscuits made by her very hands. Sometime after it washed ashore, someone gave it to My Love's mother.

At first, I thought it was badness on someone's part—bringing the basket to *me*—but I soon found out it was My Love's aunt who thought *I* should have the basket as a reminder. I wanted to grab her and scream *Why would I want to be reminded of something so awful?* But someone said, *no, she means well by it*—it was a gesture of kindness, one which might have helped seal the cracks in my age-old broken heart. For years, I held that basket in my hands as I lay in bed on my tear-soaked feather pillow—remembering it dangling from her tanned arm the moment she came into view, as I stood against the dory that day—our *last* day together. I never stopped sniffing for a hint of the shortbread cookies. But eventually, I had to drop it off on her mother's back step, even though the house was empty of people by then.

"Alright, b'ys," My Brother says, "let's let this poor auld bastard die in peace, an' fer fook's sake when I'm dyin', don't be crowdin' 'round me like this. 'Tis all bad 'nough. See ya by 'n' by."

All my nieces and nephews and their children, even My Brother's great grandchild of four or five, come to my side in single file. Some bend to kiss my clammy forehead, others touch my tender arms or shoulders while some just stand, lost in whatever their young minds have formed over the not-so-pleasant spectacle before them, saying nothing—tears pooling in their kind eyes with some running over their precious cheeks and onto their clothes or the cozy, fleece comforter they bought and wrapped lovingly around me. My Brother and his wife had raised them right.

"Alright," he says, "let's go. See ya, Brudder."

When he squeezes my shoulder, tears fly from my eyes. He looks away.

"Yeah. See ya, Uncle Din," I say, trying to laugh.

Just like that, the best friend I've ever had is gone.

When the house is empty of company, I close my eyes and wonder if Nan will be there to greet me (wherever *there* might be), or the Crooked Auld Bastard and he as happy as a lark dancing with all his children, poor Mother included, Mammy half vexed over her precious ring lost, Nan's grandfather carrying me wherever I want to go in his dory (surely there's a bay in Heaven where there's no moratorium on cod and where no one ever drowns), the Youngfella from in the Lane, or maybe even the nice man—Mr. Morrissey from the Cape Shore.

I've come to understand as long as men are in power, the world will always be at some sort of war. I learned through Mother, Nan, and My Love, even her mother, that women are more sensible than men—not always craving the need for power and control.

My musings are interrupted by a knock on the door and followed by the sight of a beautiful young girl.

"Sir?" she says, a world of doubt in her voice.

For a second, I take a deep breath and accept I've finally died and there she is—not quite the same face, but people change. I wonder what age she is at this moment.

"I'm really sorry, sir, for botherin' ya," she apologizes, "but I have a question for ya an' I'm sorry 'cause I knows you're not well."

I struggle to wipe the tears from my eyes over my mistake of mistaking her for My Love. She takes a tissue from the box on the little table next to the daybed and bends over me, dabbing my eyes.

"How can I help ya, me darlin'?" I ask, feebly.

"I know this is hard fer ya, but yer girlfriend, the one lost in the water down by The Point...she wore a ring, right—one ya used t' ask fer her hand in marriage?"

"Ya," I say, knowing another ring will soon be presented as *the* ring.

"Were there initials carved on the inside o' that ring?" she asks, awkwardly.

"I think so," I pretend to not know the answer.

"Wasn't her name Betty Cleary?"

"No," I say, "but there was a Betty Cleary moved up here wit' the crowd from Argentia, though. I 'spose ya don't know anyt'ing 'bout that, do ya?"

"I do, actually," she says, smiling. "I just read about it in a book by a local fella…what our people were put through when The Base came. Terrible what happened, but nothing compared t' what the poor Jews were put through on the other side o' the world."

"Nice t' know the young crowd cares 'bout that time," I say in a low voice—my strength leaving me as I try to speak. "Them poor people suffered, 'ndeed they did. Not a bit like the poor Jews, but they suffered, b'lieve me. That's how I met My Love, ya know."

"Really?" she asks, genuinely.

"That's right. She an' her crowd were burnt outta their home, too, an' ya talk about a lovely creature—the first time I see her luggin' sacks an' wooden crates up o'er the hill, *Old Settlement Hill* they calls it now. I set out t' make her mine. An' I did…until…"

"I'm really sorry fer your loss, sir," the young girl says. "I won't bother ya any longer."

"That's alright, me dear," I say. "What did Betty Cleary's name have t' do wit' yer visit, anyhow?"

"Oh, nothing, I guess," she says. "The initials inside the gold ring my little sister found read *B.C.* an' I've asked a lot of the old folks around if they knew of anyone by that name."

"Jesus, almighty!" I say, the loudest I've spoken in ages. "B.C. B.C. Beatrice…no, hang on, Blanche…no, sorry."

"That's alright," she laughs. "Ev'ryone in Freshwater curses."

"Bet'ny!" I almost shout. "Bet'ny! From Ireland, so she was. Clancy! Yes, that was her last name, *Clancy*. From Tipperary. Me Nan told me a t'ousand times, that story. Yes, by the Jesus! That was me great gran'mudder's name an' that's what was on the ring Nan give My Love the night 'fore she was lost t' that friggin' sea. Ya don't have it on ya, do ya?"

"I do," she says, reaching into a front pocket of her jeans.

"Show," I say, losing my breath and coughing.

The young girl passes me my mug, holds my head up a little, allowing me to clear my throat with a drop of water.

"Ya okay?" she asks.

I nod.

"Here," she says, holding a ring.

"O'er in the drawer there's a flashlight. I 'spose the batteries are workin'. Pass it o'er, will ya?"

The flashlight works and I point it at the ring. The outside of the ring is tarnished, but the inside has been scrubbed with something. In the light reflecting from the exposed gold, I see My Love's eyes, then the sky in her eyes.

"Turn it the other way," the young girl says, taking the ring and flipping it around.

My body goes from a motionless lump into a shivering mass of hysteria. My tears are hotter than ever, as the young visitor races to dry my eyes again.

"Are ya alright, sir?" she asks. "I'm sorry t' have upset ya."

"'Tis it," I say, my lips quivering and dripping of my salty tears.

"My God!" she gasps, "Are ya sure?"

"Tell Me Budder t' put it in me pocket when I'm in me coffin, will ya? That way, I'll be able t' put it on My Love's finger again when I sees her."

"I will," she says, wiping tears from her youthful face.

"Yer a good girl," I say. "I loved her, ya know. I still do. I always will."

The young girl smiles, saying how lucky I was, I am, to have had someone to love so much.

"No one ever said the like o' that t' me before, ya know," I whisper.

The girl can't respond for the gulps in her throat, and she's busy wiping more tears from her face. For the first time this day, I notice the sun has gone and a clear, dark sky offers extra peace to the night. I turn my head to the side and squint at the window facing Castle Hill.

"Mind raisin' the window fer me?" I ask.

"Not at all," she manages to get out.

When she's out of my way and back in a chair, I keep my focus on the sky, clearer than ever now that the glass is out of the way. In seconds, a lifetime of heartache disappears. I slide the ring over the tip of my pinky as I glare towards eternity.

"She never forgot," I say.

"Never forgot what?" the young visitor asks.

Even though I'm overwhelmed with content, I'm choked up more than the throes of death have already dealt me. I force a cough to try and clear my throat. I cry louder than I thought possible at this stage.

"She used t' say…she used t' say…if she ever died before me, all I had to do is look to the sky at night an' she'd be a star twinklin' just fer me."

"That's right sweet, oh my," says the young girl.

"No sweeter was ever made, me dear. Fer all the years I looked to the sky fer a sign I'd find her body, I never minded what she said. It must o' meant I'd see her or a *way* to her before I'd die. I never thought I'd have t' wait so long, 'tis all."

"Oh, my," the girl says, fretting for me. "Maybe ye'll be together for eternity, now that you see her twinklin' for you—especially how you devoted your whole life to findin' her."

I wonder if every person must wait until they're almost gone from this world before they hear words which they had longed to hear a lifetime.

"In that drawer, where ya got the flashlight," I say, "there's a couple of wrinkled papers with my hen scratches on it—words I wrote for My Love years ago. Would ya mind readin' it, so I can hear?"

"I'd be happy to do, if that's what you really want," the girl says, hesitantly.

I decide the young girl alongside me is my angel, sent to me by My Love. Without My Angel, I'd have never seen My Love twinkling for me in the lovely night sky. And I'd never have seen and felt the ring Nan gave My Love so long ago—something I never dreamed possible—a symbol confirming her belief (and Nan's) that me and My Love *were* really meant for one another.

My Angel clears her throat before reading. I close my eyes and listen, imagining My Love is listening, too. In my mind, I hold and squeeze My Love's hand.

"For My Love," My Angel reads the heading before she

gulps.

I open my eyes to see tears pooling in her young eyes.

"'Tis okay," I murmur. "Go on."

"Okay," she whispers.

My Angel begins again.

For My Love

Did I really kiss you; fall to the ground, either grass or snow?

If it was so long ago, how could I still miss you so?

I dream of your smile, how you were my best friend

I wish for a million ways to make this nightmare end

I cover your body with a quilt from the cold—move your hair from your soft face, expect you to scold

But your eyes tell me things I've waited so long to hear

I feel the squeeze of your hand, feel your breath in my ear

The warmth of your sweet voice fills my being with sin—as I long to tell you all the things I've kept in—what I wouldn't give just to hold you again

I still see you standing against the rocks of Dead Man's Cave

Burning driftwood until this life you'd soon save

Graceful, you were, as meadows rolling away from the sea

How I wish for the time back when it was just you and me

You carried your mother's homemade bread and kept right warm the strong tea—your light hair against the dark water—your smile just for me—how could anything God made be half as lovely

At night in the kitchen kept warm by the stove, memories still strong of loving you in the cove

Me, drunk on your beauty—you, lost in my eyes

Got me through thousands of nights without lies

For, surely, I did fall at your feet—oh, what love
How I pray to hold you forever when we meet again up above.

"Yer a good soul," I say to My Angel.

"Thank you," she says, sniffling but no longer crying as if she understands and has accepted the purpose of her first and last visit to my home.

"I'll soon hold her again," I cry.

I close my eyes, try to smile, and feel the warmth of My Angel's gentle squeeze of my hand. I long to open my eyes again, but I'm afraid this will be just another dream. Like the onset of the hundreds of bronchitis attacks I've had, air is sucked through my nostrils. I wonder if that was my last breath, then laugh because I hope I'm not dead and still able to wonder about anything.

My Angel's grip becomes stronger on my hands. How I'll miss My Brother; I'll save a seat on the comfiest cloud in Heaven for him until he meets me there. In the meantime, I long to see Mother and Father, Uncle Din, and Nan.

Before me, My Love appears. I am saturated in peace by her smile. To me, she extends her hand. Her hair is clean and giving the sun its light while her eyes paint the sky the loveliest blue. The ring glows from her finger and I watch Nan, grinning away, coming down the road in a car to our wedding. Mother and Father are in the front pew of our church; a little girl stands between them—our sister—and they're turned around, all smiles, too, for us. Uncle Din is standing against the back wall, sipping from a little flask, rolling his eyes, and winking at us as we enter our new life together. I take My Love's hand and pull her closer to me. Her own mother and father, even her little brother, are stood just inside the entrance to the church. I let go

My Love's hand, as her father takes it. I walk to the front of the church where the priest nods his approval of my existence.

I've found her. Finally. I've found her. A breeze stirs the curtains of my open window.

At the sound of my last breath, My Angel gasps. She hauls the fleece blanket over my face and leaves.

ABOUT THE AUTHOR

Darrell Duke is from Freshwater, Placentia Bay, Newfoundland.

Swept Away is his seventh book. The story idea was first written in 1993. In 2001, Duke wrote, directed, produced, and acted in a stage play called *Swept Away—The Musical.* His ballad, *Swept Away*, may be heard on his 2015 album, *Safe from the Storm.*

OTHER BOOKS BY DARRELL DUKE

If You Look Closely, You'll See (Byrnt Books, 1999)

When We Worked Hard (Flanker Press, 2007)

Thursday's Storm (Flanker Press, 2013)

An Irish Tale of Leaving (Stagehead, 2018)

The Adventures of Crunch and Munch: Vol. 1 (Stagehead, 2019)

The Garden Gate (Stagehead, 2021)

The Adventures of Crunch and Munch: Vol. 2 (Stagehead, 2022)

Facebook: Darrell Duke

Twitter: @DarrellJDuke

Email: stageheadbooks@gmail.com

Manufactured by Amazon.ca
Bolton, ON